MORE PRAISE FOR

Death and the Running Patterer

"The story's climax, involving a classic Agatha Christie–like gathering of suspects—some historical, others invented—is gripping and surprising . . . [The] novel is packed with fascinating tidbits and in-jokes . . . [as well as] dollops of trollops; a generous spoonful of crime and retribution; lashings of colonial era minutiae and atmosphere."

—*The Sydney Morning Herald* (Australia)

"[C]olonial Sydney comes gloriously alive and teems with a rich array of characters both historical and fictional."

—*The Age* (Melbourne, Australia)

"[An] enjoyable murder mystery . . . Adair gives us the authentic feel of the roistering days of the early colony."   —*Pittwater Life*

"Historically sound and fast-paced."   —*Australia Broome Advertiser*

"[A] meticulously researched and cleverly constructed mystery . . . Entertaining."   —*Senior Lifestyle South Coast*

D0167018

Death and the Running Patterer

ROBIN ADAIR

BERKLEY PRIME CRIME, NEW YORK

THE BERKLEY PUBLISHING GROUP
Published by the Penguin Group
Penguin Group (USA) Inc.
375 Hudson Street, New York, New York 10014, USA
Penguin Group (Canada), 90 Eglinton Avenue East, Suite 700, Toronto, Ontario M4P 2Y3, Canada
(a division of Pearson Penguin Canada Inc.)
Penguin Books Ltd., 80 Strand, London WC2R 0RL, England
Penguin Group Ireland, 25 St. Stephen's Green, Dublin 2, Ireland (a division of Penguin Books Ltd.)
Penguin Group (Australia), 250 Camberwell Road, Camberwell, Victoria 3124, Australia
(a division of Pearson Australia Group Pty. Ltd.)
Penguin Books India Pvt. Ltd., 11 Community Centre, Panchsheel Park, New Delhi—110 017, India
Penguin Group (NZ), 67 Apollo Drive, Rosedale, North Shore 0632, New Zealand
(a division of Pearson New Zealand Ltd.)
Penguin Books (South Africa) (Pty.) Ltd., 24 Sturdee Avenue, Rosebank, Johannesburg 2196,
South Africa

Penguin Books Ltd., Registered Offices: 80 Strand, London WC2R 0RL, England

This is a work of fiction. Names, characters, places, and incidents either are the product of the author's imagination or are used fictitiously, and any resemblance to actual persons, living or dead, business establishments, events, or locales is entirely coincidental. The publisher does not have any control over and does not assume any responsibility for author or third-party websites or their content.

PRINTING HISTORY
Penguin Group (Australia) Michael Joseph trade paperback edition / July 2009
Berkley Prime Crime trade paperback edition / December 2010

Library of Congress Cataloging-in-Publication Data

Adair, Robin, 1936–
    Death and the running patterer / Robin Adair. — Berkley Prime Crime trade paperback ed.
        p. cm. — (Curious murder; 1)
    ISBN 978-0-425-23703-8
    1. Murder—Investigation—Fiction. 2. Sydney (N.S.W.)—Fiction. I. Title.
    PS3601.D355D43 2010
    813'.6—dc22

                                                                              2010032717

PRINTED IN THE UNITED STATES OF AMERICA

10 9 8 7 6 5 4 3 2 1

For Julie

'Tis wonderful what fable will not do!
'Tis said it makes reality more bearable;
But what's reality? Who has its clue?

—Lord Byron, *Don Juan* (1819–24)

DRAMATIS PERSONAE
(in order of appearance)

Anonymous private soldier—relieving himself outside a pub; may lead to a sticky end.

Lieutenant-Colonel Thomas Shadforth—"Die Hard" commanding officer in the 57th Regiment in 1828 Sydney.

Captain Crotty, of the 39th—assisting Shadforth.

Captain Francis Nicholas Rossi—magistrate and police chief; a spy nursing royal secrets?

Nicodemus Dunne—paroled convict, now a news-hawker; a disgraced policeman, he still cannot avoid walking down the mean streets of murder.

Lieutenant-General Ralph Darling—aloof, embattled governor of New South Wales; foppish, but don't let those polished fingernails fool you.

Reverend Dr. Laurence Hynes Halloran—publisher of *The Gleaner*, a veteran of Trafalgar, teaching and transportation.

Miss Rachel Dormin—Halloran's protégé, a pretty free-settler.

Will Abbot—soldier turned printer; a bad type?

Reverend Samuel Marsden—gives a new twist to "muscular Christianity" as the "Flogging Parson."

Dr. Peter Cunningham—ship's surgeon who sails with an unlucky cargo.

Miss Sarah Cox—hears the siren song of a love-struck parrot.

Joseph Hyde Potts—of a rare breed, the generous banker.

The Ox—an ungentle giant with blood on his hands.

Dr. Thomas Owens—a doctor who seems more at home dealing with the dead than the living.

Alexander Harris—Dunne's free friend who uncovers vital clues.

Edward Smith Hall—crusading editor of *The Monitor*.

Madame Greene—brothel-keeper supreme who lives up to her colorful name.

Elsie—Madame Greene's too-devoted maid.

William Charles Wentworth—volatile lawyer, politician and publisher.

Blacksmith at Lumber Yard—strongman with a big mouth.

The Flying Pieman—Dunne's peddler pal William Francis King, also an athlete extraordinaire.

Private Joseph Sudds—wayward soldier whose fate convulses the colony.

Private Patrick Thompson—Sudds's partner in crime, and punishment.

Bungaree—"King" of the local Aboriginals.

"Commodore" Billy Blue—the harbor's most famous ferryman.

Cora Gooseberry—King Bungaree's queen.

Barnett Levey—a man with theater in his blood and blood in his theater.

Mrs. Norah Robinson—a very accommodating hostess.

Muller—a German typesetter.

Brian O'Bannion—an old lag from the Auld Sod.

James Bond—a young lag, suitably stirred and shaken.

Thomas Balcombe—a man for whom every picture tells a story.

Oh, and Master William Shakespeare—dead more than 200 years, he wanders through the story, scattering clues.

Death and the Running Patterer

Sydney, Australia
1828

CHAPTER ONE

Ours [our army] is composed of the scum of the earth—
the mere scum of the earth.
—Duke of Wellington (1831), quoted in P. H. Stanhope,
Notes of Conversations with the Duke of Wellington

A SCARLET-COATED SOLDIER, A PRIVATE OF HIS BRITANNIC MAJESTY KING George IV's 57th Regiment of Foot, was dreaming, drunk and disorderly, as he leaned against the bar with his head on his arms. He dreamed he was home in his West Middlesex village, safe and sweaty in the arms of his common-law wife. He hadn't seen her for years, didn't know if he ever would again.

When the regiment had marched out of its depot, bound for Sydney town, six wives were allowed to accompany each company of 120-odd men. At dusk the night before they marched, the Color Sergeant had drawn from his military cap a piece of paper for every camp follower. For the lucky ones these read "to go." Hers had read "not to go." Ah, well, luck's a fortune. Any old how, there were plenty of women here and now. Some men were still allowed to live out in the mean streets near the barracks, in miserable dwellings with their wives, old or new. For others there were harlots for hire, chances to seduce town girls who had an eye for a man in uniform—it was called "scarlet fever"—even blacks, who could be bought for a drink, a threepenny nobbler of rum. There were plenty of boys, too, for those who leaned that way.

He'd first taken the king's shilling to escape grinding poverty or a life of crime, or both—and, bugger me gently, here he was now, in the year of Our Lord 1828, in the world's biggest and most remote prison (as a guard, mind) on Sydney Cove, 15,900 miles from home.

Not that it wasn't an easier billet than some he'd had to endure in the past. God knows he'd fought in Spain at Corunna (he'd seen them bury the general, Sir John Moore) in '09 and then at Waterloo, where they'd pushed back the Frogs, screaming, "Avenge Moore!"

There had always been an answer to his soldier's prayer, "God save me from the surgeons"; he'd beaten battle wounds, his cock hadn't fallen off—not for want of trying—and yellow fever had never turned his flesh to custard.

Now he spent most of his off time in the pub. And most of his money, even the extra he made from weaving cabbage-tree hats during the dull hours in barracks and selling them to traders in the town. Tom Killett's Crispin Arms was good sport, but a bit close to the barracks. He liked the Cat and Fiddle and the Brown Bear, which stood together in the rough-and-ready Rocks. But so did too many sailors for comfort.

Once, he seemed to recall, he'd gone to the World Turned Upside Down and seen a giant Otaheitean pimp beat a man halfway to heaven for refusing to pay for a prostitute. And some publicans were reputed to sell drunks to crewless captains.

No, on a dry day he'd settle for the Labor in Vain. Its sign outside always made him smile. A crude artist had depicted a black in a tub of water, with a sailor trying to scrub him white. The rum they served there was good

Bengal spirit, not, like some you got elsewhere, too heavily cut with water, brown sugar, black Brazil tobacco and a dash of vitriol. And there were dudeens to be had, short clay pipes at a penny each, and you got your own glass and didn't have to share what was called the circling glass, a common cup passed around.

At two shillings for a pint of rum and one and six a gallon for colonial beer, a man could drink his pockets dry in a hard session. Thank God soldiers were on the stores. The weekly ration was five pounds of beef, two pounds of mutton, seven pounds of wheat (not maize) bread and two pints of rum—not nearly enough for a thirsty man.

The taproom was clean and lit with oil lamps, not tallow dips like some, but as the soldier roused from his slumber he felt suddenly dizzy. Dimly he listened to a fat old tart tell him she was just out of the Female Factory. "I got a five-bob fine or the stocks for an hour for being drunk," she said. "So I called the charley a cunt*-stable and they gave me a month in the aviary!"*

Then she broke into song:

> *I've to the Factory been, my Jack,*
> *and lost a lot of fat.*
> *And wouldn't mind going there again,*
> *for I'm none the worse for that.*

Not to be outdone, the soldier roused himself and bellowed back at her, and to anyone else who would listen:

> *I don't want a bayonet up my bumhole,*
> *I don't want my bollocks shot by ball.*
> *For, if I have to lose them,*
> *Far better I can choose them*
> *To cop a pox from any whore at all.*

He suddenly felt his belly rebel, and staggered to the door; if he puked inside, he knew he'd be barred. In an alley nearby, shadowed by buildings that leaned so precariously toward each other they almost kissed, he retched and fumbled with his balls to piss. A sound made him turn around and squint. "Hello, mate. Come to shake the snake, too?" Then he frowned as the fog of rum cleared briefly. "But your lot shouldn't be here."

He didn't get a bayonet up his bumhole, but a keen blade slashed at his throat, then across his stomach and finally across both ankles. Then a hand showered a cascade of small grains across his face and into his silently screaming, dying mouth.

CHAPTER TWO

Whence are we, and why are we? Of what scene
The actors or spectators?
—Percy Bysshe Shelley, *Adonais* (1821)

I N A PRIVATE ROOM DEEP IN THE HEART OF THE GEORGE STREET Military Barracks, the largest overseas garrison in the British Empire, three men sat over pipes and claret. Two wore the distinctive red coats that earned their wearers the name *lobster* or, from the French, *rosbif* (roast beef). In turn, of course, the British called their enemy "Frogs" or *crapauds* (toads).

The soldierly pair were Lieutenant-Colonel Thomas Shadforth, commanding officer of the 57th Regiment, and Captain Crotty, his aide, an officer of the 39th. The third man, a civilian though he retained the courtesy title of his one-time British Army rank, was Captain Francis de Rossi. He had long ceased getting upset when the English fell into the habit of dropping the "de."

The soldiers were uncomfortable with the presence of Rossi,

and not just because he was swarthy, spoke heavily accented, excitable English and had a Mauritian wife. After all, he was still an outsider, a Corsican. Not like Bonaparte, of course—indeed Rossi had fought against Revolutionary France and served the British Empire for thirty years. But he was a mystery man.

How had Rossi become, Shadforth wondered, in the few short years since 1825, superintendent of police at 600 pounds a year and collector of customs at 1,000 pounds? When, mind, a servant could be had for no more than 20 pounds with keep? As if that weren't enough, he had also been appointed chief magistrate and thus was the chief of police.

The delicious gossip, of course, was that Rossi had been rewarded for his role as an agent during King George IV's separation from his queen, Caroline, which ended in her exclusion from his coronation. The royal scandal had thrilled Britain and Europe, and the distant colony, even Shadforth himself, loved the idea of having one of its plotters in its bosom. There was also a whisper that Rossi had been a Secret Service spy, even a slave-trader in the colony of Mauritius.

As if to divert his own attention from any unseemly thoughts about his royal master, Shadforth turned to his subordinate. "The Linnets were damned slow on that exercise, Crotty," he said. "Perhaps you need another dose of Sankey?"

Crotty flushed.

"Linnets? . . . Birds? . . . What is this?" Rossi frowned.

"It's just the colonel's joke—and an old one," said Crotty, tapping the green facings on his uniform's collar and cuffs. "The 39th is commonly known as the 'Green Linnets.' And also as 'Sankey's Horse.' During a Spanish battle, regimental tradition tells that Colonel Sankey mounted his men on mules to speed them to the fighting."

Shadforth nodded, adding, "Just as we in the 57th, sir, are called the 'Die Hards.' On the Peninsula, at Albuera in '11, our regiment suffered three-quarters casualties. Colonel Inglis, sorely wounded, cried: 'Die hard, my men, die hard.'"

"Ah," said Rossi. "Of course. I knew of the 'Buffs,' the gallant 3rd Regiment who have been here, with their buff facings."

"Quite," said Crotty. "And they are also the 'Nutcrackers.' During another Peninsula battle the men heard the enemy loudly boasting that they would break the Buffs' necks. They heard the words *nuque*—neck—and *croquer*—to crunch—and voilà—nutcrackers! They got it wrong in much the same way as sailors call HMS *Bellerophon, Billy Ruffian*. And Casa Alta becomes 'the Case is Altered.'"

Shadforth jumped then scowled as a voice from a far corner said softly, "Here endeth the lesson."

If the military gentlemen were uncomfortable with Monsieur de Rossi, they were utterly frosty toward this fourth person in the room, a man who shared neither wine nor tobacco.

Younger than his companions—he seemed to be about thirty—he was tall and lean, with reddish-brown hair, startlingly blue eyes and a strong nose. He wore a loose jacket of cotton twill over trousers of fustian, a stout fabric woven from cotton and flax. No socks showed above his shoes, which were a poor man's "straights"—pointed shoes that fitted either foot, after a fashion. His footwear and clothing were the work of convict tradesmen from Hyde Park Barracks, across the town. While his appearance did not necessarily mean he was a convict, he was clearly a class below the other men.

Rossi had earlier introduced the young man to the officers as Nicodemus Dunne, a colporteur. But, they wondered, why was he here?

"What the devil is a colporteur anyway?" Crotty now asked irritably.

Dunne answered. "M. de Rossi . . . "—Rossi nodded apprecia-
tively—". . . is close, gentlemen, but I'm not a colporteur. A colporteur is a peddler of books and pamphlets, usually religious
matter. Neither am I a crier, nor a bellman. I am, in fact, a running
patterer."

The officers nodded. They knew that the role of a patterer was
to act as a walking newspaper, reciting stories and advertisements.
It was a service particularly useful for illiterates, as, indeed, most
of their soldiers were. In return, the patterer received small gra-
tuities from listeners and even more money from publishers if he
drummed up any business for advertisements or subscriptions.
But that still didn't explain why Rossi had brought him here today.
Or indeed, more to the point, why they had all been summoned.

Their nagging puzzlement was relieved only when the door
opened to admit a middle-aged, balding man who walked with
military stiffness. He carried a tall gray hat and wore an elegantly
tailored coat of dark blue woolen broadcloth cut away to tails to
reveal an oyster-gray vest above charcoal-gray trousers. These
were fitted with suspenders and highlighted boots with a mirror-
like shine to match his well-manicured fingernails. An ivory silk
scarf on a high stiff collar supported a slightly petulant face.

The four men stood instantly. "Sir," murmured the soldiers and
the magistrate.

But the patterer smiled broadly and said cheerfully, "Hello,
darling!"

His Excellency, Lieutenant-General Ralph Darling, Governor of
Britain's farthest-flung flyspeck, was not amused.

CHAPTER THREE

*The angel of death has been abroad throughout the
land; you may almost hear the beating of his wings.*
—John Bright, speech to the British House of Commons
(1855)

THE OFFICERS WERE VISIBLY SHOCKED BY THIS BRAZEN FAMILIARITY
with the governor. Were Dunne a free man—an immigrant or
an Emancipist—the governor could punish his disrespect by cutting him dead socially and making sure he received little or no
government support. Were he a soldier, he could be flogged. Even
as a ticket-of-leave man, a good-behavior convict excused from
government labor to pursue his own work—as Dunne was—his
parole could be revoked.

But, as only Rossi knew, and had earlier hinted to Dunne, Darling needed something, and badly enough to overlook insolence.
So the governor simply glowered, grunted and sat down, motion-
ing to the others to follow suit.

"Gentlemen," Darling began, "no doubt you are wondering why

I have called you together. So listen very carefully, I will say this only once. There is a mysterious and ominous development in the matter of the death of that soldier outside the public house."

"Sir," said Shadforth, "distasteful as it was—and I regret to say he was one of my men—surely it was just a murder for robbery or a drunken brawl? And he was only an officer. Why does it concern Your Excellency?"

"Because," said Darling, "of this. It came addressed to me by mail today."

He handed over an opened letter, bypassing Rossi, who seemed to know its contents. It was neatly written, with one corner folded down to contain a small copper, an English halfpenny.

The three men in turn studied the message:

The man I tore,
There will be more.
This is a clew:
First find a Jew.
Take care to choose him
Who knows the zuzim.

As several started to speak at once, the governor held up a hand. "In the interests of brevity, gentlemen, I can anticipate at least two obvious questions. No, I have no earthly notion what a *zuzim* is. And yes, this is about our murdered military man." He held up a small brass button. "This bears the emblem of the 57th. It was contained in the flap with the coin."

The governor turned to Dunne. "I have, I must say after much deliberation and with some misgivings, involved you in this because Captain Rossi is convinced you can help, as, he says, you have in the past. I'm persuaded that there is little chance of the conventional law officers or the armed forces solving the problem on their own. Someone is needed who can use more, shall we say, unconventional means." Darling then seemed to change tack. "Why were you transported?"

So, thought Dunne, the governor didn't know all about him. Or was it a trick? No one would expect him to remember the background of every one of the hundreds, perhaps thousands, of men and women he had seen paroled, but the life of every rogue was on record. And Rossi must have briefed him. Perhaps the wily old bird was using the lawyer's ploy of never asking a question unless he already knew the answer. Let's see where this goes, Dunne thought.

"I was sentenced in London to eight years for assault, although there was no serious injury, save to a gentleman's pride."

"Jove, that sounds a bit stiff!" interjected Crotty.

Very well, decided Dunne, I might as well have my say. "Stiff? Not really. In Britain's fair lands, as well as transportation there are floggings, pillories, stocks, ear-nicking, branding with hot irons." He ignored the rising color in Darling's cheeks and the warning shake of the head from Rossi. "There are still a hundred offenses punishable by hanging. At Newgate, a boy of ten was hanged for shoplifting. Two sisters—eight and eleven—were hanged for stealing a spoon. Dear Lord, a spoon!

"My heinous crime was to strike a Life Guards officer. It was during Queen Caroline's funeral. The mob only wanted to show they loved her, but the king's men called in the army. I merely protected a child who was being thrashed with the officer's sword."

"Even so," said Crotty, "eight years . . ."

"Tell us what your job was at the time," coaxed Rossi.

"Ah, there was the rub," replied Dunne. "They said I had betrayed their trust in me and that if I were a soldier they would have shot me. I was a Bow Street Runner."

The governor nodded coldly. "A policeman, yes. I will not attempt to conceal my disapproval of your actions . . . But, well, the past is past. Now we seem to need you to fight a common enemy. Your law-officer's skills as well as the fact that your new calling here, such as it is, allows you to keep ahead of news and abreast of gossip. And it permits you to see people and go places that are out of bounds to, and beyond the ken of, the captain's constables. Nevertheless, Captain Rossi will still direct his wardsmen, conductors and patrolmen to pay particular attention to the matter."

The governor rose abruptly. "I fear we may have a madman at large. Keep your eyes on your men, Colonel. Rossi will coordinate the campaign. I rely on you, Dunne, to solve the riddle of the letter. The government will doubtless smile on the continuance of your parole if you succeed. No fuss, mind. Not a word to anyone, especially not the damned press." He stalked out, trailing a "Good day."

"What about the dead soldier as a start?" Dunne asked Rossi.

"He's not going to tell you much. The hospital surgeon took only a cursory look and now our soldier's at attention in the ground. The leech did not note much, except that the victim's throat was slashed, as were his belly and, strangely, his ankles. The slashes were even and suggest that the weapon was a long, sharp knife. Now, let's be about our business."

As he separated from Dunne, Rossi paused and snapped his fingers. "There was one other odd thing. His mouth had been filled with fine grains. It was sugar."

———————

TWO THINGS WERE nagging at Nicodemus Dunne as the meeting broke up. Why, for instance, had the governor tolerated his insolence? He could think of no good reason. He had instantly regretted his rudeness; it was an undeserved slight. Still, it was done and could not be undone, so he shrugged and put the matter aside.

His main interest was in something that had *not* happened at the meeting.

In the corridor, he buttonholed Thomas Shadforth, a kindly man in his late fifties whose life was devoted to the 57th. He had soldiered there for twenty-six years, and two sons had followed him into the regiment. During the meeting, he had modestly left himself out of the mention of the bloody battle at Albuera, even though he was one of those badly wounded original Die Hards.

"Are you familiar with the 5th Regiment, Colonel?" asked the patterer.

"Certainly. Damn fine men. Fusiliers. Attached to Wellington." He barked a laugh. "And he was attached to them!"

Dunne raised an eyebrow. "Do they have an informal, affectionate name?"

"'Course they do. The 'Fighting Fifth,' the duke called them. They're also called the 'Old, Bold Fifth' and the 'Ever-Fighting, Never-Failing Fifth.'"

The patterer thanked the colonel and walked away. How strange, he thought, how very strange, that Captain Rossi should today profess ignorance of this time-honored custom of bestowing a nom de guerre on a regiment, when only the other day he had boasted of receiving his lieutenant's commission in, of all units, the 5th. The regiment might be never failing, but the police chief's memory seemed suddenly less reliable. Or was it? Was there something else at play?

Dunne discreetly opened a small notebook and, as he had been trained to do by the best thieves in the Bow Street Runners, penciled in a heading, "Persons of Interest," underneath which he wrote one name: F. N. Rossi.

CHAPTER FOUR

Whate'er men do, or say, or think, or dream,
Our motley paper seizes for its theme.
—Juvenal, translated by Alexander Pope (1709)

NICODEMUS DUNNE WALKED BRISKLY ALONG BUSTLING GEORGE Street, or the High Street as many still called it—some old settlers still even thought of part of it as Sergeant-Major's Row. His mind was already occupied with the case. He had held back from the truth about his immediate intentions in his last words with Rossi. Yes, he wanted very much to chase his Jew and talk to the surgeon, but the governor had told him to spy while he worked and he had an obligation to his listeners as well as to his stomach. So he went about his usual routine. He already had copies of the main newspapers—*The Australian, The Monitor* and *The Gleaner*—with only *The Gazette* to pick up.

Dunne's first call was, as always, on an Emancipist named Sam Terry, the richest man in the colony. Terry had been transported at the turn of the century for stealing either geese or 400 socks, no one quite recalled.

Dunne reported to Terry in a rough pub he ran in Pitt Street. There, among other business transactions, Terry took land titles as payment for gambling and drinking debts. Next door he ran a pawnshop for the poor. It was said that he held a fifth of all mortgages, more than the banks themselves, and owned rows of shops and dwellings.

He was reputed to be worth 50,000 pounds a year—that's as much as the Duke of Devonshire, marveled the patterer—so he could well afford the five shillings he gave each time to have the papers skimmed for him before anyone else. On this occasion, the dour Terry wanted only the latest shipping movements, commodity prices, news of contracts and property sales.

Next, Dunne backtracked to call on James Underwood, another former convict. He lived in a stone mansion near the Tank Stream, an infinite improvement, thought the patterer, on serving fourteen years for stealing a ewe. Underwood, too, was prepared to pay for his news, as he was too busy building ships and making gin to read the papers himself.

Dunne regaled the tycoon with a report of a duel on Garden Island. There had been no death or injury: "The combatants returned to Sydney, perfectly satisfied, in the same boat. The cause of the duel arose from a misunderstanding at cards." He then finished a selection from "Police Incidents" with the tale of Catherine Wyer, "who was charged by her husband with breaking four pounds' worth of crockery, picking his pockets and getting drunk on the proceeds and divers other scandalous outrages, to the subversions of all domestic economy. The bench sent her to the factory for one month, and Wyer said he would pay to keep her there."

But the item that most caught Underwood's ear was an announcement that Marr's Rooms in Castlereagh Street had received a new consignment of English willow cricket bats. Dunne knew that boys at play and often even the men of the two main clubs, the Australian and the military, used bats of ironbark or cedar to slog out their "notches," still so called because, paper being in short supply, the scorers notched wooden wands to tally runs.

Underwood shook his head at the story from the English papers that someone had suggested the ball be bowled *overarm*, and clapped his hands delightedly at the news that a match had been played on horseback!

The patterer next earned a handful of coins from a party of women resting in Macquarie Place, alerting them to the fact that rival apothecaries begged to solicit their attention to new consignments just received from overseas. There were household stalwarts such as aromatic vinegar for the headache, plants of Spain for toothache, essence of ambergrease, eau de luce for curing the bite of venomous reptiles, tincture of opium and its variation, mother's quieting syrup. And he told them of mysterious-to-the-male items: Venice treacle, gold-beater's skin, Grains of Paradise, colocynth essence, Dalby's carminative, even Dragon's Blood (special, at one and six per ounce). In deference to the ladies' sensibilities, Dunne dropped from the list Spanish Flies at two and six an ounce.

The pennies of bored and lounging soldiers earned them the news that a terrier at Brickfield village had killed sixty rats in one minute and that, in pugilistic news, "Three regular pitched battles took place, one for fifteen pounds, the second for ten pounds and the third for five pounds. All the parties were prisoners of the Crown who, together with seven others looking on in a like situation, were sentenced half for ten days in the cells on bread and water and the remainder for fourteen days on the mill."

Boos at these punishments turned to laughter when the soldiers next heard how Sarah Lackaday, "With locks disheveled, and fire in her eyes, threatening destruction to the whole of the police posse, a strong party of whom were put into requisition to put her at the bar. The charge against her was insolence and being excessively liberal in the use of her muscle to her fellow servants and mistress . . ." She was sentenced to "one month of the factory, where an attempt would be made to reduce her strength like Samson, by having her locks shorn off."

Their fun was interrupted by the sudden arrival of one of Rossi's uniformed men, who dragged Nicodemus Dunne out of earshot of the curious soldiers.

"The captain wants you, urgent like," he said excitedly. "He said to tell you that there's been another one!"

CHAPTER FIVE

It is evident that we are hurrying onward to some
exciting knowledge—some never-to-be imparted secret,
whose attainment is destruction.
—Edgar Allan Poe, "MS. Found in a Bottle" (1833)

THE POLICEMAN LED DUNNE TO THEIR DESTINATION, THE *New World* office. It was off the beaten track, near the Judge's House, on the better side of Kent Street, which ran behind the barracks.

Dunne had never visited the *New World* before, with good reason: it had yet to publish its first number. When he arrived, he soon realized there would be no new paper any time soon, if ever. From the outside, the building looked like a smoldering ruin. Most of the hardwood shingled roof had caved in, leaving only the stone-and-brick walls standing.

Captain Rossi stepped gingerly through the doorway to greet Dunne, who had pushed through a line of gawkers being held back by constables. Inside, surprisingly, part of the large open press room had remained relatively untouched by the flames. The fire had died down once the fuel of paper and roof batting was exhausted.

In one corner of the room stood a metal press similar to the one Dunne had seen at *The Gazette*. But that thought left the patterer's mind when, through the smoke and dust, he made out what was sitting on the exposed press bed and what, apparently, had taken the full pressure of the machine's powerful jaws.

It was what was left of a human head. An exploded human head.

Dunne gagged; it took him a major effort not to vomit on the floor. He had seen plenty of men and women die on the ship that had carried its cargo of convicts, including him. And violent death was a commonplace in the colony. Locals were used to seeing dangling hanged bodies, once eight in a row, over the walls of the George Street jail. But this, this thing, was the worst he had ever seen, a catastrophe of ruined bone and scattered, bloodied tissue. He turned away, shaking.

"Here's the rest," said Rossi quietly, pointing to the floor in the shadowy corner behind the press.

The headless body lay sprawled on its belly, arms and legs splayed. Dunne had never seen so much blood.

Rossi seemed calm as he asked, "How can you fit a head under the press?"

"Yes, well," said Dunne, collecting himself, "the assembly of type normally sits on the bed and then there's only room, between this type and the descending mechanism, for a padded frame and the paper about to receive the impression. But, if you haven't placed any type form or paper frame, or any other paraphernalia between the bed and the downward thrust—well, there must be just enough room for a head. Any locksmith will tell you that a human body can be squeezed through a window open no more than six inches. Just ask any of the thousands of burglars here."

Rossi held up his hands in mock surrender. "I didn't know you understood so much about printing."

Dunne smiled wanly, starting to feel less queasy. "You don't frequent newspaper offices without learning a little. And you should know, Monsieur, that on arrival I was assigned to *The Gazette*—before the outdoor life called."

Rossi nodded and turned his attention back to the body. "The decapitation was a clean cut. How? Knife? Sword? It's too neat for an axe."

The patterer looked around what was left of the composing room. Near the press stood a guillotine for cutting paper to size. "There." He pointed. "That blade would do the job as well as any in the Terror. And, judging by the blood around it, it did. But, Captain, the burning question—if you'll pardon my lapse in taste—is, who is our victim?"

They steeled themselves to look more closely at the shattered remains. Once the head had been eased from the maw of the press, they could see that the face was blanched from loss of blood but still showed hints of a leathery tan. The long hair was drawn back into a pigtail tied with a black lace ribbon. Dunne examined the head carefully, especially the right cheek and temple.

When they turned over the body, they found it was dressed in a shabby linen jacket over a cotton shirt. The trousers were of a rough weave and the chest-high linen apron was soiled with black drops and smears. All the clothes were otherwise clean, apart from where gouts of blood had fouled them. The boots, although well worn and often repaired, were clean and polished.

Rossi pointed to the apron and the corpse's blackened fingers. "A printer?"

"Most certainly," the patterer agreed. "But he was also once— and not too long ago—a soldier."

At Rossi's raised eyebrows, Dunne pointed to the victim's face. "What is left of the right temple and cheek is heavily pocked with deeply ingrained black specks. A soldier can never rid himself of the tiny powder burns and spots he gets there from firing a musket. I'd also wager that his teeth are blackened from biting cartridges. And the boots are army issue and kept in good order from habit."

Their conversation was interrupted by the arrival of two constables carrying a litter and a sheet of canvas. They were to remove the remains to the hospital in Macquarie Street for examination.

"If this is connected to the other murder and our murderer *is* deranged," mused Rossi, "is it possible he's left another message for us?"

The fire had spared no scrap of paper that might have offered a clue.

"Let's see what he might have been working at," said the patterer. "It's a forlorn hope, I know, but it may give us something."

There were no complete page forms of typesetting, as far as Dunne could see. Type was usually so scarce that any page had to be broken up as soon as it was printed and the characters distributed for use again. But then Rossi called out to Dunne; all he could find that looked like new work was a narrow and shallow metal tray—a galley—part-filled with lines of type.

"Can you read what the type says?" asked Dunne.

Rossi stood facing the open end of the unfinished galley. "I can't really make much of it." He bent closer and squinted. "It's gibberish to me. My eyes aren't what they used to be . . . But wait, the last line is clearer, after a fashion." He produced a quizzing glass. "It says, no, I give up. It just seems to say 'exobus SISSE.' Latin, perhaps?"

Any further discussion was halted by two new arrivals, who suddenly burst into the ruined room. The first was a short elderly man in clerical dress. He was followed by a figure who took all Dunne's attention.

It was a very young and very beautiful woman. She was tiny but perfectly formed—as far as the patterer could tell through the barriers of her walking-out ensemble, which covered her from chin to toe. Her full, high-necked red dress was frilled from knee to ankle and its leg-of-mutton sleeves ended where her white gloves began. Her tiny waist was nipped in by a broad belt that matched the long ribbons falling from a large feathered confection of a hat. Blond hair touched her shoulders.

In a town starved of women, she was a vision.

The young man was in love. Or lust. He didn't know which. Or care.

CHAPTER SIX

And when a lady's in the case,
You know, all other things give place.
—John Gay, *Fables* (1727)

RELUCTANTLY TEARING HIS ATTENTION FROM THE FAIR NEWCOM-er's solemn, handsome face, Nicodemus Dunne recognized the man as Laurence Hynes Halloran, publisher of *The Gleaner*.

From what the patterer could gather, Dr. Halloran had been an academic and schoolmaster in England and a chaplain in the Royal Navy at Trafalgar. In 1818, it seemed, his respectability had suffered a setback when he received seven years for forgery. On regaining his freedom he had opened first a school then a newspaper.

"Rossi . . . Dunne!" he said, seeming flustered. "Well, gentle-men. This is a pretty pickle. My dear, should you be here? All this, ah, blood . . ." At this he shooed his lovely companion out the door, even though she had not seemed at all distressed.

Halloran waved as she departed then turned back to Dunne and Rossi. "Goodness, my manners . . . that was Miss Rachel Dormin. She earns her living as a seamstress, but has evinced an interest in the workings of our colonial society at all levels and I have attached her to our intelligence-gathering enterprise. I believe in equal opportunity for the genders, you know."

He gestured defensively, as if expecting an attack from the other, less-enlightened males. When none was forthcoming he came back to the matter at hand. "This is terrible, terrible. I heard the news from one of your men."

"Do you know who the poor fellow is?" asked Rossi.

"But of course! He must be Will Abbot, the printer and publisher of the *New World*. I helped him to set up his endeavor."

"You would help a rival?"

"Of course. It was my Christian duty."

"Was he a free man?" asked Dunne.

"Naturally. He was an old soldier with an honorable discharge."

"Do you perhaps know his regiment?"

"As it happens, I do. I believe it was our own 57th."

At this, Rossi and the patterer exchanged glances, then Dunne went off on what seemed to Halloran to be a tangent: "Doctor, you are a man of erudition. How or where would we find out about an arcane piece of Hebraism, something that appears to be a cipher perhaps?"

The publisher preened himself. "Why, sir, it may sound immodest but you may do no better than ask my good self. I have deeply studied Hebraic lore and indeed did mission work among Jewish people in the East End of London."

"Well, sir," said Dunne, "what or who is a *zuzim*?"

"Ah," replied Halloran. "Are you familiar with this popular rhyme, which only the other day I heard some children in the street reciting?

> *This is the man all tattered and torn,*
> *That kissed the maiden all forlorn,*
> *That milked the cow with the crumpled horn,*
> *That tossed the dog,*
> *That worried the cat, that killed the rat . . .*
> *That dwelt in the house that Jack built.*

"Et cetera. Well, your mention of the word *zuzim* brings to mind that in a similar vein there is a Hebrew parable. It goes, in essence, if my memory serves me right:

> *Then came the Most Holy, blessed be He, and slew,*
> *The angel of death who had slain,*
> *The slaughterer who had slaughtered,*
> *The ox which had drunk,*
> *The water which had extinguished,*
> *The fire which had burned,*
> *The staff which had smitten,*
> *The dog which had bitten,*
> *The cat which had devoured,*
> *The kid which my father had bought for two* zuzim."

Dr. Halloran paused, pleased with his performance; then added, "The sainted Isaac Newton had the right of it when he wrote, as you will doubtless recall, '*Actioni contrarium semper et aequalem esse reactionem.*' "

Rossi looked blankly uncomfortable, but Dunne surprised both his companions (and perhaps even the shades of his childhood teachers) by nodding and saying, "Yes, I see, 'to every action there is always opposed an equal reaction.' "

"Indeed," said Halloran enthusiastically. "The Hebrew verse simply means that life is a chain."

Dunne nodded. "And there seems to be a running theme of retribution. Be that as it may, would I be correct in thinking that two *zuzim* are worth about a halfpenny?" The meaning of the coin in the governor's letter had constantly nagged him.

Halloran looked surprised. "Why, my dear sir, how did you know? Yes, indeed, the amount would be a halfpenny."

"And how widely known would the parable be?"

"Why, it would not be all that hard to stumble across. Possibly it could be found at the subscription library and reading rooms. Mr. McGarvie may well have it at his stationery warehouse. Even I have it in a volume at my office. And, of course, there have been Jews in Sydney since the arrival of the First Fleet."

Dunne nodded thoughtfully. He needed time to think about all that had happened. Even though he had found a Gentile instead of a Jew who knew the answer, the first riddle had indeed led them to a strange verse recording a cycle of faraway violence. Yet here and now they seemed involved in just such a cycle.

But where to next? Perhaps the corpse held more clues, he thought. He beckoned to Captain Rossi to follow and left Dr. Halloran idly wondering if a fire-damaged cast-iron Stanhope press would be a good investment. Although, if pushed, Halloran would have been the first to admit he had scant knowledge of printing.

Outside, the patterer hoped to see Miss Dormin again, but she had disappeared.

CHAPTER SEVEN

Riddles lie here, or in a word,
Here lies blood . . .
—John Cleveland, "Epitaph on the Earl of Strafford"
(1647)

Rossi and young Dunne walked back along Kent Street. The magistrate planned to turn off after a few blocks and return to his court, while the patterer continued across town to his ultimate destination, the hospital beside the Hyde Park prisoners' barracks.

"Why were we sent the halfpenny with the verse?" Dunne wondered aloud. "Apart from equaling two *zuzim*, what was its relevance?"

"I don't know," admitted Rossi "but I suppose it may be significant."

"Let's be logical," said Dunne. "Was the killer making the point that he was changing the parable's original currency into English coin?"

"Very well. So?"

"So, does it mean that he has also given much of the parable's wheel of death and destruction an English context? By 'English' I mean here, in Sydney. Yes, there *is* still an angel of death—our quarry. But forget the ox, the water, fire, staff, dog and cat, and reckon that, instead, there are Englishmen—here—at risk. And so far it seems it all has something to do with soldiery."

"And the kid?"

"I don't know. Maybe we can forget that, too. Or perhaps there is an English local equivalent that started the circle here."

"The victims in the verse kill each other," pointed out Rossi. "Our victims seem to have a common nemesis."

"Perhaps our angel would be happy for them to kill each other. But if they won't oblige, he will."

Rossi grunted. "You've overlooked the end of the loop—the Most Holy, who slew the angel of death."

"Yes, well . . ." The patterer had a sudden thought. "Perhaps our angel wants to be caught and punished. If so, he's not just taunting us, he's *guiding* us! So we *must* be about to receive another clue. Or there's one we've overlooked."

"Well," sighed the magistrate, "it's a poser, whichever way you look at it."

The patterer stopped in his tracks, turned to the magistrate and asked urgently, "What did you just say?"

"I simply said that it's a poser . . ."

"No, no—the last bit; you said, 'Whichever way you look at it.' "

"Well?"

"Well, indeed! Tell me, how exactly were you standing when you tried to read that last line of type?"

Rossi frowned. "Ah, I was facing the end of, what did you call it, the galley? Why, is that important?"

Dunne shook his head impatiently. "Were you at the head of the column of type or at the galley's open end? I mean, were all the letters upside down?"

"Why, no. When I come to think of it, I was at the open end and the letters were the right way up. Backward, of course, but . . ."

"Patience, Captain. The last line you tried to make out—it wasn't quite as unintelligible as the rest above?"

The magistrate agreed.

The patterer grabbed Rossi's lapel excitedly. "Let's go back to the scene of the crime and take another look at that typesetting."

———————

THE NEW WORLD was deserted, apart from one constable nearby, guarding against looting. Not that this was an automatic protection, Dunne thought as he saw the man hastily hide a bottle at Rossi's approach.

The patterer had always taken a professional interest in the colony's police. He knew that the mounted force, set up only a few years before to hunt down outlaws, was a success though accused of questionable tactics. But after more than ten years, the foot patrols labored under a welter of problems. They were under-strength, and pay and morale were low. Why, in the mid-'20s, in a force that should have hovered around eighty bodies at any one time, there had been twenty-five resignations and sixty or so sackings for drunkenness, dishonesty or other misconduct. And many constables were ex-convicts, causing suspicion or mistrust among all members of the populace.

"*Sed quis custodiet ipsos custodes?*" murmured Dunne.

"But who is to guard the guards themselves—Juvenal?" replied Rossi, earning a raised eyebrow from the patterer. "That's at least *one* piece of Latin that police chiefs know!" the magistrate said with a wink.

CHAPTER EIGHT

IN THE COMPOSING ROOM, THE PATTERER PICKED UP THE GALLEY OF type and then carefully, so as not to spill the tiny characters, centered it on a perfectly level stone-topped table. Keeping the lines of type firmly together by blocking them with a heavy metal wedge, he lightly coated the typeface with an ink-sodden dabber made of horsehair and wool covered with sheepskin. He next covered the inked surface with a sheet of paper and, with a clean padded roller, took an impression. He peeled off the proof to reveal a column, not one and a half inches deep, its lines in a very small typeface. On examination, this text proved to be an incomplete recitation of government orders, but the last line seemed to have no place in the report and the first line read, puzzlingly, "All eight point."

Dunne showed the proof to the magistrate. "It's hard enough to read now," he said. "The typeface is a very small one—it's called Ruby—so small that you can print more than a dozen lines to the inch."

Rossi looked at the galley proof and shook his head. "But that's damned odd. When *I* looked at the type I couldn't decipher the beginning, but could make some sense of the last line. Now the tables are turned."

The patterer laughed. "No wonder. You looked from the wrong end of the galley. A compositor masters the art of reading type in reverse and upside down. That's why we say, for 'be careful,' 'mind your *p*'s and *q*'s'—it's old compositors' lore, because *p* and *q* are the hardest letters to distinguish in reverse, along with *b* and *d*. You read what you thought was 'exobus SISSE' because you guessed correctly at the backward *e* and *s*. But you confused *d* in reverse for *b*, a backward numeral 2 for *S* and a reversed 3 for *E*."

Rossi squinted at the proof. "But even printed, that last line doesn't make sense. Now it reads: '32212 sudoxe!' "

"It suggests that Will Abbot didn't set that last line—and that whoever did wasn't really a printer. Oh, he understood a smattering, but not the rudiments. He simply set what he wanted to say just as he'd write it—from left to right. So it *prints* in reverse order."

"So, it is meant to say . . ."

"Exactly—exodus 21223! Given that our amateur printer made several mistakes, it may be a reference to the biblical Book of Exodus, chapter and verse."

———

As THE INVESTIGATORS were leaving what was left of the *New World* printery for the second time that day, heaven smiled on their quest for biblical enlightenment. For they spied in the distance a bulky figure emerging from the nearby Judge's House, which was now home to the newly arrived junior judge, James Dowling. The fellow steering a stately course for his carriage was the Reverend Samuel Marsden, an old man of sixty-three but still, with his great land-holdings, a leading figure in the colony even though his earlier powers were now in decline.

"Ah, capital!" said Rossi as he headed toward the cleric. "Who better to give us an opinion on matters spiritual than the gentle-man who was once assistant chaplain for the entire colony?"

The patterer hung back, clearly not as happy as Rossi to see Marsden.

"Well, you do all the talking," he muttered. "He'll ignore us if he knows I'm not free, pass-man though I may be. He even loathes men who have done their time. He'd probably like to cut me dead—literally—if I stepped out of line in any way. He's not known as the 'Flogging Parson' for nothing."

He ignored Rossi's snort and continued. "It's true. Why, as a magistrate he used to scourge suspects until they confessed. And he had a woman at the Factory chained to a log for two months."

Rossi simply snorted again and strode on, so Dunne kept silent and maintained a respectful pace behind him as they intercepted the minister.

Marsden was clearly interested in what was put to him as an official request and, after hearing the full details, agreed to help. He waved away a suggestion that perhaps he and Rossi should repair to a place that contained a Bible.

"No," said the minister. "My sight may be fast failing now, but it has only sharpened my mind. And I have lived the words of the Bible all my years. Tell me the references and doubtless I should be able to identify them."

"Well," replied Rossi, "I believe the book in question is Exodus, but after that all I have is a string of numerals—2, 1, 2, 2 and 3."

Marsden was silent for almost a minute, then said, "Hmm. As there is no Chapter 212, there are, it seems to me, only four possibilities that make much sense. There can be either two verses from Chapter 2—and they are verses 12 and 23—or two from Chapter 21—verses 2 and 23.

"The two verses from Chapter 2 I don't expect to be of much help to your cause. In verse 12, Moses kills an Egyptian for smiting a Hebrew and hides him in the sand. In verse 23, the King of Egypt dies but the children of Israel are still in bondage.

"In Chapter 21, verse 2 says that if you buy a Hebrew servant he shall go free in his seventh year of servitude. Perhaps you could draw a long bow and see some link with our system of penal transportation."

The old minister paused for breath. "Now, verse 23 may be the interesting one. Everyone has heard of it even if they don't know its provenance. It and the following verses read, 'If any mischief follow, then thou shalt give life for life, eye for eye, tooth for tooth, hand for hand, foot for foot, burning for burning, wound for wound, stripe for stripe.' That's all I can suggest to you."

After he had profusely thanked the departing minister, Rossi raised his eyebrows at Dunne.

"I don't know," said the young man. "The last verse seems to reinforce our belief that it is all about revenge, retribution, call it what you will. But does this advance our case at all?"

"I can't see it," admitted the magistrate. "But, anyway, you must admit that the reverend gentleman was very gracious and generous with his time. And you are wrong about him, you know. I believe he has a loyal band of convict servants he could not do without."

Yes, the patterer thought bitterly. They can't live with us and they can't live without us.

"Come!" said Rossi. "His Excellency will want to know. We should catch him at the barracks."

CHAPTER NINE

Seldom, very seldom, does complete truth belong to any
human disclosure; seldom can it happen that something
is not a little disguised, or a little mistaken.
—Jane Austen, *Emma* (1815)

Rossi and Dunne left the governor and carefully skirted the barracks' dusty parade ground to head for a gate onto George Street.

The barracks were surrounded by hammer-dressed stone walls ten feet high and two feet thick, which kept their fifteen-acre world private from the growing town outside. Drought was in its third year and the fountain at one side of the open ground was dry. Perhaps it always had been; Sydney, apart from ale and rum, was a dry town. The original prime source of water, the Tank Stream, had long become fouled, and fresh water was drawn now from the Lachlan Swamps four miles away to boost inadequate private wells. Carters hawked it at sixpence a bucket.

The only other movement near the parade ground came from

three soldiers on punishment detail. They were passing the shot—
each in turn bending to pick up a cannonball, straightening his
back and handing it on to the next fellow.

At Dunne's grimace, Rossi said, "You have no time for discipline?"

"Discipline, yes. Bastardry, no."

Rossi changed the subject and returned to the cause of the patterer's transportation. "Tell me, did the English really love Caroline?"

Dunne shrugged. "Mostly they were sorry for her. George was a
drunk and a debauchee. They say he only married her in return for
payment of his debts. Anyway, he was married already, wasn't he?"

"So they say." Rossi pondered for a moment how Protestant
England would have reacted to the secret bride, a Catholic widow
named Maria Fitzherbert, sharing the throne. Anyway, the marriage was a sham—not that the poor lady had any inkling. "Was he
married? Yes—and no," he continued now. "But that's as you well
know. You don't need me to tell you." His tone was chiding.

The patterer grinned and nodded. He did know the story, of
course. He had no personal memory of it—it had occurred back in
1785, after all—but he imagined that few in Britain would not know
the story, or some version of it: how the then Prince of Wales had
taken Mrs. Fitzherbert as his bride, in defiance of his royal father.

"How *did* Prinny hope to get away with the marriage?" asked
Dunne.

"Oh." Rossi shrugged. "I suppose he thought he could present a
fait accompli—and, to some extent, he did. He found a clergyman
in debtors' prison and offered him 500 pounds to clear his short-
ages. And he threw in the bait of offering a bishop's mitre. He had
his wedding."

"Did the clergyman get what was promised?"

"Do you know," sighed the captain, "I'm not sure. I imagine so.

But poor Mrs. Fitzherbert, alas. She hovered as the illegal 'queen' for years; the marriage was annulled, naturally. Then, of course, the prince in '95 properly married your Caroline of Brunswick— and you're right, it was only for money."

"Well, anyway," said Dunne, "I'm glad I have no interest in the royal family."

Rossi stared at him. "Perhaps your lack of interest is misplaced."

"Pardon?"

"Ah, well." The captain's frown closed down the conversation. As he walked away he muttered, "Ignore my meandering. Forget I said it."

NICODEMUS DUNNE WAS so preoccupied with thoughts of royal goings-on that he collided heavily with the first pedestrian he came across in George Street.

"Steady, Dunne!" said the offended target.

Only after he had apologized did the patterer recognize his victim. "Oh, Dr. Cunningham," he said. "My clumsy fault. How are matters with you?" He had not seen the ship's surgeon around the town since he had landed after his latest voyage some months before.

"I fervently wish I could go back," said Peter Cunningham wryly.

"Well, that's surely no problem. Just take a new berth."

Cunningham sighed. "If it were only that simple. No, I meant that I would like to be able to reverse my latest passage out here."

The patterer was puzzled, and it showed.

"Look," said Cunningham, "my voyage involved problems and left me with ghosts I wish I could exorcise. Surely you remember how your fellow prisoners imagined that, if they dreamed hard enough, they could perhaps go back to a time before the law took them. I've seen new arrivals walk backward onto the deck on landing—because they fancied that they were boarding to return! That's all I'm doing, hoping to turn back my last passage on *Morley*."

"Specifically, why?" asked Dunne.

"Well, since I left the navy, I've made five voyages to Australia as a surgeon-supervisor. I've cared for 746 prisoners and over these nine-odd years, I've lost only three."

"That's outstanding, miraculous. Is it not the best result ever? Why are you concerned?"

Cunningham grimaced. "Because some say a disease slipped ashore this time, carried by some soldiers' children—a disease that had never before been here: whooping cough."

The patterer knew there had been a fiery epidemic. "But no one could blame you."

"One of the victims was the son of a very important personage," said Cunningham. "He died."

"Oh." There was little more that Dunne could say. He changed the subject. "Well, I must away. I'm off to the hospital—don't concern yourself, I am well. I must consult a doctor on another matter."

Cunningham raised an eyebrow. "Be careful there. Don't get too close to anyone." Before Dunne could satisfy his curiosity about this odd remark, the surgeon had nodded and walked off.

CHAPTER TEN

. . . for a bird of the air shall carry the voice, and that which hath wings shall tell the matter.

—Ecclesiastes 10:20

Ox-wagons and an occasional carriage stirred the dust, but most Sydneysiders walked about their business. The patterer watched as a smart curricle went by, whipped along at a cracking pace by a young dandy and splashing through a mess of fresh dung and urine—to the consternation of a pedestrian who received the spray and shook an angry fist.

In this part of town, shops and houses of business, some dilapidated, some neatly painted and adorned with flower beds in window boxes, punctuated stands of more impressive private houses in the latest Georgian style.

Enterprising street traders noisily hawked oysters, apples and pies, their cries mingled with the exotic calls of parrots perched on shoulders and shopfronts. Parrots were everywhere in Sydney. People flocked to Cumberland Street hoping to hear a bird recite the Lord's Prayer and the Ten Commandments. Even in the colony's first breach-of-promise case, the patterer recalled, the court heard that a shy young suitor had taught a parrot to sing, "My heart with love is beating." Although that case had been heard several years before, the patterer had experienced a more recent reminder of the rather bizarre circumstances of the case.

This jolt to his memory had come one morning when he slept in late in his rented room in a cottage behind Government House. The cottage was one of two built by Mr. Francis Cox, a ship- and anchor-smith, for his wife, Frances, and their four children. Dunne paid one pound a week for board and fifteen shillings for food. On that particular morning, the clatter of his landlady, Mrs. Cox, in the kitchen downstairs had helped awaken him, but the sound that finally drove him into awareness of the advancing day was a strange voice. "My heart with love is beating," he finally decided the high, scratchy voice was saying. Again. And again.

Intrigued, he pulled on a banyan, the voluminous and thus discreet Indian silk dressing-gown that society regarded, alone among male *robes de chambre*, as suitable for a gentleman to wear before ladies. Dunne was, when he could afford to be, quite a dandy, although he usually wore simple working-man's dress, so as to merge into his general audience.

Dressed in his banyan, he made a rather grand entrance into the kitchen and found Mrs. Cox with her daughter, Sarah—and a gorgeously plumed parrot.

Sarah was an equally splendid creature, a young woman in her early twenties, with raven hair and a generous figure. The patterer was, he knew full well, not the only man to admire her. Three years earlier, in May 1825, she had sued Captain John Paine, a ship's master, for breach of promise. Miss Cox had agreed to marry Captain Paine, but he began pursuing others, first a young heiress, then a rich widow.

In court, Paine faced the accusation of having injured Sarah's reputation. She told the jury that she was a respectable girl who "kept good company and was never out late at night." The court believed her and awarded her 100 pounds plus costs. His Honor had upheld her honor.

One fact of the case was indelible in Nicodemus Dunne's memory: Captain Paine's failed defense had argued that Miss Cox had other beaus—and had produced as evidence the parrot sent to her by a rival suitor. It had been trained to say the very words that had woken the patterer.

"You kept the bird, I see," he said to Sarah, who was now better known as the consort of the lawyer who had represented her in court, Mr. William Charles Wentworth, firebrand publisher of *The Australian.*

"For sentimental reasons, Mr. Dunne," she said with a smile.

At that moment, a small child rushed into the room, panicking the parrot.

"My daughter, Timmie," said the young woman proudly, at the same time as she deftly rescued the bird.

"How she has grown!" said the patterer, who, in truth, had little idea of what a child's physical progress should be. "How old is she now?"

"Three years come Christmas," said her grandmother proudly. "Doesn't time fly?"

———————

BIRDSONG OF A different kind dragged Dunne from his reverie back to his slow promenade to the hospital. Shrieks of peacocks came from the gardens of a handsome mansion a block away. Often, the birds' shrill cries were drowned out by the wails of men being scourged at the Government Lumber Yard nearby.

With the smell of hops from Matthew Bacon's Wellington Brewery at his back, Dunne skirted the bold begging of a black man wearing a tattered corporal's red coat, a cocked hat and a brass nameplate that proclaimed him to be "Bungaree, King of Sydney Cove." The patterer could also see a group of blacks down an alley, fermenting the head-splitting grog they called "bull" from sugar bags soaked in a pail of water with old potatoes. There were other ways to make bull. Some publicans would let the "Indians" scrub out rum and brandy casks. The first rinse was still rich in alcohol. This bull was pay enough for their work.

A guarded coffle of government men shuffled to work dressed in a motley of gray, brown and yellow overalls. They held their leg irons clear of the ground in unconscious mimicry of ladies lifting their skirts. They were passed by a wagon groaning under its load, bound for a building site. Its full cargo of 350 bricks was hauled by twelve convicts—cheaper to run and more expendable than animals. They had pulled the cart from the kilns at Brickfield Hill a mile away, one of the five trips they had to do each day.

The idea of using convicts as beasts of burden wasn't new, thought the patterer. In earlier years, an enterprising Scot thought to introduce to Sydney the sedan chairs that carried people through the narrow streets of Edinburgh Old Town. He had planned to use assigned convicts as chair-men, but the scheme never caught on.

Between the barracks and the Cove stood the office of *The Gazette*. The patterer cribbed from all the papers but found *The Gazette* the most staid and pro-government, thus the least interesting, even though it had the most colorful history.

Nicodemus Dunne had never known the first editor, a Creole convict printer named George Howe. As George Happy or Happy George, he had been sentenced to death for shoplifting, then transported to Sydney and assigned to start *The Gazette* in 1803.

Happy George's son, Robert, who had succeeded his father in 1821, could hardly be called "Happy Robert," mused Dunne. The patterer had not seen Robert since an announcement—and Dunne recalled its odd wording—that he had appointed an editor because he was "debilitated by mental anxiety and domestic disquietude." Dunne decided that having been whipped in George Street by a certain Dr. Redfern for an insult printed in the paper could not have helped.

Although he rarely saw the new editor, a retired Wesleyan missionary named Ralph Mansfield, he idly wondered now if Mansfield had any knowledge of Hebraism that could help elucidate the clue in the letter. But when he entered *The Gazette* to grab an early copy—he usually took a dirty spoil rather than pay the proper nine pence—there were only printers on hand.

The composing room that day was probably the brightest interior in the town. Dozens upon dozens of candles were ranged over the type-cases to light the way for the compositors who were laboriously hand-setting every letter. A "printer's devil" was employed to change the candles regularly and make sure the candle grease did not trickle into the tiny type or onto the copy being set.

Two sweating men were working at the iron Albion press applying vertical pressure on the paper- and ink-coated type, which was regularly refreshed from ink-filled paddles. They printed only one side of the paper at a time. After each impression, another devil, called a "flyboy," whipped the sheet from the press and pegged it up like laundry for the tacky ink to dry.

Dunne was always impressed by the strength and rhythm of the pressmen, who could at best strike 240 impressions in an hour. Thus, a circulation run of a four-page edition could take up to twelve hours to print.

It all looked too much like hard work. So the patterer tucked his *Gazette* into the leather satchel that already contained latest copies of the three rival newspapers and left. Walking and talking were easier.

Rather than go straight to the hospital, the patterer went on to one of his best paying regular engagements, although it was one that always puzzled him. Ever since he had become free to work for himself, he had visited each week the Bank of New South Wales in George Street near the military barracks. He did not query the bank's strange location, sharing a building with the dismal Thistle Inn.

The oddness of the assignment lay in the fact that he was required to read a round-up of commercial news, much of it rather out of date, to a solemn audience of one man who never took notes. This was out of keeping, Dunne always thought, with the general efficiency of the bank. It had come a long way in the eleven years that had passed since it began trading as the colony's first bank, in cramped rooms in Macquarie Place opposite the site where the obelisk from which all distances were measured now stood. This location was known, widely and slyly, as "the center of the universe."

Certainly, the Bank of New South Wales could boast of being at the center of Sydney's business universe. Its only true rival was the Bank of Australia, begun in 1826 by wealthy pastoralist John Macarthur and his fellows. Most colonists spurned this institution, which was widely derided as the "Squatters' Bank," and stayed loyal to the Wales.

But no one was more loyal to the bank than the man to whom Nicodemus Dunne now, and always, reported—Mr. Joseph Hyde Potts. He had started as the bank's first employee, as porter and general servant, but Mr. Potts now used his penmanship, calligraphy and cleverness to draft official documents, even to design banknotes.

As he had done since his first day, Mr. Potts always slept on the premises, ever watchful but hoping never to have to use the rifle and case of pistols he kept handy. Only once had the iron chest that served as a vault for money and valuables been threatened. On that occasion, Mr. Potts had to see off a drunken burglar who climbed down the chimney.

This day, as usual, he and the patterer shared the cane-bottomed couch that welcomed visitors and customers while Dunne served a digest of London stock markets, fat lamb prices, wool sales, bills and bonds, land sales and shipping movements: much the same fare that Sam Terry had demanded.

Dunne could never quite fathom why the bank—which surely had its own intelligence sources as quick as those of any newspaper—needed him. But Mr. Potts always assured Dunne of the value of his news and paid him the handsome sum of six pounds a month for his trouble. Also odd was that this client insisted that the fee be paid into an account opened for the patterer, but the credits always showed up and Dunne shrugged it all off as merely a banker's eccentricity.

CHAPTER ELEVEN

Fair Cloacina, goddess of this place,
Look on thy supplicant with a smiling face.
Soft, yet cohesive, let my offering flow,
Not rudely swift, nor insolently slow.
—Ancient Roman prayer to a deity, entreating success
over the cesspit, or *cloaca* (translator unknown)

*E*VERYONE CALLED HIM SIMPLY THE OX. OR THE OX OF THE ROCKS, THE
violent Sydney village in which he lived and worked. The name
suited him, for he was tall and powerfully built, and after all he did work
as a slaughterman.

But The Ox was puzzled by another nickname. God knows, he thought,
why they called this place a "house of ease." In other ordinary language it
was a privy, an outhouse, the jakes, a shithouse. But house of ease?

He had even heard older people call it the "hole of the siege." And in his
case, "siege" was a good word. Because, again, for days he had been laying
siege to his bound-up bowels. And losing.

In the word of the apothecaries he haunted he was "costive," as it was
delicately called, constipated. Yes, he ate well, he thought, though perhaps

not as well as he had in the service. Now his teeth—missing, broken, worn down or decayed—left him unable to chew his food properly, even though his diet was as good as that of any other working man: maize bread and mutton or, when he couldn't afford that, Norfolk Island mutton. (That's what transported men called the despised substitute, goat.)

And there was always the chance of bullock's head brawn, boiled calf's head, cow's heel or calf's feet broth. You couldn't eat too much meat. That wasn't the problem. He'd always been known to his messmates as "old cannonball guts." They'd reckoned only a charge of gunpowder would move him.

No, he had tried everything in search of the sovereign remedy for his condition. Nothing worked—pray God it wasn't a sore! He couldn't afford to consult a leech, so he regularly plagued the twenty or so apothecaries who hung up their mortar-and-pestle signs throughout the town.

He'd loudly complained about his predicament in so many places that the whole colony must know of his failures. Castor oil was three and six a pint down the drain; Epsom salts were the cheapest chance at nine pence a pound, but they didn't succeed; senna leaves at one shilling an ounce were no answer; rhubarb root at the same price had the same negative effect; ipecacuan powder at two and six an ounce had a result but with the wrong orifice—it simply made him vomit.

During this latest visit, the apothecary had desperately suggested he consider the gum resin called asafoetida, until the disgusting smell convinced The Ox otherwise. So he was frantic enough to grasp at any help when he left the shop, even though the apothecary had promised to think of something and send word to him.

He had walked only a few hundred yards along George Street when he felt a tug on his coattails. Looking around and then down, he saw a barefoot urchin of streetwise teenage years.

"Bugger off," The Ox said, raising his fist to give the lad a cuff. He was surely a beggar wanting a penny, a child of the streets or even a stray from among the child offenders in the Carters Barracks at the southern end of town. There were hundreds of masterless children at large.

"No, sir," said the dusty boy. "Something for you." He held out a small envelope.

"Who from?"

" 'Pothecary, sir. 'Pothecary sent it. For you, sir. Said it was urgent."

Sure enough, the envelope was addressed to The Ox by name. He took pride in his ability to read.

"Said you could pay later," piped the scrawny street sparrow.

That idea appealed to the big man and he looked down at the boy. "Did you get anything for your trouble?" he asked.

"Threepence, sir."

"All right. Then here's a tip from me—bugger off!"

Much amused and hopeful, The Ox headed home.

———————

HOME, WITH ITS privy out the back, was a dingy room in a dilapidated house in The Rocks, near Cribb's Lane. The narrow thoroughfare, made by a butcher whose yard was nearby, was nondescript and anonymous to most outsiders. So if The Ox wanted to give directions to it, he simply said it was near a hotel, Jasper Tunn's Whale Fishery.

Now he was back at the siege-hole, reading a note from the envelope. It told him that the accompanying powder would work most efficaciously if swallowed while he was at stool in the squatting position. He prepared to take his medicine.

He sat over the latrine pit. In Sydney, if you were fortunate, cesspits emptied into a drain or the mess seeped into the surrounding soil. Many, *however, overflowed or even leaked out under adjoining buildings. Some people simply emptied their chamberpots into street gutters or even threw their contents onto the street out of a window. The warning cry, "Watch under!" was so common that human emissions were generally known as "chunder."*

The only people sanguine about the unwanted abundance of dung were the men called rakers—usually Celestials—who collected nightsoil to spread on their market gardens. Fullers of cloth would seek urine but it was rarely pure.

Hoping finally to end his lonely vigil, The Ox obeyed the note's instructions. He was ready. Optimistically, he had set beside him what were called arse-wipes—paper was scarce in poor households, so arse-wipes were usually old cloths or even small piles of dried cut grass. Some men, old salts come ashore, stuck with their maritime habits and used a sponge and a bucket of seawater.

In accordance with the instructions, The Ox had a beaker of water, half-filled, into which he mixed white powder from a spill of paper in the envelope. He swirled around the mixture then, as instructed, swallowed it in one gulp.

He sat awaiting results. Which soon manifested themselves as increasing pain in his belly, pain that he felt spreading to his muscles and extremities. He tried to call out for help but his throat was too painful, as if it had been scalded, and he found breathing difficult.

Before he lost consciousness, he felt himself lose control of his bladder and his bowels began—finally—to empty. The pain was beyond endurance.

Waking briefly from his faint—he didn't know for how long he had lost his senses—he knew that his agony was worsening. The icy chill settling throughout his limbs did not diminish his pain.

As he jerked against the privy wall then slid to the dirt floor, his bowels, mouth and nose voided blood. The Ox was dying, not even as quickly as one of his slaughterhouse victims.

THE SMELL OF *feces, human as well as animal, was usually unremarkable in much of the town. Even the grandest manor might have runnels of noxious waste flowing, not so freely, close beneath polished floorboards and Turkish carpets.*

But no near neighbor could for long ignore the stench of The Ox's violent last relief at the siege-hole. When a nose-holding fellow lodger finally investigated and pushed open the privy door, he turned tail and ran, yelling for help.

At first, he believed that the figure on the floor was alive. It still seemed to be moving and a low groaning sound arose from it. But the movement simply came from Lucilia cuprina, *the blue-black blowfly, and perhaps 60,000 of its cousins at work, as did the drone that accompanied their feasting. They heaved on the carcass as they searched for new parts in which to plant their eggs, the millions of eggs that would soon hatch into maggots.*

Someone was dead, awfully dead.

IN AN APOTHECARY'S *shop in Pitt Street, not far from Sam Terry's houses, the pill-and-potion purveyor looked up and smiled as a customer, whose clothes he recognized, came in. A scarf worn high hid the newcomer's face.*

As the apothecary wrapped the customer's purchases, he said, "So that's two ounces each of peppermint and magnesia lozenges, each at five pence per ounce; that's one shilling and eight pence. And four shillings for a lancet—you can't be too careful with boils—that's a grand total of five and eight pence." He added, *"Did that mixture deal with the rat?"*

The customer nodded. "I fervently hope so. Good day to you."

———————

So IT WAS that Nicodemus Dunne, when he finally arrived at the hospital in Macquarie Street, had not one but two interesting bodies to survey.

CHAPTER TWELVE

O, that it were possible,
We might but hold some two days' conference
With the dead!
—John Webster, *The Duchess of Malfi* (1623)

ALONGSIDE THE HYDE PARK PRISONERS' BARRACKS, SYDNEY'S general hospital loomed large, three graceful blocks in the classical colonial colonnaded style. As Nicodemus Dunne walked east up King Street, past St. James's Church, he acknowledged that the pleasing pile nonetheless deserved the rather unbecoming label bestowed on it by the public, the "Rum Hospital." This was not because its patients were all victims of the ardent spirit (although many undoubtedly were), but because the whole massive enterprise had been floated, so to speak, on an ocean of rum.

It was no secret to Dunne or any other resident that the hospital had been built a dozen years earlier only because its contractors were given a monopoly on importing the colony's rum for three years. Even then the construction cost them little; the government supplied convict builders, working bullocks and oxen for rations.

The patterer had never met the most widely known of these contractors, Dr. D'Arcy Wentworth, who had died only the previous year. He was better acquainted with one of the late doctor's sons, William Charles Wentworth, a businessman, explorer and lawyer who published *The Australian*, baited the governor and wooed Miss Sarah Cox.

Old D'Arcy's past was now discreetly veiled over. He had been acquitted at least twice of highway robbery in England before going into exile in Australia—where he found fame and fortune, helped immeasurably by the chance to sell 60,000 gallons of rum. He had even taken up the running of the new hospital, with Dr. William Redfern (the choleric gentleman who had flogged the hapless *Gazette* editor), a surgeon who had been sentenced to death, then to transportation, for involvement in a Royal Navy mutiny.

Entering the hospital's northern wing, Dunne felt the apprehension that such institutions elicited in all people. These were places you were lucky to escape from alive; all advice was to stay out— especially if you were sick!

Tales of privations from the hospital's early years still chilled Sydneysiders. The convict staff had been accused of theft and rape. The rations, certainly, were only cheap meat and flour; those unable to stomach this diet had to trade with citizens on the street outside. The room designated the kitchen had instead become the death-house. And dysentery victims, the most numerous patients (after those with venereal disease), had to stagger to outside privies.

The patterer was still inwardly shuddering at the ghosts conjured by the mere proximity of the place when a hearty voice echoed through the main entry. It came from behind an outstretched hand, unseasonably heavily gloved.

"Hello, I'm the doctor. Have a lozenge."

The speaker was a very tall man of forty or so years, with a shock of curly brown hair escaping from a wide-brimmed hat. He had a shy, discolored smile. The patterer knew him by sight as Dr. Thomas Owens, but apart from that he was an unknown quantity. His origins were unclear and he seemed to prefer keeping it that way. But that sort of secrecy was common in the colony, and the patterer had heard that Dr. Owens's abilities were unimpeachable.

As he spoke, Owens held out a paper bag filled with diamond-shaped confectionery. "I always offer these to visitors entering the hospital," he said cheerily. "These are peppermint," he added, pointing, "and your tastebuds and olfactory organ will appreciate the relief they offer in the face of the noxious miasma that invariably inhabits a house of sickness. These other lozenges are of tolu, a stomachic agent of fragrant balsam. Even I, inured as I am to grisly sights and effluvium, find tolu useful to settle an interior unnerved by exposure to corruption. Do not hesitate to tell me if, or when, you require one of those."

Dunne duly took a peppermint and sucked it thoughtfully as they walked along a corridor flanked on one side by a ward of coughing, occasionally groaning patients and on the other by a room that, incongruously, was filled not with people but with stuffed birds and animals.

"Don't believe all the stories you hear," said Owens suddenly, seeming to read the patterer's initial gloomy thoughts. "The hospital has been reformed in many ways. Those taxidermy subjects are the only things we *want* to see dead!" At this he peeled off his gloves.

"Oh, we have had to share with other birds of a feather in this institution. Why, until a few years ago the central wing was occupied by judges and officers of the Supreme Court. Truly a case of putting *habeus* and *corpus* together, what?" When Owens clapped his hands, Dunne noticed he had scaly and scarred palms and fingers, no doubt what they called "doctor's hands," with localized sepsis caused by the bacteria commonly transmitted from patients.

They arrived at the dissecting room, a large area well-lit both by tall windows and by candles and oil lamps in wall sconces and portable holders. A workbench along one wall was littered with glass phials on stands, chemical retorts and similar alembic apparatus.

Dunne's gaze took in the glass-doored wall cabinets and shelves. These exhibited metal basins, bleeding bowls, clamps and probes, and various saws and knives. Some of the most fearsome instruments were also works of art, their handles decorated with sharkskin, mother-of-pearl or tortoiseshell. There were also trepan sets for drilling into the skull.

Apart from these instrument cases, the only other furniture was three long, wide tables. These were scored along their tops by long, deep grooves that led into drains over enamel buckets. The dominance of the tables in the room was accentuated by the sinister magnetism of the bodies resting, under blankets, upon two of them.

"We don't have many visitors here," said Owens. "Living ones, that is," he added slyly.

But Dunne wasn't listening to the doctor's black humor. He was mesmerized by the outlines on the tables. One blanket obscured two distinct mounds. He pointed.

"Is that . . . mine?"

CHAPTER THIRTEEN

The voice of the dead was a living voice to me.
—Alfred, Lord Tennyson, "In the Valley of Cauteretz"
(1864)

"INDEED IT IS *YOUR* BODY, AS YOU SAY," SAID DR. OWENS ENTHUSIAS-tically. "Its companion is another gentleman recently brought here. I have performed postmortems on both. Two in a matter of days. Dear me."

"Do you handle many?" asked Dunne.

"Oh, we would only deal with, ah, cases of suspicious death—those the coroner cannot comfortably rule as having 'died by visitation of God.' And we are allowed to anatomize the bodies of prisoners hanged at the jail. That keeps us on our toes, mind. They hang up to fifty poor devils a year, y'know. What remains ends up in an anonymous lime pit.

"It is rough justice, Mr. Dunne. As is even flogging, to my mind. That's one of our more unfortunate duties, y'know—to supervise, witness, the scourgings next door at the barracks or down at the Lumber Yard." He snorted. "As if they need a surgeon to tell them that even after four strokes the cat draws blood. Why do they need to be told what a canary of a hundred strokes will do?

"But enough of that. About the first murder, the soldier at the public house, I can tell you little that you probably haven't heard already from Captain Rossi, who, as you know, has discussed it with me. Now, of course, the body is lying in the Sandhills cemetery. At the time, we studied the exterior of the man only briefly, the cause of death being so obvious: calamitous loss of blood following a cut to the throat. Expiry was almost instantaneous. The lacerations to the abdomen and ankles were profound but largely superficial. But I'm sure you've already been told this."

"Yes," said the patterer. "Although one thing has been troubling me. What did Captain Rossi mean when he said there was sugar in the man's mouth?"

"Well, that *was* interesting. Of course, by the time he was examined it had largely dissolved, but there's no doubt his mouth had been filled with what was clearly fine-grained sugar. Not the irregular pieces people make by scraping at a sugar cone, highly refined stuff. There's something else in line with that—but I will delay mentioning it until a more appropriate, logical time."

Dunne was puzzled but decided to let the matter lie. "Is there anything else you can tell me about the victim?"

"I can tell you he was attacked from the front and also, from the fatal wound I deduce that the killer was Bollocky Bill."

"You know his name?" asked the patterer incredulously.

"My apologies," replied Owens with a laugh. "I was slipping back into the idiom of my military days. Bollocky Bill was the derisory name given to the soldier who broke the rhythm of any cooperative function, say arms drill, because of his left-handedness. He ballsed it up. Your killer was sinister, literally. But that's all we know."

The doctor waved at the covered, complete body nearby. "By the way, this other fellow also died hard. He said he wanted to and he did indeed."

The younger man frowned. "What's your meaning?"

"Well, he was poisoned in a most painful and pitiful manner. In point of fact, he ingested enough arsenic to kill a team of horses or a plague of rats."

The patterer was curious. "Why did you say he wanted a hard death? Did he leave a farewell note?"

"In a manner of speaking, yes. A note was found near his body that gave explicit instructions on the method of administering the poison. You certainly, however, don't expect a man of his class and background to take that particular way out of this vale of tears."

Dunne felt a sudden tingle of anticipation. "What of his background and class?"

"See for yourself." The doctor turned down the blanket and they looked down on a tall middle-aged man with a trunk built like a barrel. Dunne tried to avoid staring at the long cut from breastbone to belly, which had been roughly sewn up. He understood vaguely that this was the primary cut in anatomical dissection. Indeed he had even read that early surgeons named the knife to perform this crucial leading incision "Follow me."

The corpse reeked of the vinegar with which it had been washed. But, said Owens, this was a distinct improvement on the earlier encrustation of excrement and dirt. The skin was white under a pelt of dark hair, except for the hands, which were deeply tanned up to the wrists. The face, too, had a curious tan: It ended about an inch above the eyebrows and just below the chin at the Adam's apple.

Owens watched the patterer keenly, with the hint of a knowing smile. "Think about the coloring," he said. "It is unlikely to be what is commonly called a farmer's tan, or a laborer's tan—these arms, neck and brow have not seen sunlight for years. But what if I said to you that I have often seen such solar pigmentation—when the face is always shaded by a military cap's visor, the arms by unchangeable uniform sleeves, the neck by a high collar . . ."

"You're saying that he was a soldier?"

"Indeed. And not just any soldier. Observe!"

Owens dramatically and triumphantly pointed to the corpse's shoulders. On the left was a tattoo, the Roman numerals "LVII," and on the right the words "Die Hard."

Dunne shook his head in disbelief. "Die Hard" and "LVII"—the man was yet another, the latest, the third, dead soldier of the 57th Regiment!

CHAPTER FOURTEEN

Death hath a thousand doors to let out life:
I shall find one.

—Philip Massinger, *A Very Woman* (1655)

"YOU MENTIONED A NOTE," SAID THE PATTERER TO DR. OWENS. "May I see it?"

The doctor gingerly produced from the side bench an envelope, a spill of paper and a single small sheet bearing a short message. All were still soiled with excrement and were terribly malodorous.

Wishing he had another lozenge, Dunne read, "To work efficaciously, swallow all at once in small water while at stool."

Even before his brain registered the meaning of the words, he recognized the writing—it was the same script used by the author of the letter to Governor Darling, the letter that had begun the quest. And the patterer realized now what the backward-slanting characters had always indicated: The writer was left-handed.

Distantly, Dunne heard the doctor saying, "We examined the

vital organs and it was, without a doubt, arsenic, commonly used as vermin bait. And available at any apothecary's—you can buy a pound for two and sixpence."

Owens looked pained when the patterer asked if he was sure of his analysis. "There is no doubt about such matters these days." He explained that the detection of poisons had advanced greatly since the pioneering work in Spain fifteen years earlier by Dr. Mathieu Orfila. "Once doctors could not do much more to identify a poison than interpret a victim's symptoms, or even rely on smelling the breath or vomit. For instance, prussic acid is apparently given up to the investigator by a distinct odor of almonds. But heart's-ease—useful in itself—when crossed with some other plants can give a false scent of prussic acid . . . Anyway, there were arsenic grains in the envelope."

The doctor's paean of praise for advances in chemistry washed over Nicodemus Dunne. He was stunned by the latest development. Bodies everywhere! He felt like a crow in a field of carrion. He took quick notes on the unexpected corpse, but also realized that he should concentrate on pursuing the case of the dead printer.

At a nod, Owens turned and lifted away the blanket covering the remaining body and its head. The trunk and limbs had been cleaned with a disinfectant but Dunne still caught the scent of growing putrefaction.

The doctor first remarked that the larger body part was not marked in any significant manner, then went on: "The deceased was a well-nourished male in his forties, almost six feet tall—allowing for the head, of course. The body tells us little else. Now, the head . . ."—and here Owens prodded the scorched and shattered mass with a silver instrument—". . . tells us much. I will come back to the injuries but, first, a few general remarks . . . Only one eyeball, the right, remains intact." He paused. "Y'know, once an anatomist would have shone a lamp onto it . . . a very old-fashioned concept, of course."

"What was the point of it?" asked the patterer.

"Oh, the desire that the light might bring up the reflected image, from the moment of death, of the killer. Some thought the eyeball retained such an accusation."

"Is there any basis of truth in it?"

Owens, the modern man of science, waved away this talk of past superstitions. "Most certainly not, but old beliefs hold on. To the matter at hand: He *has* most probably been a soldier"—at this Dunne nodded, pleased—"as the powder burns on the right side of the face indicate. But more of that later."

"And his teeth?" prompted the patterer.

"Certainly, they are blackened by powder and by chewing tobacco," Owens replied. "A printer, like many tradesmen, often chews plug tobacco or snuff instead of smoking because their close manual work makes it difficult to keep a pipe alight or to take snuff nasally.

"And here's the completion of the thought I left dangling earlier, when we discussed the mouth of the first victim and the sugar found within it. With our man now, not all the brown or black, hard and viscous matter in *his* mouth was a mixture of tobacco and cartridge spillage over years. No, the cause wasn't Brazil's best twist or the army's finest black powder. Because of the proximity of the fire, his mouth contained a melted mass that looked like treacle. It was burnt sugar. Sugar, again," he repeated, as if Dunne needed the point emphasized.

"In greater detail," the doctor continued, "a portion of the frontal bone, immediately above the left eye, was burst in. The orbital

margin of this bone was also destroyed, as was a corresponding part of the roof of the orbit . . . The separated piece of bone was broken into several parts and pressed in on the dura mater covering the brain . . ."

"Whoa!" interrupted Dunne. "In layman's terms please, Doctor."

"Very well. There was massive injury above the left eye and bone from it pressed in on the dura mater—the tough, fibrous membrane outermost of the three coverings to the brain and the spinal cord. To continue, the skull was fractured and the comminuted—very well, pulverized—portion of bone forced into its cavity, at least a quarter of an inch within the internal surface of the frontal bone."

Owens pointed to the front of the skull. "When the brain was examined, the anterior part of the left hemisphere, corresponding to the external injury, was covered with a thin layer of extravasated blood—that is, forced out from blood vessels to diffuse through surrounding tissue. I don't imagine you would wish to see the specimen of fluid found there of a semi-purulent—suppurating—nature?"

The patterer shook his head. So many new thoughts were running through his brain that once again he was not paying full attention to the doctor, who was now saying, ". . . it is somewhat extraordinary that the ball did not do more damage."

Dunne whispered, "What ball?"

The doctor cocked an eyebrow. "What ball? My dear sir, the printing press doubtless crushed the skull nastily, but it alone did not kill him. Oh, dear me, no. He was probably dead before that Shot, sir, shot! Here's the ball."

Dunne leaned against the one vacant dissection table, his mi weighed down by this amazing new knowledge, his hand v the ammunition that Owens had casually tossed him. It wei about an ounce but felt like a cannonball.

He heard the doctor explain that the powder burns on the *left* side of the face were not, of course, from musket use, but from a weapon held close to the head. The killer would have been either left-handed if shooting from behind, or right-handed if firing from in front. The only certainty: The shot came from low down.

Dunne hurriedly thanked Dr. Owens then left the hospital, hoping to catch Captain Rossi at his office. The business could not wait until tomorrow.

That was Sunday. Which meant church. And cricket, of course.

CHAPTER FIFTEEN

È sempre bene
Il sospettare un poco in questo mondo.
(It is always better, in this world,
To be a little suspicious.)
—Lorenzo Da Ponte, libretto for Mozart's *Così fan tutte*
(1790)

SEVEN BLOCKS BACK ACROSS THE TOWN FROM THE HOSPITAL, ON George Street, magistrates' courts and a police office now stood under an elegant dome at the southern end of an area called Market Square, which had been laid out eighteen years earlier.

Admiring the building for which he was headed, the patterer mused that, ironically but in the best traditions of the colony, this home of thieves had been designed by a criminal, a pardoned forger named Francis Greenway.

The courts had risen, but the cluster of milling people through which Nicodemus Dunne worked his way still had unfinished business in the area. When the locals had completed their day's duties, there would be an almost carnival atmosphere in and around the markets, which stayed open until late on Wednesday and Saturday nights. As well as stalls offering fruit, vegetables, meat and poultry, there were general stalls to tempt visitors, who were also entertained by jugglers, dancers, gypsy musicians, wandering food-sellers and peddlers. And there would be, of course, pickpocketers and pimps procuring for the town's many brothels.

Some of the crowd were already bent on having a drink or more at nearby hotels. They would "work and burst," a wry saying that meant that after a week's labor they would spend all their earnings on one long binge.

Others would pause to be entertained—rather than educated as the authorities intended—by the sight of wretches sentenced either to the large wooden pillory or to the stocks nearby. Dunne saw that this time the four stocks, wooden frames with holes for imprisoning ankles and wrists, were empty. Sometimes the stocks were even used as flogging restraints, when the iron triangles were too busy.

The pillory, bars atop posts with apertures for prisoners' hands and heads, and wide enough to accommodate two victims, now confined only one poor soul. One of his ears was bloodied, having been nailed to the frame, an additional punishment meted out for anything ranging from perjury to selling underweight bread.

It was small comfort, but Dunne knew the prisoner's ordeal would be over by nightfall. He would be free of the strength-sapping and muscle-wrenching suspension and inactivity, and from the intermittent showers of market refuse from jeering bystanders. The patterer had once heard the punishment described as "a civilized crucifixion."

At least prisoners here were not left out overnight, he thought, even if only to protect them from the rats in the marketplace or those from the abandoned burial ground next door, which bred among the often-exposed old graves, disturbed only by thugs and robbers. A fence kept out rooting pigs, but not these rats, which literally rose from the dead.

Deep in his gloomy thoughts, the young man bumped into Captain Rossi on the steps of the columned entrance to the law offices.

"Ah, Dunne," said the policeman. "Can we meet in half an hour in the taproom?" He pointed toward the Market House Hotel.

This suggestion suited the patterer. He had neglected his pattering work of late and welcomed the opportunity of a captive audience again. In the crowded bar he was soon busy.

To a group of sunburned men in long smocks, clearly farmers in town with their produce or animals, he retold from one of his newspapers the story of the bloody and brutal end to a dogfight at Brickfield village. Two bull terriers had forced a stalemate when they sank their teeth into each other and neither would let go. To prove his charge would fight on in any circumstances, one owner had chopped off the animal's feet. He lost his wager.

Dunne then sold an advertisement to a drinker. He helped him with a prepared document that needed only names and dates filled in. There was always great call for this form. The stock advice read:

I the undersigned do hereby Caution the Public, not to give credit to my Wife _____, as I will not be answerable for any debt she may contract, she having left my house on the _____ instant, without any cause whatsoever, and which she has repeatedly done.

At the end was room for a name and date. The newspaper's rate was eight lines for two and six plus a penny per extra line. The patterer charged the man for ten lines; two shillings eight pence. He could keep sixpence of that for himself, and charge the man threepence for taking the notice to the printer and making sure it appeared.

Next, he related to drinkers how "Jeremiah Gerraty, in possession of a proboscis highly carbuncled, was charged with reveling in Bacchanalian joys, till Morpheus muzzled him and laid him on his back in the middle of George Street. For this, two hours' lounge in the stocks."

To a group of women smoking and drinking together, away from their men, he shared the authorities' regret that "We have no bathing place for the fair sex of Sydney. At present females are debarred from this enjoyment, which in many cases is necessary to restore health."

The women showed more interest when he alerted them to the fact that J. Wyatt's cheap wholesale and retail warehouse had just received Leghorn bonnets at twenty-five shillings and upward, children's beaver hats and bonnets with feathers, twelve and six each, and ladies' white stays, ten to twenty-five shillings per pair.

As always lately, he avoided relating any of the small stories that referred, with details officially played down, to the three recent murders.

He had finished his recitations and ordered his first glass of beer when, over the sea of straw, beaver and kangaroo-skin hats, he saw a familiar face heading his way. Nicodemus Dunne was pleased. He liked Alexander Harris, an educated and intelligent man who described himself as an emigrant mechanic, and whose shrewd opinions the patterer valued.

As he approached his friend, Harris politely refused an invitation to drink from a man he did not know who was already at the bar. When the man had gone, the mechanic declared, "I can't help observing a remarkable peculiarity common to them all—there is

no offensive obtrusiveness about their civility; every man seems
to consider himself just on a level with all the rest, and so quite
content either to be sociable or not, as the circumstances of the
moment indicate as most proper."

"That's quite a mouthful, and rather a philosophical turn of
mind for a Saturday in a taproom," Dunne remarked. Yet at the
same time he wondered if this were true.

Harris nodded. "I only have a moment, but, yes, I have been
thinking greatly on my fellow man, hoping that the lot of all may
improve. I simply cannot get out of my mind a disturbing experience I just had in Bridge Street, at the Lumber Yard. I had to pass
the triangles, where they had been flogging incessantly for hours.
I saw a man walk across the yard with blood that had run from his
lacerated back squashing out of his shoes at every step he took. A
dog was licking the blood off the triangles . . . and the scourger's
left foot had worn a deep hole in the ground by the violence with
which he whirled himself round on it to strike."

Harris ended this grim tale and excused himself for it, just as
Captain Rossi bustled through the low doorway.

"Great news, sir!" Rossi said as he motioned for a nobbler of
rum. "We are finally making progress. And I have very special
news for you, something very pleasing, I'm sure!"

At this, Harris made a discreet departure.

Intrigued though the patterer was at the prospect of Rossi's
news, he insisted on first relaying his own startling intelligence
from the hospital visit, about the unsuspected death by firearm and
the emergence of yet a third victim, the poisoned army veteran.

In truth, these were the only positive new factors he could grasp
and juggle. Of course, he had suspicions, riddles and puzzles.
Something about the *Gleaner* publisher Dr. Laurence Halloran's

avowed Christian charity toward the dead rival publisher did not ring quite true. Even Captain Rossi's clear ignorance of his old regiment seemed rather odd. And what, nagged a voice at the back of his mind, had Dr. Cunningham meant by his hint to avoid close contact with anyone at the hospital? Did he in fact mean a medical colleague, Dr. Thomas Owens, perhaps?

But Dunne was also conscious of the overriding dictum of the Runners, passed down from their founder, Henry Fielding: Never take anything at face value; suspicions, hunches and doubts are useless without proof. Sound advice, mused the patterer. So he would take all the evidence with a grain of salt—even the mysterious grains of sugar.

He turned to Rossi. "So, what's your news?"

CHAPTER SIXTEEN

Each lordly man his taper waist displays,
Combs his sweet locks and laces on his stays,
Ties on his starch'd cravat with nicest care,
And then steps forth to petrify the fair.
—Bernard Blackmantle (C. M. Westmacott),
The English Spy (1825)

"I HAD INTERESTING CONVERSATIONS WITH DR. HALLORAN AND Miss Dormin earlier," Captain Rossi began. "The publisher tells me that the man Abbot was originally an American printer who had supported the loyal—to the Crown, that is—forces in the war of 1812, before having to leave his home and business for Canada. He ultimately enlisted in, or was pressed into, the 57th."

The patterer raised his eyebrows but was not surprised.

"But, my boy," Rossi continued, "the very important intelligence is that we can now more accurately estimate the time of the murder. The doctors, I gather, could not be sure of that because the fire distorted the usual signs, such as rigor mortis. We do have a witness, however, to shed new light on the case: Miss Dormin! That's why she came to the scene with Dr. Halloran, to tell us. But she became upset, and left abruptly. When she had recovered, she was able to tell me that she saw the printer, alive and well, on the morning of the fire. She was a visitor to the shop, by arrangement, to collect a manuscript—I believe they call it 'copy.'"

"What else did she say?" asked Dunne, trying not to appear eager for any crumb about the young lady.

"I suggest you ask her yourself," replied Rossi, with a smile. "She will attend morning service tomorrow at St. James's. *Bonne chance!*"

———————

Nicodemus Dunne left the taproom determined not to rely simply on luck. He headed diagonally across George Street to the huge emporium on the corner of Market Street known as the Waterloo Stores.

He had once done a signal service for the proprietor and now in turn needed help. The stores sold everything imaginable, but Dunne particularly needed a new outfit of smart clothes, if only for a short time. He knew his day-to-day outfit would never do for Miss Dormin, and even his usual Sunday best was not good enough.

Big Cooper was only too happy to oblige. Daniel Cooper was called "Big" to distinguish him from the several Coopers prominent in Sydney life and trade. The stores were an institution in the town, their co-owners, Cooper and Solomon Levey, known to all. During a shortage of coin, the business had even issued its own paper currency, called Waterloo Notes.

So Big Cooper handed the patterer over to a tailor and habit-maker, who had trained in London before stabbing a co-worker with pinking shears and being transported. His instructions were to lend the young man a suitable ready-to-wear wardrobe.

SUNDAY DAWNED WITH the promise of a fine day and Dunne whistled softly as he washed, shaved and dressed carefully in his Bent Street room. Mr. Cooper's man had excelled himself. As the Patterer headed south to morning service, few acquaintances would have recognized him.

His dark green fitted coat was double-breasted, with a rolled collar, skirts that fell to his knees and tight sleeves puffed at the shoulder. His trousers ended in suspenders under a pair of gleaming boots. The crown of his top hat widened at its peak, and its brim was turned up.

His work uniform was, albeit briefly, a thing of the past, replaced by the mirror image of a fashion plate. He would not, his tame tailor told him, be out of place in such European publications as Harriette Wilson's *Paris Lions and London Tigers*, a bible of the beau monde.

Dunne had never heard of this volume; apart from her fame as a courtesan, he knew of Wilson only as the author of her colorful *Memoirs*, news of which had famously caused the Duke of Wellington one of her conquests, to challenge her to "publish, and be damned."

Admittedly, conceded the young man as he strode toward St. James's to the beat of an ivory-topped cane, the tailor had archly warned that this style was really several years old, but he had added that, as they were a world away, few would know the difference. The suit would pass muster.

"Muster," Dunne thought idly, was quite the word of the day. All convicts were mustered for compulsory church attendance, and the rule applied to pass-men, too. While controlling the men and women in captivity posed few problems, keeping a religious rein on the scattered parolees was a harder task.

But the patterer, though not religious, rather liked the change of pace and the gentle ritual involved. And he liked the music, if not the fire-breathing sermons from the archdeacon, the Venerable Thomas Hobbes Scott, although he had to admit that the man appeared to earn his 2,000 pounds a year. New St. James's was usually a bit fancy for Dunne, too: He preferred the older St. Phillip's, between the barracks and The Rocks, where convicts usually predominated on its 800 seats.

As he reached the church, he reflected that it was yet another triumph for the convict architect Francis Greenway, standing opposite his Hyde Park convict barracks. These and his other town works were everyday pleasures for residents' eyes. But, thought Dunne, perhaps the most enduring memorial to Greenway's genius was Macquarie's Tower, the colony's first lighthouse, a graceful beacon that guided shipping through the stark headlands guarding Port Jackson.

And another aloof creation was a majestic building, largely out of sight for townspeople, across the sprawling Domain. With crenellated parapets, medieval towers, soaring lancet windows, yet suddenly Tudor arches over carriageways, it had been described as "Gothic picturesque." Newcomers on arriving ships admired it from the harbor and were sure it must be indeed the grand viceregal castle. In fact, it was the governor's stables, far nobler than the real, decaying Government House. One critic had bitterly described it as "a palace for horses while people go unhoused."

It was so typical of Sydney, pondered the patterer as he turned into the redbrick pile of the church. Not everything was as it appeared. This was particularly true of the sedate St. James. Christian amity and charity were often far removed from its four walls. He recalled the startling services in recent months, after the archdeacon was more than usually outraged by attacks in Mr. Edward Smith Hall's *Monitor*.

One Sunday evening, Hall arrived to find the way barred to his family's pew; it had been locked on the church-leader's instructions. The editor, unperturbed, climbed into the pew and broke the lock. The following week, armed beadles stood guard. Hall and his family sat on the altar steps during the service and refused to budge.

Finally, one evening they found the pew boarded up. "Like the deck of a ship," in the words of *The Monitor*, which Dunne repeated to amused listeners.

On this Sunday, when the patterer looked around the church there was no sign of Mr. Hall—but when he looked right he saw Miss Rachel Dormin. She was wearing the same cut of dress as she had during their first brief encounter, only this time in more sober blue, suitable for Sunday.

The sweet message of redemption, punctuated by thunderous threats of damnation from the red-faced minister, wafted past the patterer's consciousness. He had eyes and thoughts only for the face demurely cast low, apparently in prayer and reflection. Then she caught his eye, and he could have sworn that she winked.

CHAPTER SEVENTEEN

There is nothing makes a man suspect much,
more than to know little.
—Francis Bacon, "Of Suspicion" (1625)

A S THE SERVICE ENDED, THE PATTERER MADE SURE HE WAS OUT THE
door first, so that he could "accidentally" cross his quarry's path.

"Why, Miss Dormin," he said, raising his hat. "What a pleasant surprise. Do you remember me? I was with Captain Rossi when you and Dr. Halloran visited the unfortunate *New World* office."

"Mr. Dunne—of course! Though I barely recognized you. Clothes, indeed, maketh the man."

"My tailor," said Dunne, "tells me I would grace Harriette Wilson's *Paris Lions and London Tigers.*"

Miss Dormin looked perplexed until her escort explained the reference, then said, "Ah, I was not familiar with the allusion—pray, are you a lion or a tiger?"

"I suppose I am a kangaroo now."

She laughed delightedly.

The patterer made his next move. "May I walk you to your next destination?"

She smiled. "With pleasure, although you may be soon bored. I am at rare liberty this morning and simply plan to stroll gently until pleased to stop." She took the arm he offered and looked up, serious now. "I talked to Captain Rossi and he spoke most highly of you. He rather more than hinted that you are someone special, an important ally in the search for the printer's slayer."

Nicodemus Dunne flushed and stammered a modest reply.

"Poor Mr. Abbot," the young woman continued. "As I told the captain, I saw him on both the evening before his death—and the next morning. Sadly, beyond the conventional courtesies, we exchanged barely a word. Business is often like that, isn't it?"

"Yes," he replied, and he felt a shiver as she tightened her grip on his arm.

"I delivered to him some matter to be set into type, on the understanding I could pick it up the following morning, to be passed on to the next journal on a list." Such a round-robin procedure was common, and saved an advertiser from having to write out the material more than once.

"Very economical, I'm sure," said the patterer. He knew full well that the most sensible system would be for one printer to set the matter and, if their press times did not coincide, share the laboriously set type with rivals. Sometimes this happened, but spirited, often bitter competition usually ruled out cooperation. "Tell me," he added. "You saw nothing suspicious that morning?"

"Not a thing. But the death and then the fire must have happened soon afterward. Goodness, do you think the killer was there, hiding nearby, when I called?"

"I can't dismiss the possibility, in all honesty," said Dunne quietly. "Let us hope not. But, away from that, do you recall the content of the copy you were transporting?"

"Indeed. It was a government order. Dr. Halloran had had it set for *The Gleaner* and I knew it was Mr. Abbot's turn, before Mr. Wentworth's *Australian*."

"Would you recognize that text now?" asked Dunne. He took out of his pocket the galley proof he had pulled in the *New World* office and showed it to her.

She studied the text and said, "It's very tiny type, isn't it? Dr. Halloran once showed me the case with it in. It's called Agate or something, no?"

"I really meant, are the words familiar?"

Miss Dormin nodded. "Oh, yes. I know I probably shouldn't, but I can't resist sneaking a look at the copy that comes my way. This seems to be the beginning of the government order. However . . ." She broke off and frowned. "I don't understand the ending, such as it is."

The patterer hesitated. "What exactly did Captain Rossi tell you about the fire and what we found?"

"He said I was not to tell anyone yet about having been at the scene. I asked why, for goodness' sake, and he said it was for my own protection. I asked what he meant and he said he had to confide in me that there may have been other slayings connected to this one and that the killer may think I know something I should not. He said, however, that I could talk to you. He added that I could trust you implicitly."

That was when Nicodemus Dunne nodded, took a deep breath and made Miss Dormin his partner in crime. Detection, that is.

The moment he opened his mouth to tell her all, he knew, of

course, that he should not have revealed anything about the investigation. The governor would have been furious, but what chance did duty to a past-middle-aged general stand in the face of the wide-eyed interest of a nubile beauty?

An imp in the patterer's brain rationalized his capitulation to Cupid with the indelicate words, coarse but true, of love-blinded men throughout the ages: A standing co—. No! In deference to Miss Dormin, he would censor these words! Rather, he would concede that a *tumescent male member* has no conscience.

Dunne was uneasy thinking even in those terms, but admitted their validity. He consoled himself with the idea that it had been Captain Rossi who had opened the door to the young lady's curiosity. Come to that, he thought almost indignantly, why had the captain encouraged her? Was he, too, smitten—and sniffing like a dog after Rachel Dormin?

So, omitting the most distressing details, the patterer told Miss Dormin how it now seemed that three men, connected by the thread that they were current, or past, members of the 57th Regiment, had been murdered most foully. He admitted he did not know why. Suddenly hoping that he had not gone too far (and unable to think of anything else that could show him in a good light), he begged her to put the matter out of her mind and try to enjoy the rest of their time out together. Miss Dormin agreed.

On one subject the patterer kept his own counsel. He judged that his fair companion held a certain colonist in high esteem. He guessed that she knew of Laurence Halloran's transportation. But, given her recent arrival, she may not have known that two years before he had been jailed for his constant condition—debt—or that a year even further back his schoolmaster son had faced complaints of unseemly behavior. She must know that only this year the governor had appointed Halloran Coroner for Sydney, then dismissed him for threatening a defamatory attack on the colorful Archdeacon Scott.

What she did not know, however, and Dunne was convinced of this, was that Halloran was facing final financial ruin; his business was in trouble that would be terminal if yet another new rival flourished. How would a man described as having a "disturbed mind" and a "sense of persecution" react to such a threat? He had been heard to say that he would have to "kill off the opposition."

And now someone had done just that. Which was why in his notebook, under that heading "Persons of Interest," Nicodemus Dunne carefully wrote the name of the ailing *Gleaner*'s Laurence Hynes Halloran.

CHAPTER EIGHTEEN

I do desire we may be better strangers.
—William Shakespeare, *As You Like It* (1599)

B Y THE TIME THE PATTERER HAD POURED OUT TO HIS FAIR COM-
panion a digest of the perplexing details, their walk had taken
them farther south along Elizabeth Street, away from the church.

This was not the most fashionable pedestrian promenade. That
was in the other direction, toward the water and Mrs. Macquarie's
Point—an earlier vice-regal lady's favorite resting spot—and the
Government Domain. But Dunne had his reasons.

Etiquette dictated that the gentleman must keep the lady on
that side of him where she would be least exposed to crowding or
receiving thrown-up muck, mud or dust from the gutter and roadway. Though unsaid, it meant that a chamberpot emptied from
a window above would, hopefully, miss the lady. Also unsaid,
because memories had dimmed, was that walking on the street

side had originally had the benefit of leaving free the sword-arms of most men.

Here, there were few pedestrians, no bedrooms above with threatening chamberpots and there was no likelihood of lurking attackers crossing swords with Dunne's walking stick. Still, he kept to convention and walked at Rachel Dormin's right-hand side. Such courtesies had been drummed into him by his foster parents, who insisted that his mother—about whom they protested no other knowledge—expected him always to act like a gentleman.

To their left as they strolled, Dunne's long gait easily adapting to his petite partner's pace, stretched Hyde Park, up to forty acres saved from grazing and brickmakers' clay-quarrying to become a park, a project that was still in progress.

Bound to the north by the Domain, south by the brickfields, east by what had once been First Fleet pioneer "Little Jack" Palmer's Woolloomooloo Farm, and west by the town proper, the park was dedicated to serving the recreations and amusement of the populace. It had once been an exercise field for troops, and even for a decade the first racecourse.

Today the southern end was occupied by two separate groups. Strictly speaking (and the ones speaking most strictly were proponents of the official church line of Sunday observance) there should have been little or no activity. But, in fact, the authorities turned a blind eye between the end of morning prayers and the beginning of evening services.

Thus the first group toward which the patterer steered Miss Dormin was a jolly party of adults and children who had just set up a picnic and amusements. There were, for the children, a swing on which to seesaw and running in sacks. For adults, there would be a blindfold wheelbarrow race in which husbands or bachelors would push their squealing partners or sweethearts. A table was loaded with food and drink.

"What on earth are they doing?" asked Miss Dormin, pointing to a line of people waiting to poke their heads in turn through a horse collar.

"Oh," said the patterer, "it's to see who can pull the ugliest face—it's called 'grinning.'"

"Some of those men look familiar."

"That's because you are looking at a wayzgoose."

"A what?"

"A wayzgoose—a printers' picnic. You recognize some of those gentlemen from *The Gleaner* or some other journals you've visited."

"What an odd word, wayz . . . whatever! What does it mean?"

"Well, originally it was about a master printer entertaining his craftsmen at St. Bartholomew–tide, on or about August 24. In Europe, this marked the beginning of the season of working during the day by candlelight. Here, of course, it could mark the start of the season of relying less on candles.

"*Wayz* is an Old English word meaning 'stubble.' So a wayzgoose was a bird that fed on a field of mown crop stubble. Goose, if you can obtain it, is still the traditional main dish at a printers' picnic. And Sunday is one of the rare times they can take a few hours off to celebrate. Anyway, strictly speaking they can all say that, after a fashion, they are keeping Sunday observance. The men are all members of a chapel—that's what their craft guild is called. It harks back to early printing's strong links with the church. A printers' leader is even still called the 'father of the chapel.'"

Dunne excused himself and approached a compositor he knew. When he returned, he explained, "I wanted to know if there were any other American printers in town who may have known more about Abbot's life. The answer was that there are none. But I learned that he was an extremely skilled typesetter and press-man. And . . ."

He noticed that Rachel Dormin had been humming a doleful air. "What tune is that?" he asked.

"Oh, it is just a sad song I once heard. Your mention of a celebration aligned to the saint's day brought it to mind. It could be regarded as odd to picnic and play at any time connected with that saint or his day. It should perhaps be sad remembrance."

"Why so?"

"That was the day in 1572 when Catherine de Medici instigated the St. Bartholomew's Day Massacre and thousands of French Huguenots died."

"And your song is about that?"

"No, not that, but about something else that was evil. It was about a dank debtors' cell in the Fleet Prison in London. Inmates sitting on the straw-covered floor with their legs in irons called it 'Bartholomew Fair,' as a parody, a gallows humor allusion to the famous real fair of that name held every year at Smithfield."

Dunne remembered the fair, and the grim prison, from his Bow Street days. Then Miss Dormin began to sing, quietly but sweetly:

Cutpurses, cheaters, bawdy-house doorkeepers,
Room for company at Bartholomew Fair.
Punks, aye, and panderers, cashiered commanders,
Room for company, ill may they fare.

She ended on a clear, long note. "They sang that because they were in the vile cell for the crime of debt. They felt that other, real criminals should not be free."

The patterer shook his head. "How on earth do you know all that?"

"Oh, I had an aunt who lived in Farringdon Street. I would hear the singing as I passed the jail and she explained it all. How she longed to leave that sadness." She waved a hand in an arc encompassing the town. "Perhaps all in Australia should regard St. Bartholomew as their patron saint—especially the prisoners here."

"Why do you say that?"

Miss Dormin frowned. "Recall how St. Bartholomew was martyred. He, too, was flayed."

She looked across at her companion. "Do you know what is the strangest thing?"

Dunne shook his head.

"Well," she continued, "it is that always, from the time I was a little girl, I wanted to go to a magic island. Here is too vast to comprehend. Perhaps what I had in mind is something more like that small island to the west of Jack-the-Miller's Point and Dawes's Battery. Perhaps it is enchanted."

"Perhaps it is," said the patterer with a grin, trying to lighten the mood. "But you might have trouble communicating with its main inhabitants. They're goats."

Considering the young woman's sudden change of mood, as well as not wanting to speak unproven ill of the dead, Dunne refrained from telling her what else the man at the picnic had told him: The late Mr. Abbot was rumored to have had a special reason for becoming self-employed. Gossip had it that he had been dismissed from *The Gleaner* for attempting blackmail. But, thought the patterer, what valuable secrets could Abbot have known? How could he have made such threats? And how did the story tally with Dr. Halloran's avowed desire to help the man?

CHAPTER NINETEEN

No, no—surely not! My God—not more of those
damned whores! Never have I seen worse women.
—An Officer of Marines's first impression of female arrivals on the convict transport *Lady Juliana* (1790)

ACROSS TOWN, ON THE FRINGES OF THE DISREPUTABLE ROCKS, A
fat but very strong woman approaching middle age had
completed an energetic caning of the pale, bare buttocks of an officer of the proud 57th. As he eased on his regimentals, she bade him
a courteous farewell and took the gold coin he had handed her to
the downstairs parlor. She wiped her brow, for she had found the
exercise more than usually exhausting.

Madame Greene (she had no other known name) *was* a madam
and she *was* always green. That is, she conducted a brothel and, by
a strange compulsion, always appeared from head to daintily shod
toe in garments of various shades of green. Lately she had even
begun to dye her hair green.

She was a very lawless lady and very rich. The latter condition and the importance of her services more than counterbalanced the former. Madame herself was no longer an active whore—she did not count punishing naughty soldiers as whoring—but from the front room of her big house in Harrington Street she controlled a platoon of prostitutes just as strictly as any army officer from the nearby barracks drilled his soldiers. Except on such occasions as that very morning, when she would come out of retirement to perform delicate extra services for special clients, her role was to act as commander-in-chief.

Madame really ran two brothels. One, in back rooms, was for the lower orders willing and able to pay only a few shillings for a quick roll. The other, upstairs, was more lavishly appointed and was reserved for the gentry, officers, well-to-do merchants and professional men, who could pay more for their pleasures.

Madame herself was almost respectable, just another trader in an essential commodity. Prostitution was frowned upon officially, but permitted in fact. There was a decided imbalance in Sydney town between the numbers of men and women. There were few free immigrants of the fairer sex and only one in seven convicts was female. Overall, the ratio of male to female was three to one. The government acknowledged tacitly that the men needed sex with women, and so turned a blind eye to them paying for it—if only to avoid the unmentionable alternative, men having sex with men.

So Madame Greene's only problem was keeping up her ranks of girls. She sighed often about the misconception that there was a constant supply of experienced whores on every transport that arrived. The truth was that most women who were now "on the town" had not been whores before coming to the colony. Prostitution was not, in itself, an offense punishable by transportation.

Madame recruited distressed women by any means. If they

went along with her plans for them, she pampered them. If they resisted, she had "breakers," men who raped them into submission.

Few questioned her methods, or her background. She liked to describe herself as a free arrival, not a convict, in the First Fleet. She always said she arrived in 1788 on the transport ship *Friendship*. What she did not explain was that she completed the voyage in the belly of her mother, a prisoner impregnated by a crewman or a marine guard—her mother had never been sure which.

Young Greene soon worked herself up from being on her back to being on top. Her business boomed. Now she even rented out her top-story rooms for people to view in comfort the prisoners being turned off the gallows of the jail-yard below. It was one good reason to call her establishment the "High House."

The now saddle-sore soldier had been her only customer that day. Normally business was suspended on Sunday mornings, which gave the girls time to rest from the attentions of what Madame described as "hop-harlots" and, once a fortnight, to receive a medical examination. It was not an official requirement, but the mistress of the house was sensible about such matters. Venereal disease was among the colony's greatest scourges, so she kept her girls as clean as possible. Hard though it was, she tried to persuade them, and their customers, to use what were delicately called "preservatives."

She did care, of course, about the unfortunate by-product of a client tumbling his seed in the wrong place at the wrong time. It put a girl out of the line and was a nuisance. It could be, and usually was, remedied. But even worse was the threat of diseasing someone who might be very angry and vengeful, and no longer a source of gold.

Madame Greene's musings on the subject were, appropriately, interrupted by a maid (who really was one, in both senses) tapping on the parlor door and announcing, "Ma'am, the pox doctor is ready to leave."

Madame shook her head and tut-tutted. "Elsie, love, don't call the medical gentleman that. It's rude. Send the bugger in!"

She liked this doctor. Some of the other medical men in town either wanted to sample the wares or else were sniffy about the business. Like that Jim Bowman. Well might he have cleaned up the Rum Hospital and got rid of the rogues and rapists there, but he didn't approve of her and refused to call. She wasn't surprised when he became inspector of all hospitals, too high and mighty for any ordinary work, and married an Exclusive. She didn't miss his airs. Nine years or so, it must be now. Lord, she could harbor a grudge!

Dr. Thomas Owens, black medical bag in his gloved hand, entered and bowed. "Dear lady, your flowers are blooming."

"Good, I should hope so," said Madame Greene. "As one professional to another, would you care to see my latest prick-sheaths, just arrived from Europe?"

Owens winced at the crudity, then gave an enthusiastic nod. She produced a polished casket, rather the size and shape of a cigar box, and opened it to reveal its contents. With the keen eyes of connoisseurs, both admired the treasures. Most poor men in the colony, or those few who cared, would use prophylactics, or "yard-cases" as they were also crudely and boastfully called, made from pig's or sheep's bladder, shaped and sewn tightly with tiny gut stitches. Madame intended her prized consignment for her gentlemen. Instead of intestine, these were made from fine, fabric-thin soft leather or proofed silk. There were gay silk ribbons for tying them securely. Surely they would bring several guineas each.

"Look at 'em," she said proudly. "The very best French riding coats."

Owens smiled. "You know, of course, that the French call them *redingotes anglaises*?"

"They would, wouldn't they?" She snorted. "Bloody Froggies! Any old road, these splendid preservatives of mine will help take care of any misguided poxed meat-wands."

Owens paused, then nodded grimly. "Certainly the plague of the disease must be defeated at every turn." He rose abruptly, extending a paper bag. "Have a lozenge."

Madame Greene absently took one and popped it into her mouth. She didn't feel like a comfit, in fact. She even toyed with the notion of delaying the doctor's departure and seeking his counsel. For even though she was only forty, she was feeling progressively unwell. Of late she regularly had an aching head and muscles, felt nauseous and passed water a lot.

When she looked in the mirror she saw that her skin was clear and her eyes bright, but that her face was paler than it should be. She was faithfully taking the medicine Dr. Owens had earlier prescribed for her, but it didn't seem to help. She was, if anything, worse.

Madame was usually proud of her looks (apart from her weight) and energy. She loved theater and appeared at masques, concerts, balls—any entertainment where they were likely to ask her to dance and sing.

With a smile and a bow, the doctor was gone. She had missed her chance. Rather sadly, she chewed and sucked on the sweetmeat. Then she winked at Elsie. Oh, well—she had risen to be queen of the High House, the best bordello on Gallows Hill. Stuff 'em all!

CHAPTER TWENTY

When to the sessions of sweet silent thought
I summon up remembrance of things past,
I sigh the lack of many a thing I sought . . .
—William Shakespeare, Sonnet 30 (1609)

Miss Dormin recovered her good humor as she and the patterer walked away from the wayzgoose and across the park. Farther south, approaching the park's extremity, they found a large open space being used for a game of cricket, about which endeavor she professed to Dunne her ignorance.

"You underestimate the influence of a feminine touch in this game," said the patterer.

"Do I, sir? How is that?"

"Well, let's examine the match before us." He pointed to a player who was carrying a wide bat, wearing a tall black top hat and facing the bowler. He explained how this man's headgear indicated that he belonged to a military side. The fieldsmen and bowler were in more motley attire; some were barefoot and hatless while

others wore straw hats or kerchiefs on their heads. Long blue ribbons around hats or waists identified the soldiers' rivals. "They
are civilians," said the patterer, "as their informal garb indicates.
There's nothing casual about their play, however. They invariably
win over the soldiery."

"I fail to see the feminine influence," Miss Dormin reminded
the patterer.

"Ah, well. As to that, consider the manner in which the attacking player bowls. He is not allowed to perform his action with the
arm raised above the shoulder—that would be called overarm.
Now, in England about five or so years ago, a young lady was
bowling, under shoulder level of course, to give her brother batting
practice. This young lady, a Miss Christina Willes—or Willis, it
escapes me—soon discovered that her skirt was a handicap to her
action. So she bowled *over* the shoulder—and claimed his wicket!
Her brother was impressed with the new delivery, but was barred
by officials from using it in competition. If the method is ever recognized, you may claim that one of your sisters showed the way."

Miss Dormin suddenly pointed to one of the fieldsmen. "Why, if
it is the military team's identifying garb, is one of the civilian players wearing a black top hat?"

Dunne consulted another spectator and soon reported back. "It is
as I suspected. When that man in the hat bowled earlier, he claimed
three wickets with consecutive deliveries, a rare occurrence. The
tradition is that the third man to fall honors the bowler by handing
over a hat as a trophy. Thus the feat is known as a hat-trick."

They stood in companionable silence, watching the match.

We must make an attractive couple, thought Dunne, as he felt
Miss Dormin's gloved hand in the crook of his elbow. He wondered

if she could feel his heart, so near. He glanced surreptitiously sideways; why, this profile, through the fluttering loosened ribbons, was as perfect as the other.

Then something extraordinary happened. The batsman cleanly connected to a delivery and the ball scooted along like a bouncing cannonball—right toward the patterer and his companion. Dunne shot out a foot in front of the young woman to deflect the oncoming ball, but his heel caught in a pothole.

She, however, reacted more successfully. In one fluid movement and without even relinquishing the hold on her escort, she flicked off her bonnet and, reaching down, neatly scooped up the ball into its crown. The players and spectators applauded.

"That, sir," said Miss Dormin, as she rolled the ball back to the nearest player, "*that* is a hat-trick."

He laughed as they turned away from the cricket match and back toward the heart of the town.

"I know *what* you are," said Miss Dormin suddenly as they strolled. "But *who* are you?"

So Nicodemus Dunne told her about how he had been brought up in the southern English port of Weymouth by a kindly guardian who treated him well. His foster-father was a retired senior army officer. No struggling retiree on half-pay, he seemed a wealthy man who knew important people in London. The young Nicodemus had more than once seen communications coming to the house bearing what seemed to be royal seals, and he knew from overheard conversations that his foster-parents had close links to a General Garth.

They had never told Dunne anything about his true parents, whom the boy had never known. All he did know was that he was born in the year 1800. After a time, anyway, his curiosity faded. The Dunnes were generous and had him educated broadly.

The patterer told Miss Dormin that Dunne Senior had wanted him to enter the army. That ambition failed in the face of his foster-son's keen interest in the legendary Bow Street Runners. This was the police force molded by justice of the peace Henry Fielding, famed as the author of the comic epic *The History of Tom Jones, a Foundling.* (Dunne at times idly wondered if he himself had been a foundling.) Henry's sightless brother, John, who later took over leadership of the Bow Street Runners, was the celebrated "Blind Beak," a magistrate who claimed he could identify 3,000 miscreants by their voices alone.

Miss Dormin frowned as the patterer repeated the story he had told Governor Darling and the others at the barracks about his own fall from grace. He explained that since transportation, after four years of much lighter service than most convicts were subjected to, he had been given his ticket of leave. This was because he was classified as a Special—the name given to some educated felons. Before parole, he was assigned to work at *The Gazette*, where he had first met Captain Rossi. In about a year, Dunne told her, he would be emancipated—if he kept his hands, and his nose, clean.

"Will you go home?" asked Rachel Dormin. She emphasized the word *home* the way so many English in Australia, even convicts, did, Dunne thought. Home: You could almost see it with a capital *H*, the manner in which it was often rendered in the newspapers. The yearning in so many people was almost palpable, no less so in those exiles for whom "home" meant nothing better than a poverty- and disease-riddled rookery such as St. Giles.

He recalled that there had been cheers, and even tears, when he read to gatherings from a poem contributed to one of his newspapers. It had ended:

> *Tho' boundless leagues from dales and moors*
> *Under a foreign sky,*
> *And stranded far on unknown shores*
> *An Englishman I'll die.*

The patterer shrugged and answered his companion. "Where or what is home to me now?" he asked, giving the word a neutral intonation. "I would not be welcomed at the Dunnes' hearth—if they are still alive. I fear they felt that I had disgraced their name. Indeed, I gathered that my offense went somehow even deeper. No, perhaps I will try and make a fresh start here, although as an Emancipist that can be difficult."

"Why so, if you have paid your debt to society?"

Dunne sighed. "Oh, my dear young lady! It appears you have not been here long enough to learn that the class divisions in the colony are as complex—perhaps more so—as those in Britain, or even as the caste system of the Hindoostani.

"You," he said with a gesture, "are doubtless 'Sterling,' freely come from Britain. Other free men and women, born here, are 'Currency.' Why these odd names? It seems they were coined—and you will pardon my pun—by the pay officer of the 73rd Regiment in Governor Macquarie's time. Currency circulating locally was considered inferior to the pound Sterling.

"Not all Sterling are equal, however. At the top of the tree are the 'Pure Merinos,' such as Captain Macarthur and the Reverend Marsden and all other members of the pastoral elite. Their aim is to keep their bloodlines pure from contamination by lesser mortals; like their animals, they boast of no cross-blood in their human flocks. These people lead the master class called the 'Exclusives.' The military, officers only of course, are top-drawer, too. Exclusives even look down on free men in trade, let alone the one-time prisoners who have stayed on and succeeded, such as Mr. Terry and Mr. Underwood. Even powerful men not in trade but in the professions, men who appear to be and are indeed perfectly respectable, can be snubbed at the mere hint of a convict stain.

"Why, take Mr. Wentworth, whom you have encountered at *The Australian*. Gossipers whispered—not too loudly; D'Arcy had a fierce disposition, as does his son—that the old man 'volunteered' for exile here after trouble with the law. The Brahmin caste shut many doors to the father and they still do the same to his son William. And imagine the obstacles for a convict who is Irish *and* Roman Catholic!"

"It is quite bewildering," said Miss Dormin. "I'm sure I will never work out who everyone is. I'm not even quite sure who I am!"

"Why, it's simple: I judge you not only suitable for the label of Sterling—you are also a 'Jimmy Grant,' an immigrant." Then the patterer added mischievously, "Of course, if you married a settler over the Blue Mountains, you would be linked to a 'Stringybark' and your children would shoot up as 'Cornstalks' or, by their healthy outdoors coloring, be known as 'Nut-browns'!"

As the young woman blushed, the patterer apologized. "Forgive my chatter, I beg you. Let me be suitably chastened and serious. Please tell me, what brought you all the way to Australia?"

Miss Dormin hesitated. "I suppose it all began as a promise of new life. And ended in death."

CHAPTER TWENTY-ONE

. . . the agonies which are, have their origin in the
ecstasies which might have been.
—Edgar Allan Poe, "Berenice" (1835)

Rachel Dormin's story, Nicodemus Dunne decided, was one of optimism and quiet courage in the face of tragedy and sadness.

She told him how she had arrived in the Cove on a late summer's afternoon in 1826. Her ship dropped anchor and she and her fellow passengers were rowed to the King's Wharf.

Why had she essayed such a voyage? Surely she had not done so alone. Long an orphan, she explained, she had no family left after her aunt died. This lady bequeathed her 150 pounds, leaving an equivalent sum to a local church charity. And, indeed, Miss Dormin received the welcome windfall on reaching her majority during the year before her voyage. (So, reckoned Dunne, she is twenty-four.)

Life was so promising. She had completed her informal inden-
tures with a well-regarded London milliner and costumier. With
her inheritance she had the wherewithal to establish, if she wished,
her own business, and could enjoy her passion for the theater. "You
must come and see me contribute to Mr. Levey's entertainments at
the Royal," she added as an aside.

And, she explained, there was another reason for contentment:
love. "I was newly engaged, to a young man in the wool-importing
business." She paused. "So you can see that I more than understood your references to pure merinos. I expect I could exchange
more than pleasantries with the pastoralists here. And, by the by,
I have no doubt that Captain Macarthur will be viewed by future
generations as the father of the Australian wool trade. Whereas,
in fact, Elizabeth—Mrs. Macarthur—did all the hard work, while
he was off gallivanting overseas. And the Reverend Marsden and
Mr. John Palmer, strictly speaking, owned merinos here before
Mr. Macarthur ever did."

The young woman suddenly giggled. "You know that he and I
have something in common?"

"I can't imagine what."

"Well, surely you know why his enemies sneeringly call him
'Jack Bodice'? It's because his father was a corset-maker!"

The patterer could only gape at the arcane knowledge pouring
from the lips of this seemingly most unlikely source. "And your
engagement?" he prompted, to return to safer ground.

"Oh, he was offered a new position, to go to Sydney with the
Australian Agricultural Company. It seemed a godsend. He had
found he was stricken with phthisis, and the doctors believed the
dryness and heat here would be beneficial."

Dunne nodded. Phthisis was the dreaded lung-wasting disease

that invariably consumed the sufferer. What a burden for both young people. And who did not know of the Australian Agricultural Company? With a capital of a million pounds it held a similarly vast number of acres north of Sydney, past the Coal River secondary punishment settlement. There were many people who thought the harbor there would eventually become as important as Port Jackson, filling ships with the promised bounty of wool, olives, wines and coal. In 1825, the endeavor had begun, to great fanfare, with the arrival from England of two ships carrying 25 men, 12 women, 726 sheep and 8 head of cattle. The patterer reflected that the land was not living up to the great expectations.

"It was a wonderful chance," said Miss Dormin. "He left and I agreed to follow, once my affairs had been settled. I was fortunate to gain a position as companion to a wealthy lady who was returning to the colony alone. Thus I acquired a chaperone—and a first-class passage cabin worth between seventy and a hundred pounds. Even steerage would have cost me twenty-five. Oh, what a bonus! I laid out fifty pounds on clothing—and cloth to sell here; I believed ladies would be starved of European finery—plus books to read on the voyage and such food and drink as would not be provided. So you can see that I sailed with much of my legacy intact."

"Did you have a fair passage? My own was hideous—200-odd days stop-start via Tenerife, Cape Verde, Rio and Cape Town."

"La, sir, we took but half that time! We went straight to Rio then dropped down to ride the winds for a straight run out." Then Miss Dormin frowned. "We had a safe and uneventful voyage and I was the happiest of women—until I set foot on Australian soil.

"All went well until the actual landing. At the headlands we were boarded by the pilot, who was later joined by the quarantine physician, which was my first sight of our esteemed Dr. Bowman.

We had aboard no notifiable sickness, so we were free to proceed to an inner anchorage. It was also my first chance to see King Bungaree. He boarded and was paid the golden tribute he demanded. With a glass of rum! I only learned later that he called on all newly arrived vessels. It is my last pleasant memory of that day."

The patterer broke in. "If it upsets you to talk—"

Rachel Dormin shook her head. "On landing, I was directed to the Australian Hotel, where my fiancé had arranged for me to await him. Alas, all that awaited me was the news that my husband-to-be had died not long after his arrival and was buried."

"Surely his consumptive disease had not advanced that quickly?" asked the patterer.

Rachel Dormin paused and sighed. "Ah, no. It was a related illness of the respiratory organs. They called it pertussis. Another *p* word—for pain."

She hurried on. "I knew no one. The lady with whom I traveled had already been met and had gone inland. I had my luggage, much of my inheritance and my professional skills. Oh, and I had this . . ." She reached deep into her reticule and produced a small leather-bound portfolio. "It is my lucky charm; I carry it everywhere practicable."

She opened the bindings to reveal a painting, small but far from a miniature, of a ship under full sail. Inset, in an oval outline in one corner, smiled a small portrait. It was clearly of Miss Dormin.

She pointed. "The ship portion was a gift, painted by a fellow passenger. I had my likeness added later, here. If circumstances had been different I would have added my fiancé's face." At this she broke off.

Dunne wildly clutched at straws to change the subject. "It is indeed a fine painting, but obviously not by a sailor—see that whip?" He pointed to a trailing red-and-white pennant. "I believe it should be flying forward with the wind."

"You are very observant. Yes, it is so, he was an amateur dauber." She laughed. "But I trust the added portrait is more true to the fruit?"

The patterer peered at the likeness and nodded. Yes, "J. L.," whose tiny initials signed that part of the work, was very professional. As good as any Dunne had seen. "You never forget a voyage like that, do you?" he said, covering the artwork once more with its protective sheet of paper. Written on that layer, in artistic script, were the words "A memento of the *Azile*."

"No, you certainly do not," agreed Miss Dormin briskly, taking the painting back and securing the wallet in her bag. "Nor its aftermath."

The patterer was still curious. "Forgive me, but how did you manage to, shall we say, survive—and prosper?"

"Oh, a friendly soul introduced me to Reverend Halloran at *The Gleaner*, and I returned to dressmaking. I accept private commissions and also do much work for Mrs. Rickard's Fashionable Repository. I board with a respectable family near her shop. Then there is the theater, and other projects keep me busy." She broke off. "Oh, speaking of Dr. Halloran, there he is over there. He has offered to give me luncheon. I am unhappy to interrupt our promenade but I have promised him—and I did not know I would meet you today."

"Perhaps tomorrow?" said the patterer as, after a pretty curtsey, Rachel Dormin turned to cross the road to meet her approaching host. Dr. Halloran apparently could not see the young man, and so was unaware of his bitten-back curse, which belied the salute offered by his doffed topper. Dunne decided that he would miss that hat when it went back to the Waterloo Stores in the morning.

HE COULD NOT have known that, even had Miss Dormin desired it, he would not meet her the next day. For that matter, nor would he return his borrowed finery to Mr. Cooper.

Overnight, yet another death would claim all his attention.

CHAPTER TWENTY-TWO

Good things of day begin to droop and drowse,
Whiles night's black agents to their preys do rouse.
—William Shakespeare, *Macbeth* (1606)

WITH HONORABLE (AND EVEN DISHONORABLE) EXCEPTIONS— children, the aged, the ill, or any of Madame Greene's hard-working horizontal helpers—on that Sunday night Miss Rachel Dormin may well have been the first Sydneysider to go to bed. Alone. It was nine P.M.

A sensible young woman, aware of a very busy day ahead, she first cleaned her teeth with a brush and baking soda (imported powders were too expensive) and washed her face, using her Castile soap sparingly.

After her ablutions, she brushed fingers through her hair, then rummaged through bottles, bowls and vials cluttering a shelf of the commode on which the washbasin and ewer stood. She pushed aside violet-scented hair powder, orris root perfume, salt of lemons for fabric stains, a bottle of Godfrey's tonic for unsettled stomachs and oil of cloves for toothache—although, unlike most settlers, she had been free of this plague.

She found what she wanted: a pomatum of specially mixed cream, which she proceeded to massage onto her face, neck, hands and wrists. Ah, she thought, if only Mr. Dunne—Nicodemus . . . she played with the name—could see what a girl has to do! She frowned. Perhaps he *would* see, one day.

After turning down the blankets and sheets on her narrow bed, Miss Dormin raked up into a bundle the scattered twigs lying on the mattress. Cabinetmakers made varnish from this plant's seeds; every good housewife knew that the twigs killed bedbugs. All apothecaries sold the plant: hemp. The young woman believed the botanical name was *Cannabis sativa* . . . or was it *indica*? No matter, she knew it provided fabric and cordage—and could yield the euphoriants *bhang* or hashish. Soldiers and sailors had brought such drug habits here. She had seen the results.

She opened the window and breathed deeply to relax. She had her bag packed and clothes laid out ready for work. Tomorrow was just another day, one she was confident would proceed to her liking.

As always, she said her prayers. Only then did she lie down, carefully cross her arms upon her breast and compose herself for rest.

———

ELSEWHERE IN SYDNEY, not everyone found sleep easy or desirable. Not even during the small hours of the morning.

Mr. William Charles Wentworth, for example, usually spent his weekends at home with his young family at Vaucluse House, his grand property six miles east of the town, passing weeknights in Sydney in a room near his legal chambers. But late this Sunday night, he slipped out of the house as soon as its other inhabitants had settled down and strode to an outhouse where he had earlier saddled his horse. He walked the animal out of earshot of his family, then mounted and trotted toward the town.

Always an irascible man, he scowled and muttered angrily as he rode. He had no fear of being bailed up; the dragoons of the mounted police, called "goons" behind their backs, had pushed the banditti far beyond the town. There were official assurances that even the most feared outlaw, Irish convict "lifer" John Donohoe, was roaming the Blue Mountains. Wentworth knew Donohoe was a folk hero. They sang of him, discreetly:

Bold Donohoe was taken for a notorious crime.
And sentenced to be strung up on the hanging-tree so high.
As Donohoe made his escape to the bush he went straightway.
The people were all too afraid to travel night and day.

Wentworth snorted. They called him "Bold Jack." Bold, indeed! He had not always cut such a dashing figure. Why, at first he had been reduced to robbing slow-moving bullock trains on foot because he did not have a horse.

Still, the lawyer felt more than a certain sympathy for the twenty-two-year-old. Caught for his rather pedestrian crimes, he had been sentenced to death but had escaped between jail and gallows. Now he was a bigger menace than ever.

So, although Wentworth felt safe on the road, he still carried, in a pannier at the front of the saddle, two long-barreled pistols.

———————

THE REVEREND DR. Laurence Hynes Halloran was out and about in the same dim streets toward which lawyer Wentworth was riding.

He had no chance of slipping from his home. To say he was a family man was an understatement, for although they did not all live with him, he had twelve children by his first wife (who had died during her last confinement). He was still a strong and virile man in his sixties and had fathered several more children with his second wife, Elizabeth, whom he had married four years before, less than a year after donning widower's weeds.

As he left the house now, he vowed to Elizabeth that an emergency concerning *The Gleaner* called him away at such an ungodly time. His duty in the following hours would not be pleasant, he knew, but he had seen worse on the blood-sluiced decks of battleships.

———————

AND, IF THEY had stirred and found an empty bed, the household of editor Edward Smith Hall could have been reassured by the note explaining that he, too, had urgent overnight business at his paper, *The Monitor*.

———————

WHEN DR. THOMAS Owens left the Rum Hospital carrying his doctor's bag, the public clock (a legacy of Governor Macquarie's passion for punctuality) atop the nearby Hyde Park Barracks stood at three-thirty A.M.

Had the hall porter been awake, he would not have remarked

on Owens's movement at such an uncivilized hour. The doctor was often out on medical rounds at all times of the day or night. Even if the porter had followed Owens outside, he would only have noted idly that the sawbones (he was an old sailor; this was what he called all surgeons) headed north along Macquarie Street before disappearing into the depths of the dark.

———

CAPTAIN CROTTY, A flowing cape over his green-faced uniform, acknowledged the sentry's salute as he strode past the guardroom and vanished toward the port.

"Taking the long road round to Madame Greene's, I'll be bound," muttered the redcoat. "Lucky bastard!"

———

BUT THERE WOULD be no Madame Greene on duty to greet any nocturnal visitors to her bordello. She left her parlor and moved quietly down Middlesex Lane, past the jail. As she turned right and crossed George Street, heading south toward Bridge Street, her outline was spotted by the same guard who had seen Captain Crotty leave the barracks.

He called the sight to the attention of his mate. Not that they intended to do anything about it. Their job was to check people getting into, or out of, the barracks. What people did in the streets outside didn't matter a rat's arse. But it was interesting nonetheless. The oddest people flitted through the town at all hours. This bulky figure staggered slightly and paused periodically, as if for air.

"Just a bloody Indian full of bull," said the second soldier dismissively, as they stamped off on their rounds.

―――――――

IN AN UPSTAIRS bedroom at Government House, Eliza Darling sat up with a start at an unexpected noise. It sounded like the stairs creaking. There it was again. She considered whether to call Ralph softly (he was only "Ralph" in their most private lives; at other times he was always "General" or "the governor") from his bed-chamber next door.

No. She decided it was only her imagination. She had not been sleeping well lately, she acknowledged with a sigh. But Ralph, well, he slept like a baby. A baby; she sighed again, deeply. It was little more than a month since one of her—their—babies, Edward, had died in the whooping cough epidemic that had swept the settlement. The Darlings had a large brood but that did not stop the loss hurting her deeply. She tormented herself with the thought that, had she not agreed to come to the colony, her child would not have died.

She kept up a brave face and few noticed any change in her fine features and gracious air. She had publicly said of the loss only that "a few selfish tears will fall, but God knows best, and I can say, I hope with resignation, His will be done." Privately, she thought she could see new gray in her dark hair and lines around her bright brown eyes, even though she would not be thirty for two months.

Ralph, well, Ralph was a quarter-century older. He had his military career and his work here, unhappy though it had become. When they were first offered the colony she had jokingly called it "Bottomless Bay." Now he was depressed by opposition from the Emancipists and almost obsessed with identifying with the Exclusives. And she felt empty. It was, indeed, all "bottomless" for both of them.

Suddenly there was another sound. Eliza shivered. Intruders!

The noise was at the front door. Now she realized that it was coming from outside, a thought that drew her from her bed to the window. In the flickering flare of a cresset torch, she watched the guard turn and pace to one side.

Apparently having waited for this move and now out of the soldier's line of sight, a figure in a dark cloak darted from the doorway into the bushes, then disappeared.

Eliza Darling recognized the figure. She had been married to it for eleven years.

———

ALL THESE WANDERERS moved furtively. But other, even more shadowy, creatures of the night were watching closely.

CHAPTER TWENTY-THREE

He got a hundred on the back and you could see his
back bone between his shoulder blades. The doctor
order him to get another hundred on his bottom. His
haunches was in such a jelly the doctor order him to be
flog on the calves of his legs . . . The flesh and skin blew
in my face as they shook off the cats.
—Joseph Holt, exiled Irish rebel (1800)

I*T WAS THE MIDDLE OF THE NIGHT, PERHAPS THREE HOURS AFTER* S*UNDAY*
had turned into Monday, long before the rising sun would kiss into
bustling life the Lumber Yard on the corner of Bridge Street and the town's
main artery, George Street.

While it was, in truth, a yard filled with stacks of milled timber under
covers, the huge enclosure was much more than a storage space. Behind its
high walls was a square ringed with low buildings. These were workshops
that supplied the government with much of the sinews of the settlement's
daily existence. There were sheds for nailmakers, shoemakers, carpenters,
tailors and a forge for blacksmiths.

Guarded by bored soldiers and prodded along by "trusty" convicts acting as overseers, the convicts were marched from and back to their respective barracks every workday. They wore overalls marked "PB" for Prisoners

Barracks at Hyde Park and "CB" for the Carters Barracks at the southern end of the town. The latter jail took its name from the human "draught animals," convicts who were yoked to pull brick-carts and similar wagons. The men worked at the Lumber Yard from sunrise to sunset, a twelve-hour day at this time of year.

While the yard rang with voices and the clangs and bangs of industry during most days, it should always have been deathly still, almost grave-like, during the dark hours.

But this early morning there were unexpected noises, sounds other than the normal murmur of the Tank Stream, trapped and running slug-gishly in a channel beside the yard, or the rustle of foraging rats. The air was filled with the slaps of a hard object erratically striking a softer surface, irregular grunts of expelled breath followed by hissing intakes, and scuffling sounds of restless feet, almost the swish of a dancer. None of these noises, however, was loud enough to escape over the thick, high walls and shut wooden gate.

In any case, although the yard was only a few hundred yards away from, and almost in the line of sight of, the occupants of the main guard-house at the redcoats' barracks, the soldiers there took no interest in the closed workplace. And any passing constable on watch patrol would only see that the gate remained safely undisturbed.

Those noises that were somehow in rhythm with the dancing feet seemed to be interrupted regularly by muffled moans and sobs, and raspy, tortured breathing. The first range of sounds came from a scourger wielding a cat-o'-nine-tails; the noises in counterpoint came from a man being flogged to death.

I<small>F IT WAS</small> an odd time for a flogging, the equipment involved was standard in a time and place where the punishment was commonplace.

Convicts casually called twenty-five lashes a "tester" or a "Botany Bay dozen" to show disdain for the punishment; a "canary," as well as being a nickname for a yellow-clad convict, described a hundred strokes—because the whip and the victim supposedly "sang" together. Such punishment could be meted out for a misdemeanor as minor as insolence to a jailer.

The least lashes administered was usually twenty-five; the average was fifty. Many men suffered up to 500; some died, if not of the physical wounding then of heart attack at the pain and shock, or even the raw fear. One prison commander ordered 26,024 strokes in 16 months; another once handed out 1,500 before he took breakfast.

Although a victim could be imprisoned in a pillory or in the stocks to receive the flagellation, or even simply be lashed to a tree, the most common official restraints were the triangles.

This prisoner in the Lumber Yard was confined thus. Three iron poles, each eight feet long, were planted in the ground to form legs that tapered to a common point higher than a man's upraised hands. Similar sets stood throughout the settlement.

The scourger now wielded the cat's nine long cords, knotted rockhard at each end and attached to the leather-bound handle, but to an irregular rhythm. In the shadow of the tall walls and with not even a new moon, the darkness dampened the standard army rate of three or four strokes a minute. The only light came, weakly, from a softly glowing whale-oil lantern set on the ground. It was sufficient to show that the victim was stripped to the waist, obviously male and tall. His tormentor remained a phantom figure.

The cruelty of the cat alone was not punishment enough to satisfy the bloody-minded torturer, who regularly dipped the tails into a nearby bucket of wet sand and lime, called the "pepper pot"—to load the knots with what felt like thousands of red-hot needle points.

After twenty minutes, the method of punishment surprisingly changed.

The torturer threw the cat aside, exchanging it for a smaller, lighter weapon called a tawse, which was usually reserved for chastising juvenile offenders. It was a broad leather strap split at the end into narrow strips. Normally this would not break the skin, only raise bruising and welts. Schoolteachers often used the tawse.

This new attack had a strange variation, however. Before applying the tawse, the scourger attached a small blade that glittered even in the dim lamplight to one tail of the smaller whip. Only then did the thrashing continue, now at a more rapid rate.

Fifteen minutes later, the flogger's onslaught stopped and the yard fell still. The gagging groans and tortured breathing had stopped. Sweaty fingers felt for a pulse in the neck of the man on the triangles. Nothing.

The killer detached the blade from the tawse tail and now used it to slash at the suspended man's throat, then moved down to hack wounds first across the belly and then across both ankles.

The gag was ripped from the dead man's face, sending a frothy spray of blood and spittle from the suddenly open, slack lips. He had bitten through his tongue. Into the drooling livid mouth, bloody fingers rammed a handful of crumbs shaken from a small bag.

The final indignity was yet to come. Unbuckling the corpse's belt the scourger tore down the wet breeches—like many men being whipped, the victim had lost control of his bladder—and with two strokes of the blade slashed off the exposed penis, then shoved the gory mess into the open mouth.

Carrying the tawse and the doused lamp, the killer slipped carefully through the gate, closed it quietly and melted away into the velvet night. There was no one to hear the last whispered, bitter message delivered to the mutilated man dangling on the triangles: "Bon appétit!"

CHAPTER TWENTY-FOUR

What bloody man is that?
—William Shakespeare, *Macbeth* (1606)

Nicodemus Dunne and Captain Rossi stood in the early Monday-morning sunlight closely watching Dr. Thomas Owens examine the body on the floor of the Lumber Yard.

The hive of industry was quiet. The busy bees—an early coffle of convict workers arrived for the week's first shift—were crowded, restless, in a far corner. They were excited by the break in their hard and monotonous routine but trying not to show it. They had been warned that any talk would be rewarded with fifty lashes. To start with. Later coffles were being turned back.

A convict overseer stood nervously beside the tableau of victim and investigators. He explained he had been the second arrival, at six A.M., and had discovered the mess. The body lay now in a tacky pool of congealing blood at the base of the flogging triangles. Ants scurried through the gore, carrying away lumps of torn flesh. Someone had clearly unhooked the still-shackled wrists from the iron supports only recently.

"What do we know?" asked Rossi, studying the discarded whip.

"Well," said Owens, dusting his gloved hands, "we know he wasn't one of ours."

The police chief raised an eyebrow. "I mean," the doctor continued, "that he is black but he is not an 'Indian,' not one of our sable brethren."

"Of course he's not," snorted Rossi. "He's either a West Indian or from Mauritius. I've seen plenty of both." Dunne looked up; he had always meant to ask the lawman about his time in Mauritius.

The overseer cleared his throat. "Captain, he is—was—from the Indies, true, but a free man, one of our blacksmiths. Head one, in fact."

"So he wasn't a scourger?" the patterer asked. The thought of a revenge killing had soon presented itself.

"Lord, no. He only *made* the triangles. He really was a smith. A real craftsman, he was. A specialist, too. He usually only made shackles and chains for lags. It was like a gent going to his tailor. Here, I'll show you what I mean. Hey!" he shouted at a guard. "Send one of those over here."

When "one of those," an ironed convict, clanked over, the overseer indicated the leg shackles. "I know you gents have seen them before, but have you looked close?"—Dunne did not tell him how closely he had looked in the past—"Works of art these are, all done by our dear departed."

He pointed. The rings of iron plate, called basils, which went around the man's ankles each comprised of two half-circles that, put together, fitted the size of the leg. The ends of the irons were flattened and had holes to take linking rivets. When the circlets were fitted to a convict, they were riveted together. This man's irons were linked by about two feet of chain. A length of rope from the chain's center link to the man's belt stopped the chain dragging on the ground. Yes, Dunne remembered it all too well.

"Beautiful," said the overseer, dismissing the prisoner. "He—that's our smith—was in Mauritius before he came here. That's where he learned his craft, shackling slaves. Proud of his work, he was. Said they fitted so snug there was no chafing and he never hurt no one."

He paused. "Or maybe only the once," he corrected himself. "He felt badly about one soldier here—too heavy the shackles was; fifteen bloody pounds, they say." He dropped his voice conspiratorially. "But I reckon it wasn't all his fault. He was only doing what Dumaresq wanted, only obeying orders."

Dunne and the others of course knew the name Dumaresq. Several brothers of that name—their sister was Mrs. Darling—had followed the governor on his posting to Sydney three years earlier. The Dumaresq in question was doubtless the one who had been put in charge of the Lumber Yard.

"Was he by any chance a soldier?" asked Rossi.

"Of course he was a soldier, didn't I just say so? Oh, you mean the smith? Yes, he had been, but that was years ago, before the century turned. He was always proud he'd been in the 45th in Grenada. Over the governor, he said."

An oddity suddenly pricked Dunne. "How were you second arrival yet the one who found him? Who was first?"

The overseer shrugged. "Why, he was first, of course. Always was. He came always a few hours early at the beginning of the week because the forge would have been cold on account of Sunday. At other times the fire would have been banked overnight."

"So," said Rossi, "he was killed between, say, three A.M. and six A.M.?"

Dr. Owens nodded. That tallies with the body's rigor and the fact that there's as yet no putrefaction. And the lividity, from its levels in the lower limbs, suggests that he has been down from the triangles about—what is it now, nine A.M.?—only since about sunup."

"Yes, sir," agreed the overseer, "I unhooked him."

"That raises the question: Who hooked him up?" said Rossi. "He must have been a strong devil to handle the strength of a smith."

"Maybe our killer had an accomplice," suggested the patterer.

"Indeed, sir," interposed the overseer. "But there are tricks to every trade and flogging's no exception. I've seen a man suspend himself—God's own truth, sir!—so no manhandling of a reluctant or dead weight was called for. You persuade him, with the cat or the tickle of a blade, you see, to stand on a box or the like and throw his hand bindings or manacles over the top of the triangles. Kick his legs from under and he's hanging like game."

Rossi nodded. "However he was suspended, he was ironically—hah!—ironed around the wrists and ankles like the felons he catered for, no doubt by his very own handiwork. But, first, what exactly killed him?"

Owens blew through pursed lips. "We'll know for certain when I have had him up on the table, but I'm pretty sure the whipping didn't—by itself, that is. Men of his strength usually take it better than that. I've seen proud lads take 500 lashes and walk away. Of course, our man was old—well into his fifties, I'd guess. And his wounds were not the work of a professional scourger. Some of these are cat marks, and you can see where the tails have bitten deep. They've been dipped in wet sand to rough them up before each stroke.

"Now while that's pretty professional, some wounds are just strap marks, although they often end in lacerations, as though something sharp was attached to the strap, a blade of some sort. I'd hazard that our flogger got tired with the cat and moved to something lighter. Which suggests someone untrained in the black art."

"But what *did* kill him?" pursued Dunne. "Did he, er, choke on the . . ." He gestured at the amputated member the doctor had removed from the victim's mouth.

Owens shook his head. "No, not that. That was done last. The leather gag would not have helped, for I see that his nose has been broken in the past and he would have had trouble breathing through it at the best of times. No, I suspect he had a seizure. See, his face is empurpled. And one other thing—two, really—the cat tails and the other slashes left their marks mainly on the left of his back and curl around onto the left side of the belly. And the deepest heel marks of the scourger belong to a right foot."

"Which means?"

"That we are looking again at our old friend Bollocky Bill."

And, as Owens beckoned to two hospital handlers to approach and remove the body on a litter, he added, "Oh, and of course there were slashes to the throat, midriff and ankles. Just like the first victim outside the tavern. And, as well as having his private parts placed where they shouldn't be, the poor fellow was also given a ration of another old friend we've met before—but with a difference."

He smiled at his companions' frowns. "There is sugar again in the mouth, but very unusual sugar. It's bright green."

There was a long silence. "I think," said Rossi at last, "that we need to hold a council of war."

As the official party of investigators left the Lumber Yard, Dr. Owens to escort the body to the morgue for examination and his companions to return, if only briefly, to their normal lives, Nicodemus Dunne paused and took the captain aside.

"That strange remark by the overseer," he said. "I meant to pursue it back there, but it slipped away in the excitement."

Rossi looked blankly. "What remark was that, pray?"

"You must have heard it. He said that he—meaning the blacksmith—had served with the 45th Regiment in Grenada."

"So?"

"But he added that the man had boasted of having served *over* the governor—and the familiar way it was said indicates the reference was to *our* governor. What could be the possible meaning?"

"Oh, that." Rossi waved his hand dismissively. "I had a short word to the overseer about that. He must have misunderstood. I believe the smith never rose higher than corporal."

The patterer persisted. "All this is supposed to have happened before the turn of the century. You know His Excellency well. When did he begin his career as an officer? Did he buy an elevated commission?"

Rossi looked affronted. "No, he did not. He stepped onto the lowest rung. He became an ensign in the 45th—in which his father was also a soldier—in May '93. It was in Grenada or Barbados, I don't recall. He's come a long way since then, hasn't he? And even if that smith did happen to serve in the regiment at the same time as the governor, I ask you, what would a rising young officer have to do with a lowly noncommissioned officer—especially a black one?" He looked keenly at Dunne. "My advice to you is to put the matter out of your mind. Forget about it."

Captain Rossi started to walk away and the patterer shrugged and followed. But, and but . . . He still felt as though something had eluded him. Strangely, it was almost as if he had asked the wrong question.

CHAPTER TWENTY-FIVE

For now we see through a glass, darkly . . .
—I Corinthians 13:12

CAPTAIN ROSSI HAD ARRANGED FOR THE THREE MEN TO MEET that afternoon, when Dr. Thomas Owens could report on the results of his closer examination of the blacksmith's corpse. They would rendezvous at the Hope and Anchor Tavern.

But which one? It could all be very confusing. Due to some ancient dispute now lost in the mists of time, and no doubt in an alcoholic haze, drinkers bestowed the name on two widely separated establishments. One was in Sussex Street and the other on the northwest corner of King and Pitt streets.

The Sussex Street rival perhaps had the best claim to the name; after all it was closer to the sea, as an anchor should be. Nevertheless, the Hope and Anchor in King Street had its devotees, who often tried to avoid confusion (but just as often created more mental mayhem) by referring to it by its previous name, the Bunch of Grapes, or even an earlier name, the Three Legs o' Man.

Rossi and Dunne arrived at this tavern at the appointed hour and were served in the taproom by a powerfully built young man perhaps in his early twenties. He had a drooping moustache, which accentuated his generally sad demeanor.

"Gentlemen?" he queried in a well-modulated, cultured voice. Rossi ordered a brandy and the patterer a porter, just as Owens bustled through the door and joined them at the bar. The doctor surprised his companions with his order: "Adam's ale, please." He explained that he was drinking water because he had a lady patient to see and alcoholic breath might distress her.

Dunne was not convinced. "You, Doctor, water?" He laughed. "I recall you once warning me off the very stuff! You said it could carry disease, as miasmas and suchlike do. Why, you declared that the Tank Stream was not the only fouled water here, that most well water was unsuitable for drinking."

Owens looked down his long nose. "If it has been boiled—and I am assured that it is served here thus—then it is quite safe. Anyway, there are worse things than dirty water."

"Would you care to elaborate on that?" asked the patterer, intrigued by the doctor's serious tone.

"No," said Owens flatly. And the topic was dropped.

The doctor then confirmed that the smith had received injuries during flogging (obviously from a tyro thrasher) but had actually died of apoplexy. And yes, a number of the cuts came not from whip knots but somehow from a sharp blade, which had also been used to cut off the penis and inflict wounds mirroring those on the first victim.

"And the intriguing matter of the usual sugar in the mouth being green?" asked Rossi.

"Analysis showed normal sugar with the simple addition of copperas, or ferrous sulphate, also called green vitriol. It's used in dyeing."

"Dying?" repeated Rossi, startled.

"With an *e* in the middle, Captain—meaning for coloring." Owens then changed the subject suddenly. "I'm hungry," he said. "Does that go for anyone else?"

"Any pies, William?" Dunne called to the barman. The man left his counter and walked to the corner of the room in which stood a brightly painted handcart. The upper part of the cart had compartments for pies and gravy pans and below was a glowing charcoal brazier. He returned to his customers with three pies and accepted the nine pence tendered.

William Francis King made most of his pie sales outside the pub. Between shifts tending bar, he tramped the streets of the town and beyond, trundling his pie-cart. Behind the bar this day he wore rather conventional clothing but, when hawking, he affected an eye-catching outfit. He was as well known a character throughout the small settlement as Paddy the Ram, Old Mother Five Bob, Garden Honey or any of the other perambulating peddlers: oyster-sellers, butchers, fishmongers, fruit-traders, bakers, even apothecaries. He cried his wares on street corners, outside the barracks, at horse races, cricket matches, bull-baiting and dogfights.

It was an odd life for a man of King's background. The well-educated son of an influential Treasury official in London, he had been intended for a career in the Church. Somehow, no one in the colony seemed quite sure of the dark secrets involved, he drifted, or was bundled off, to Botany Bay. He had been a schoolteacher here briefly. But again events—some people said it was boredom, others yet another secret setback—deflected him, this time into serving beer and pies.

His main fame rested, however, on his powerful body, which carried him on endeavors that constantly amazed settlers and made (or lost) money for gamblers betting on his success or failure.

He would don an eccentric costume with either a tall hat or a jockey's cap and stout boots, and would capture the public's attention by walking the thirty-two miles from Macquarie Place, in the heart of the town, to Parramatta—and back—in six hours. He could even beat the coach to Parramatta.

He had once carried a boy on his back to the same outer town in three hours; and once lumped, on his back and at a run, a ninety-pound goat for a mile and a half in twelve minutes.

Nothing they saw William Francis King doing could surprise the citizens of Sydney town. Thus, and little wonder, he was known far and wide simply as the "Flying Pieman."

King was modest about his exploits. "I'm not in the same class as Walking Stuart," he had once replied when congratulated by the patterer on some extraordinary piece of pedestrianism.

He explained, after Dunne professed ignorance, that John Stuart, who had died six years earlier, was the son of a London draper. As a young man, he had gone to work for the East India Company in Madras. After resigning over an argument he soon earned the epithet "Walking" by doing just that, throughout Hindoostan, Persia, Nubia and across the Arabian Desert. He then trekked through Europe from Constantinople to England. Later, he walked across known America and Canada.

He was the Pieman's hero. "Thomas de Quincey," King told

Dunne earnestly, "said that Walking Stuart as a pedestrian traveler saw more of the earth's surface than any man before or since."

The patterer was not sure how good a judge of reality Mr. de Quincey might be. After all, his claim to fame was far from down-to-earth: authorship of *Confessions of an English Opium-Eater*.

Nonetheless, Nicodemus Dunne appreciated the merit in Walking Stuart's athleticism. And William King's ability was no pipe dream either.

————————

THEIR PIES (AND some further liquid lubricants) gone, the three companions turned to further digestion of the fruits, so far, of their investigative labors. They retired to the comfort and privacy of a bench against one wall.

Captain Rossi leaned back against one high wooden divider and summed up: They had three murders (they could not believe that the death of the man known as The Ox was due to suicide), all connected by the victims' service in the same regiment. The fourth killing, in the Lumber Yard, seemed different, despite similarities. The captain's listeners agreed.

Then the patterer raised a thought: "I have been wondering what the convict overseer meant when he referred to the late blacksmith regretting some work he had performed."

"Can you take any notice of anything a convict overseer says?" grunted Rossi. "They're usually the scum of the system. They're generally lags themselves who get a year's remission on their sentences for every two years they're willing to drive the poor devils under them. They're distrusted on both sides. And with good reason."

"Still," said Owens, "it's worth considering. What did the keeper say? Yes, that's it; he said the blacksmith—a hard man, mind you, no doubt made insensitive by his work—nonetheless had felt badly about how some shackles he once made were too punishing for a prisoner. And not just any prisoner, mind you. He specified that it was a soldier."

"Soldiers seem to bob up everywhere," said the patterer. "So, clutching at straws, can we link our earlier beliefs and conclude that the motives are revenge for some injury or injustice done by the action of a soldier?"

"Or done *to* a soldier by the system?" added Owens.

At that moment they were interrupted by a voice that carried clearly over the wooden divide between their bench and the next. All the voice said was, "Try suds."

CHAPTER TWENTY-SIX

Though this be madness, yet there is method in't.
—William Shakespeare, *Hamlet* (1601)

"I BEG YOUR PARDON, SIR!" CALLED CAPTAIN ROSSI BACK TO THE interrupting voice, testily.

A figure appeared around the partition and the patterer recognized his friend Alexander Harris.

"I beg *your* pardon," Harris said to Rossi, after acknowledging Dunne with a nod. "I couldn't help but overhear some of your conversation. It appears such a serious matter, and I believe I may be able to help you."

"He is my good friend and an honest man," said Dunne, introducing Harris to Rossi and the doctor.

"That may be," said Rossi coolly. "Still, the damage is done . . . Very well. If you will swear to keep the problem to yourself, perhaps you can help. And, God knows, we need all the help we can get.

But please, gentlemen, I beg of you—no more collaborators. If the governor ever found out . . ."

And so Rossi outlined the task, once Harris had promised to be discreet.

"What did you mean by your remark that 'suds' could perhaps throw light on our quest?" asked Owens, first to raise the obvious question. "What does soap have to do with it?"

Harris laughed. "Nothing of the washing variety, gentlemen. No, I was referring to a person, one of considerable renown: Sudds, with an extra d—Private Joseph Sudds."

His companions showed great interest. It was a safe wager— almost as good as backing the Flying Pieman—that almost all in the colony, even those in the outblocks, had heard of, and had an opinion on, Joseph Sudds.

The three men with Harris certainly knew of the cause célè- bre surrounding the name. Two years earlier almost to the day, Sudds and a fellow soldier named Patrick Thompson, both of the 57th Regiment, had stolen fabric from a town shop—and calmly awaited arrest.

The thinking behind this strange behavior was not particularly original; disgruntled men serving in the Buffs had done it before. If history repeated itself, Sudds and Thompson expected to receive a sentence of seven years' transportation, which in Sydney meant to a secondary punishment settlement, such as Moreton Bay to the north. They would hope to receive tickets of leave after a few years in jail and then become Emancipists, freed settlers.

At the start, such soldiers were right; a civil court leaned that way. But Governor Ralph Darling, fearing a flood of imitators, stepped in and changed the sentence to hard labor on the roads in the ironed gangs, then a return to service. The men were thrown into jail and barely five days later Sudds died. Mr. Wentworth's *Australian* and Mr. Hall's *Monitor* accused the governor of murder and sought his impeachment. The battle still raged on, long after the regiment had first drummed the men out.

"But why," asked the patterer, "does the unfortunate Sudds come into our calculations?"

"Here's why," said Alexander Harris triumphantly. "Simply because the governor had ordered that the pair be shackled with irons many times heavier than usual—each set made an extra stone's weight. That is surely what the overseer was referring to when he said the dead man—and you say he was a smith at the Lumber Yard?—was so sorely haunted. That's why the matters came together in my mind when I overheard you."

"Jove!" said Rossi. "You may have something there." He jumped to his feet. "Will you all wait here? I'll dash to my office and get a file that should refresh our memories of the case and may tell us more."

The others agreed.

While Rossi was absent, Harris told the patterer he would be interested to see the puzzling proof pulled from the type discovered in the burned-out printery where Abbot had been murdered. Owens also evinced curiosity. Dunne produced the sheet, which was becoming creased and even more difficult to read.

"I was a compositor once myself, you know," Harris remarked. "In London years ago."

The patterer had not known, although he was aware of other matters in his friend's life. The son of a parson, Harris had confided that he had fallen into the ways of atheism and drink and among fallen women. Yet his closest secret—and a dangerous one to reveal—was that he had enlisted in the army but had deserted. He had just managed to slip away to Botany Bay.

Now he examined the printed slip proffered. "Rather small, isn't it?" he remarked. "I refer, of course, to the typeface."

"Ruby, I think," said Dunne.

Harris shook his head. "No, I mean that it was wanted by the author in a larger size. See the first words, 'All eight point.' That makes no sense in the subsequent copy"—Dunne looked again and agreed—"because it was simply a reminder by the compositor to set the material all in eight-point type. Which he obviously hasn't. You know that there are about seventy-two points to the inch, thus Ruby is five-and-a-half point and Nonpareil six point." His discourse plowed on. "There's a newspaper setting record, you know—152 lines in two hours."

Owens showed mild interest. "How is changing the sizes done?"

Harris was happy to have an attentive audience. "Why, the compositor simply changes to another case. I'm not referring to 'uppercase,' as we know capital letters, and their brethren 'lowercase' pieces of type. By 'case,' I mean the whole wooden case that contains many complete sets of that particular style of type. Our man seems to have put aside his case of eight-point letters requested and taken up before him a case of the smaller Ruby. That's how the case is altered.

"I've forgotten many of the names, but the really small ones are usually used for pocket books—dictionaries, for instance. Breviaries, too; indeed, that's why one type is called Brevier. They have lovely names. They differ from place to place, you know."

The patterer did not know and he could see that Owens was becoming bored by the former compositor's loving recital of his lost craft's arcane detail.

"There are in America bourgeois and minion, which is our emerald. Nonpareil occurs in both countries, then there is Agate—or our type you mentioned, Ruby . . ." Harris rambled on but could throw no fresh light on the printed message. The discussion ended with the return of Captain Rossi.

The chief of police was happily waving a fat folder of documents.

"Here, gentlemen, is the official report on the matter. We can analyze it fully in the light of all we have discussed. In the meantime, I have sent a message to the barracks for another possible missing link—information on the men directly involved in the drumming-out. If we now believe that the blacksmith may have been a target for some sort of vengeance, who else may be seen to have persecuted Sudds?

"So let us start at the beginning." Rossi opened the folder. "Ah, yes. It seems it all started on September 20 two years ago, between eight and nine P.M. The two soldiers visited the shop in York Street, beside the barracks, of a Mr. Michael Napthali. They walked out with twelve yards of calico, valued—it seems surprisingly low—at five shillings. They were arrested and charged with theft. Their plan worked as desired at first. Quarter Sessions delivered the sentences anticipated. But then, as we know, His Excellency took it out of the hands of the civil court and imposed his own much harsher punishment."

Rossi cleared his throat with a sip of refreshment. "On October 22 just before noon, they were brought onto the parade ground and suffered much indignity and discomfort, and there was much more of the same, even worse, to come. But let Private Patrick Thompson tell us in his own words . . ."

Owens gasped. "You mean he's here? In the flesh?"

CHAPTER TWENTY-SEVEN

Smooth the descent and easy is the way
(The Gates of Hell stand open night and day) . . .
—Virgil's *Aeneid*, translated by John Dryden (1697)

"I'M AFRAID NOT!" CAPTAIN ROSSI LAUGHED AT DR. OWENS'S SUG-gestion that Private Thompson might be about to show himself. "He went to Emu Plains, then to Moreton Bay, I believe, and to Nor-folk Island. There's talk he will eventually be sent home to Ireland. He's the relatively lucky one of the pair of miscreants. However," he said, flourishing a document, "here is a transcript of his examina-tion in April 1827, taken on the prison hulk *Phoenix* in the harbor.

"It is interesting to see that there is an aside to the examina-tion stating that Sudds had been a—and I use the exact words—'remarkably well-conducted man previously, but Thompson's character was not so good, and it is believed that it was owing to his evil advice that Sudds engaged in the scheme.' But I digress."

He handed the document to the patterer. "Perhaps you would oblige me by reading it aloud?"

Dunne knew that the captain was self-conscious about his accent, so he obliged and brought new life to Patrick Thompson's words.

"'We were taken,'" he read, "'to the parade ground, and the regimentals taken off us, and a General Order read to us by Brigade Major Gillman, by the order of His Excellency General Darling. After the Order was read to us, a set of irons was put on each of us. The irons consisted of a collar, which went round each of our necks, and chains were fastened to the collar on each side of the shoulder, and reached from thence to the basil, which was placed about three inches from each ankle . . . I could not stand upright with the irons on. The basil of the irons would not slip up my legs, and the chains were too short to allow me to stand upright. I was never measured for the irons; and Sudds's collar was too small for his neck, and the basils for his legs, which were swollen, were too small.'"

Dunne paused and shook his head in dismay before continuing. "'There was a piece of iron that projected from the collar before and behind, about eight inches at each place. The projecting irons would not allow me to stretch myself at full length on my back. I could sleep by contracting my legs. I could not lie at full length on either side. After the yellow clothes and the irons were put on us, we were drummed out of the regiment, the Rogue's March being played after us by two or three drummers and fifers. We were not drummed out in the usual way, which is to put a rope about the neck, cut off the facings, and place a piece of paper on the back, with a description of the offense that the party may have committed. Instead of this we had the irons and the yellow clothing . . . '"

"What about Sudds?" interrupted Owens impatiently.

"Soon, Doctor, soon. He is coming to that now." The patterer continued his grim recital. "'The night of the day of punishment, Sudds was so ill that we were obliged to get a candle from the under-jailer in order to keep up a light during the night. I gave him some tea, which I had purchased. A fellow prisoner said he did not think he would live long. I then asked Sudds if he had any friends to whom he would wish to write. He said he had a wife and child in Gloucestershire, and begged that if he did not get better by the next night, I would read some pious book to him, adding, "that they had put him in them irons until they had killed him."'

"That they did," said the patterer quietly, handing the statement back to Rossi, who grimaced.

The group sat in silence until Dunne roused himself and commented, "It was all over in days. Sudds was taken to the jail hospital, such as it is, then to the general wards. He died less than a week after being so cruelly restrained."

Dunne paused to scan the other papers in the file. "There is no doubt that Governor Darling directed Captain Dumaresq to have particular irons fashioned at the Lumber Yard. It also seems that Dumaresq took the finished shackles to His Excellency for inspection. It's fair to assume the governor approved what he saw, and no one argues that these weren't the ones subsequently used."

Rossi sighed. "He wanted to make an example that would most discourage other soldiers from imitating the scheme."

"He certainly achieved that," said Owens coldly. "I see that Mr. Hall in *The Monitor* says the irons were such as had never before been heard of in this colony, even for the most atrocious murderers."

The patterer agreed. "They were carrying an extra fourteen or fifteen pounds, three times more than shackles on men in the usual road gangs. But let these sad events now inform our intellects, not our passions. It seems that Mr. Harris has steered us on a promising course. Apart from the case of the man known as The Ox, our victims' neck, belly and leg slashes may be seen to mimic the fall of the cruel shackles on Sudds and Thompson. The dead printer's decapitation could be seen as a reference to a spiked collar."

"Tell me," interrupted Owens suddenly. "Why was Sudds so ill suddenly, unlike Thompson? Ill, indeed, unto death. What does your report say?"

"Well," replied Rossi. "Fellow soldiers told that for quite a while his eyesight had been failing, also his hearing, and said that he had found it painful to walk. Some, including the governor, stated he had dropsy." He consulted a document. "The medical officer at the jail declared that dissection showed no apparent disease to account for death. He said Sudds had 'wished himself to death.'"

The patterer had a sudden memory of his meeting with Dr. Peter Cunningham—was it really only a few days ago, at the beginning of this adventure?—and how that doctor had alluded to the prisoners' conviction that they could will themselves to escape, to reverse their destiny. Could Sudds indeed have "wished" himself to some sort of earlier freedom? Even if the price of his return passage was death?

He jerked his mind back to the present and saw that Owens was shaking his head as he said, "Dropsy? Perhaps. It sounds, however, as if he may have suffered from a diabetes."

"Interesting," said the patterer. "But does it take us anywhere?"

Owens prompted, "Diabetes; which is known as . . . ?"

A pause. Then the patterer ventured, "Well, I've heard it commonly called the sweet-water sickness."

"Why that?"

"Why? Well, because the sufferer's water—his urine—smells sweet."

"Quite so," agreed the doctor. "It does. So you have a condition that may be described as *diabetes mellitus*. The first word comes from the Greek *diabainein*, meaning 'to pass through,' and *mellitus* is, of course, Latin—'sweetened with honey.' Now," he continued. "What is another common name for a diabetes?"

"Well, it's also called sugar diab— My God! Sugar!"

"Exactly," said Owens with a smile, which faded slightly as he added, "But why the blacksmith's mouthful was dyed green, and the others' not so, I confess to be a puzzle."

"No matter," said Rossi enthusiastically. "It seems someone is avenging the death of Sudds by imitating the pair's bodily confinements and by referring to his true illness. Now we have to find out who it is."

"But," said Alexander Harris, "where do all our victims fit into the scheme of things?"

"Perhaps this will help our cause," answered Rossi, suddenly standing up and waving wildly. He had seen a redcoat appear at the tavern door. The man advanced and handed over an envelope, after which the captain dismissed him.

Rossi tore open the seal and scanned the papers inside. "I asked Colonel Shadforth to have a search made of the victims' recent history in the regimental records. At about the time of the drumming-out seemed a logical starting point. I understand their discharges, honorable ones, were granted soon after that event."

As he began to read, he tut-tutted. "The colonel has gone back even further. This first note refers even to the time of the theft that began this sorry saga. So, what does it say? . . . Yes, in the middle of

September—that's about a week before the theft?—The Ox, as we call him, the printer Will Abbot and the soldier knifed in the alley were detailed to guard duty. Well, that's quite normal. Sudds, too, I see. No Thompson."

He turned a page. "What's this? Perhaps the colonel thought it of interest. It seems that on the following day, three of the guard were paraded for breaches of dress regulations and general good order—uniform irregularities—and for losing equipment. They escaped with reprimands."

"Which three?" asked Owens.

"The Ox, Abbot . . . and Sudds." Rossi studied the group.

Only Harris, the secret ex-soldier, offered an opinion. "Happens all the time with soldiers," he said. "Although they're generally smart enough before and after a spell of guard. Still . . ."

Rossi added, "Sudds—and we've heard what a good soldier he seemed—was rebuked for losing army property, to wit a cane. A cane?" He was puzzled.

"Ah," said Harris. "It could make sense. He was turned out well when inspected at the start of the guard duty and so he took the stick." He was met with blank stares. "Oh, the smartest soldier inspected for the guard may be excused turns at serious sentry-go and is made orderly of the guard, a light duty. Light, because it means he can carry a swagger-stick instead of a musket. They call it 'taking the stick.'"

"Well, it's not quite the information I wanted," said Rossi. He found a new page. "But perhaps this is. The adjutant has made these notes after interviews with men who recall that Rogue's March. And listen to this!" In his excitement, he had forgotten his shyness about his accent. "The prisoners' regimentals were taken off—remember, that is a prime humiliation—by a private soldier.

The name listed here is that of none other than the man who was to become our first victim, outside the alehouse! Next, one of the men who played the march and drummed Sudds out of the regiment was . . ."—he paused for effect—". . . our late lamented printer, Will Abbot!" He looked exceedingly pleased with himself.

The patterer was reluctant to temper the captain's delight but felt he must. "What about the poisoned man, The Ox?"

Rossi grimaced. "He was in the regiment at the time, and he may have observed the ritual, but there appears to be no evidence that he took an active role. Yet I insist he is linked by the killer's handwriting."

"Agreed," said Dunne. "However, there's a weakness in our theory. Or a terrible threat lurking. Our four victims so far are but a handful of the possible targets for an avenger. Granted, the blacksmith could be held as particularly culpable, but why not other drummers and fifers? Why not the unsuccessful jail doctor? And there are more important figures who could be—and are being—held responsible for Sudds's death . . . Captain Dumaresq, who oversaw the manufacture of the accursed devices, and the Brigade Major, who took the parade for the Rogue's March. Perhaps most important of course, there is His Excellency, who started it all by thwarting Sudds's plans then ordering the draconian punishment. They're all still alive.

"And where, and why, has the killer been leading us with the mysterious verse and the printed clue? The Hebraic doggerel? Well, I agree we have an angel of death and there has been a fire, a slaughterer and an ox—but nothing else mentioned applies even remotely. So far, anyway. The line of printed warning—if such it is—taken from Exodus? Again there are 'wound' and 'burning,' and 'stripe' could stand for flogging. But no eye, teeth, hand or foot."

Nicodemus Dunne shrugged. "No, gentlemen, I concede that Sudds almost certainly has something to do with it, but there's another dimension that we have not yet entertained."

"Well," said Rossi briskly. "Perhaps tomorrow will bring us a change of fortune."

The meeting adjourned.

CHAPTER TWENTY-EIGHT

A solitary shriek, the bubbling cry
Of some strong swimmer in his agony.
—Lord Byron, *Don Juan* (1819–24)

THE NEXT DAY, THE PATTERER MET THE FLYING PIEMAN GOING TO the seaside. Depressed by his lack of inspiration in the murder investigations, he thought it was more a case, as in the nursery rhyme, of Simple Simon meeting a pieman. He tried to shrug off his sense of failure with a welcoming smile.

Both men were obviously at leisure: William Francis King, though in full fig, was not towing his gaily painted pie-cart and Nicodemus Dunne was not carrying his satchel stuffed with newspapers.

Dunne was in the habit of swimming, or at least splashing about and sunning himself, at Soldiers Point, which nosed out into Cockle Bay two blocks west of the army barracks. Sorry, he thought, not Cockle Bay; now it was all to be called Darling Harbor. The name

Cockle would satisfy him, though—a cold fish in a hard shell was a perfectly apt description of the taciturn, aloof governor.

Seabathing was the best way to keep clean in Sydney. Lack of water and difficulty heating it made tubbing a distinct luxury. And, of course, many people—even doctors—believed that too much washing was unhealthy. Better that risk than stinking, Dunne had decided long ago. And many women (not Miss Dormin, he was certain) reeked almost as badly as the men.

Today he had gone to Soldiers Point, but soon left. There were, well, too many soldiers rowdily enjoying the clear waters. He had moved north to a quieter strand beside another headland that had similarly exercised the naming rivalries of the citizens. Some called it Cockle Bay Point. Others, and the patterer was among them, preferred the more colorful, even romantic Jack-the-Miller's Point. The name honored the pioneer miller on the point, John Leighton. Now there were other windmills; Miller could have owned the whole point, but he had refused to fence the area, the main condition of his land grant, and so lost it to others.

It was after Dunne had walked along Kent Street, passed the stone quarry and headed on toward the limekilns (dross from which threatened to pollute the bay) to reach the sandy stretch that he had come across William King, who was decked out in his best formal Pieman uniform. Quaintly dressed in a fashion that had expired years before, he wore red knee breeches meeting skin-tight white hose. Over these he wore a pale blue jacket, and his head was topped by a tall hat that seemed to almost have a life of its own, due to cascading, trailing streamers of many colors. Sometimes he wore a simple jockey's cap rather than this extravaganza, but he always carried a long, stout staff that was decorated like the topper.

When he reached the beach, the patterer stripped to his under-drawers and slipped into the chilly water. It was always calm for swimming here, but he knew of people back home (there, he thought, I've said it) in Devon and Cornwall who deliberately bat-tled out through the heavy seas that thrashed the shingle beaches, then rode the waves ashore using only buoyancy and body move-ments. Some, he believed, even skimmed to the shore on slabs of driftwood. He didn't know if anyone here had tried it on the beaches to the east, such as the one called *Boondi*, which was native for "sound of the surf." He was certainly not sure enough of his swimming ability even to consider testing the theory.

"Aren't you coming in?" he called to his companion, who stood stock-still and fully dressed well away from the water's edge.

King shook his head so hard that the ends of his moustache flapped and the ribbons on his hat rattled. "I have taken a vow never to meet the sea waters. I hate the sea. Anyway, I can't swim."

Dunne was intrigued. With his athletic prowess and great strength, the pieman should have been as at home in the sea as a seal.

The patterer bobbed closer to shore, but when he was only several body-lengths from the sand, still in water that was well over his head, the cramps struck. This cannot be happening, he thought . . . I have not come into the water on a full stomach; all I had was a pie hours ago and then a lozenge pressed upon me in the street by Dr. Owens . . .

In his panic, he thought he must be suffering a heart seizure or apoplexy. Whatever it was, he lost control of his limbs and his ability to remain buoyant, and began to sink, barely able to thresh the surface. And he was powerless even to stop the slight current dragging him into deeper water.

As he bobbed up briefly he saw the figure of the pieman, agitated and waving his arms, on the shore. He could not stop gulping more water as he sank again. Then suddenly something hard struck his head. Desperately trying to fight to the surface, he saw a large stick with something streaming from it—seaweed? Was this to be his funeral wreath?—and grabbed the wood with one hand.

The stick moved and he managed to go with it. His feet, knees, some body part, touched blessed bottom, then he felt strong hands drag him ashore. A scarlet haze enveloped him.

The patterer vomited copiously, and gradually the cramps and the red dizziness eased. He saw beside him the pieman, grinning with relief—and soaked from moustache to toe. The beribboned staff that had been used to reach him was another soggy reminder of the adventure.

"That was courageous of you," said the patterer. "You could have drowned, too."

William King shrugged. "I only waded in as far as possible. My staff did the rest. I couldn't leave you to drown. I just couldn't do that. Not again."

Dunne frowned. "Again? I don't understand."

The pieman sighed deeply. "Some know the story. You might as well know it, too. Soon after I arrived in the colony, I fell in love with a convict lass. She was assigned and wasn't free to marry, so we hatched a plan. I paid ten pounds for cabin passage—for one, mind you—on a bark set for Van Diemen's Land. I sent aboard my luggage, one big box. You have probably already guessed that my girl was hidden inside, as comfortable as possible. And I had bored airholes in the sides. The idea was that I would release her when we were far out to sea. I came ashore to attend to some business, but when I returned the ship was gone!

"I took a horse and rode, a crazed man, along the winding road to the South Head. I could see the bark heading out to sea. There was no way I could attract its attention. I harbored hopes that someone would hear my love and release her. There was no way I could overtake her. Then later I heard the ship had been lost. Do you wonder that I hate the sea? I drowned her, alone."

Jesus! thought the patterer. What must it have been like for that poor girl, carried to the depths in her box, a ready-made coffin? He remembered the fear in a storm of every convict battened below in chains. You knew you would never escape. He shivered, not just from his damp near-nudity, but at the memory.

The pieman was weeping.

"Come come," said the patterer awkwardly, clapping his friend's back. "Let's get out of our wet things and walk a bit to dry off."

Wearing only their drawers and shoes, the pair roamed casually toward Lieutenant Dawes's Battery. King's wet clothes were draped on his staff and they carried this laundry between them.

A scream and the sound of bodies crashing together broke the calm. The noises came from a clearing in scrub near the shore below Leighton's flour mill. King and the patterer set off at a run.

CHAPTER TWENTY-NINE

And finds, with keen discriminating sight,
Black's not so black—nor white so very white.
—George Canning, "New Morality" (1821)

THE SCENE THEY DISCOVERED WHEN THEY FOUND THE SOURCE OF the screaming horrified Dunne so much that he froze for a moment. A white man was pummeling, with fists, boots and a cudgel, two black figures on the ground. By his familiar build, tattered red coat and skewed bicorne hat, but particularly his gleaming brass plate, the patterer recognized one of the victims as King Bungaree. He couldn't yet identify the other fallen man.

Nearby, two men—who were clearly white—held a black woman pinned to the ground. They had torn off her robe and, while one subdued her struggling, his companion, trousers down around his ankles, pawed at her viciously.

The pieman was the first to react physically. Swinging his long staff, he cracked the rapist across the spine. With a second stroke he smashed the face of the man restraining the woman, breaking his nose and teeth, perhaps his jaw.

The patterer moved behind the man attacking the black figures, hitting him with a rock. The man fell senseless.

While the pieman guarded his moaning opponents, Dunne helped the black men to their feet. One was indeed King Bungaree, and now it was clear who his companion was—a huge, though very ancient West Indian they called "Billy Blue" or just as commonly, "the Old Commodore." He wore a top hat and an old naval uniform, a nod to the lofty rank he had never even remotely held (although he claimed to have fought with Wolfe at Quebec and Cornwallis at Yorktown). In truth, he had washed up in Sydney after stealing a bag of sugar in London. Apart from a relapse as a rum-runner, he had prospered as a waterman and harbor watchman for Governor Macquarie, who had bestowed on him the elevated title when the old lag's ferry fleet grew from one boat to eleven.

Even now—although Dunne knew Billy had told the recent census that he was eighty—he was far from retired. From his home across the cove at Murdering Point, the Old Commodore and his sons plied for hire as ferrymen. Often he would play on his great age, boast of his service in the Royal Navy and cajole a sympathetic passenger into helping out with the rowing.

After making sure that the commodore and the king had survived relatively unscathed, if shaken, the patterer turned to where the pieman was comforting the woman. Who was she? he wondered.

"She's Gooseberry," said Bungaree, as if reading his thoughts.

Dunne nodded. He knew Bungaree had more than one wife. There had been Boatman, Broomstick, Onion and Pincher. This, then, was Matara, also known as Cora Gooseberry.

She was sitting up now, rocking and weeping, clutching together her ripped clothing. She soon began to search in the dirt for the clay pipe she had dropped in the melee. A good sign, thought the patterer. The rest of the point was still now, the welcome calm broken only by the screech of gulls and the swishing and clicking of the windmills' sails.

While Bungaree spoke to his wife, Billy Blue explained to their rescuers what had happened. He spoke perfect English, a legacy of all his years at sea. To the surprise of many, Bungaree had also polished his own knowledge of the colonists' language while under sail. With Matthew Flinders almost thirty years earlier, he had circumnavigated the Australian coastline, acting as an interpreter.

The commodore told how he had tied up his skiff at the point and begun working in the hut nearby. With his boys, he ran the town side of his ferry service to and from there. Bungaree and Gooseberry had arrived and begun to cook a meal, which they invited him to share.

Dunne could see the leftovers and guessed they had cooked a *dampier*, named after the English explorer and buccaneer, but now more often called a "damper," made simply from flour, salt, sugar and water kneaded together and cooked in the ashes of a dying fire. Beside this ruined fire, the patterer identified what looked like the popular dish baked koala, which was actually a joke; it wasn't native bear but instead a pielike, hollowed-out gourd filled with opossum meat.

He was surprised that there were no grog bottles—Bungaree was known to be a fearsome drinker. Instead, they appeared to have taken tea. Tipped over beside the fire was a large, empty, blackened tin. Most probably it had once contained preserved boiled beef that the French, who invented it, called *boeuf bouilli*.

Settlers used the empty tins to brew tea and called them billy—for *bouilli*—cans.

The men, Billy Blue said, had attacked without warning.

Dunne and the others now turned their attention to the vanquished intruders. The one Dunne had hit was still unconscious, the trouserless rapist was temporarily crippled on the ground and the one with the broken face moaned and bled.

The patterer looked down at them closely. "They're not much more than lads," he said, shaking his head sadly. One attacker had started to blubber. "Probably the dregs of those they turn out from the Carters Barracks when they're old enough."

"Old enough for trouble," said William King.

Dunne nodded.

"So what do we do with them now?" asked the pieman. "In particular, how do we stop a revenge attack on these blacks—or, for that matter, ourselves?"

"Well, you can forget the constables," said the patterer. "They'd want too many details, and that means names, that is if they were interested." He paused. "These animals probably wouldn't recognize us when we're dressed—certainly not when you're in your usual garments. So you see, there was a bright side and a benefit to your going into the sea."

The pieman frowned. "And the king and the commodore? And Cora?"

The patterer pondered, then snapped his fingers. "I have it!" He loomed over the three young men, who were now struggling to their knees. "Do you know what The Ring is on Norfolk Island—and here?" he asked, slapping one upturned face, hard, to concentrate their attention.

The now-toothless youth nodded, wide-eyed.

"Aye," said Dunne. "And you know its punishment for its ene-mies? Just to remind you, we cut open their bellies and stuff in sheep guts instead. I'm a Sydney Ring-master and we'll always find you. Take your friends and get out of here. And if I hear of you tampering with anyone—white or black—you're deader meat than any man left ironed on Pinchgut and forgotten." He kicked one in the rear as they staggered away.

"Steady," said William King. "There's enough violence in this town. You can't be judge and executioner."

The patterer shook his head. "How else could we have stopped them? And how would they have been punished? If it got to court, what would they have been charged with? 'Taking liber-ties with blacks?' Anyway, it would only be our word—and I'm merely a pass-man—against theirs. No one would listen to three old 'Indians.' If you are concerned about that business of The Ring . . . Well, there *is* such a convicts' secret society—God knows they need someone to help them—and I've known men who are members. But that's the closest I've come."

He had a sudden sobering thought. Was the killer he was seek-ing perhaps someone who could justify his actions with similar logic: that there were times and places that called for summary justice?

To clear his mind, he turned to the two black men. Only then did he notice that Bungaree's left arm was hanging awkwardly in its uniform sleeve. "You're sorely hurt."

"No, sir. My arm is double-jointed after an old break. Another fight."

The pieman pointed to Cora Gooseberry, who was now more composed and puffing on her pipe, which she had recovered and relit from the embers of the fire. "Is she all right?"

Bungaree nodded. "They wanted to rob me, too, but all I had was a handful of dumps I was paid on the last two ships I met. If they think I have gold, they're wrong. All I ever get is dumps. But I thank you, sirs. If you ever need friendship, my people will help you." He saluted smartly and led his queen back toward the town.

The Old Commodore raised his top hat and held out a huge hand to Dunne and then King. "I, too, am grateful. I owe you a great debt. Call for my services at any time. Just send word to me." He turned and limped off toward his boat.

THE PATTERER AND the pieman were silent and subdued as they dressed and began to walk away from the battleground. Both had been badly shaken by the fight.

Dunne tried to lighten the mood. "You know, some people say that the name Miller's Point really refers to Governor Phillip's secretary, Andrew Miller."

William King thought about that then shook his head. "That can't be right. Too much of a mouthful—that would make it Andrew-the-Secretary's Point!" They both laughed, but soon fell back into their earlier gloom.

The patterer finally mused aloud, "I didn't really know it until just now, but I could easily kill someone. I was angry enough."

The pieman nodded. "You don't even have to be angry. Look at me. I *did* kill someone. And the people you talked and drank with the other day . . . deliberately or accidentally they may have killed. Captain Rossi was a soldier, Thomas Owens is a doctor—both can cause death. Even the governor was a fighting soldier once. Death's nothing to them."

A vagrant thought, lurking in the back of the patterer's mind, itched suddenly, but he couldn't scratch it to life.

King pushed through a herd of wild goats blocking their path. "They're a damn plague—like the parrots everywhere."

Dunne nodded distractedly. Parrots. Again, like his itch of a moment earlier, he had an uneasy feeling that, for some reason he could not capture, these birds were vitally important.

The patterer shrugged. If the birds had flown from his mind, not so the images of Miss Rachel Dormin, who had invited him to watch her that evening in a theatrical performance.

CHAPTER THIRTY

Judge not the play before the play is done:
Her plot has many changes: every day
Speaks a new scene; the last act crowns the play.
—Francis Quarles, *Emblems* (1635)

AT THE THEATER LATER THAT EVENING, MR. BARNETT LEVEY reassured a rather breathless Nicodemus Dunne: "Rest easy, dear sir, it's not over until the fat lady sings!"

The patterer was puzzled by this remark but did not comment. A late reading of news to a demanding but well-paying patron had made the young man late (although happily not too late) for that evening's performance at the Sydney Amateur Theater, which was noisily crowded.

Dunne knew Mr. Levey well; at thirty, he was much the same age as the patterer and he was the brother of Solomon, the partner of Mr. Cooper in the Waterloo Stores. Solomon was a successful Emancipist, freed after having been transported for seven years for stealing ninety pounds of tea (a charge he still denied). Barnett

Levey, on the other hand, was the colony's first free Jewish settler. Dunne belatedly realized that he could have sought him out in his quest for the meaning of *zuzim*.

The general merchant, builder, banker, grain merchant and bookseller was a busy businessman, but his true love was his theater—at which he wore many hats: owner, entrepreneur, often master of ceremonies, even performer of comic songs. And, of course, he oversaw the sale of drink in the bar of his Royal Hotel, which fronted his business and the theater.

As he entered the auditorium that night, the patterer reflected that, strictly speaking, there should have been no one there at all. Technically, the theater did not exist, for Governor Darling had so far refused to give Levey a license for his playhouse. But the diminutive, rotund young man defiantly mounted his theatricals as "at homes," "divertissements" or "concerts," legitimately part of the Royal Hotel's entertainments. Tonight's performances had, for instance, been announced as an "olio," an approximation of the Spanish word *olla*, meaning "stew" or "hotpot."

In actual fact, Levey's rift with Darling ran deeper than a simple disagreement over greasepaint and scenery. When Levey had proudly erected his Colchester Warehouse in George Street, with the architectural help of Mr. Francis Greenway, he had added a windmill to the top story.

If the governor was not impressed, the populace loved the confrontation. Tear it down, Darling ordered. Levey refused and pointedly had the freeman's friend, Mr. William Charles Wentworth, write a letter on his behalf. It informed His Excellency that Levey would demolish his windmill when the government pulled down its own nearby. Stalemate.

As a safeguard against official sanction, Levey called his theater "amateur." Similarly, he took no money at the door. But Mr. Levey did accept bookings at five shillings for box seats and three shillings in the pit.

As far as the patterer was concerned, a Theater Royal existed in everything except name. Barnett Levey had told him that the pit and boxes could accommodate 700 people, while the stage had, in the entrepreneur's words, "a due quantity of trapdoors for entrance and exit of the usual number of ghosts for the grave of Hamlet."

There had been theaters in Sydney before, of course. The debtors' rooms in the jail had once passed as a playhouse, and another theater had flourished near the Tank Stream, accepting rum and parcels of flour or meat for entry. One patron became overly enthusiastic about obtaining *his* pound of flesh, killing an officer's greyhound and passing off the meat as kangaroo. Officials ordered that theater be pulled down, anticipating Governor Darling's present view of "our prison population being unfit subjects to go to plays."

The patterer struggled to find his way through the darkened room and the crowd milling before the stage. There was a reek of rum, beer, perfume, unwashed bodies and pipe and cigar smoke. This was not helped by the strong smell coming from the footlights and other whale-oil lamps that needed trimming.

He finally joined Captain Rossi in a box. The policeman smiled. "Well, what brings you—as if I didn't know—to the Goose?" While most Sydney drinkers properly called Levey's hotel the Royal, local thespians and their supporters often referred to it as the Goose and Gridiron, a play on Swan and Harp, a name often given to a theatricals' tavern, and the coat of arms of Britain's venerable Company of Musicians.

Dunne put a finger to his lips as a comic began a fresh patter.

"Have you heard about the Irishman, the Scotchman, the Welshman and the English officer, all captured as spies by the Froggies before Waterloo? No? Well, the French captain said, 'You're all going to be shot at dawn . . . '"

The audience booed.

"'. . . So you're entitled to a last request.' The Irishman said, 'Begorrah, I'll have a thousand United Irishmen singing "The Wearin' o' the Green."' The Scotchman said, 'Och, man, I'll listen to 2,000 bagpipers playing as loud as they can.' The Welshman said, 'I will hear three thousand bards on Welsh harps.'"

The comic paused for effect. "Then the English officer said, 'I say, old boy, do you think you could shoot me first?'"

The audience roared its approval.

"I don't understand it," said Rossi.

"Never mind," said the patterer. "Tell me, have I missed Miss Dormin's performance?"

"I'm sorry, lad, but you have, by a whisker. She was grand in a scene from *Othello*. Oh, when she said, 'She turn'd to folly, and she was a whore . . . O, I were damn'd beneath all depth in hell, but that I did proceed upon just grounds to this extremity,' it was quite a sight and she brought the house down. I'm sorry you weren't here."

A new act hushed their conversation. A small man, noted in the program only as "Mr. Palmer, tragedian," began excerpts from *Macbeth*. As he finished, "Hear it not, Duncan; for it is a knell that summons thee to heaven or to hell," some alchemy summoned two constables onto the stage and they began to drag Mr. Palmer away.

Over boos and protesting pig-noises from the angry crowd, one constable appealed to Captain Rossi, explaining that the actor was a prisoner out on a pass from the barracks only until nine, and that the time had passed. Rossi consulted his watch, sighed and nodded.

"*Exeunt* pigs and Macbeth," muttered Dunne.

Two members of a low act, rushed on by Mr. Levey to calm the crowd, sang a couple of ditties designed to appeal more to the battlers in the pit than to any ladies and gents in boxes. They sang:

In St. James's the officers mess at the club,
In St. Giles's they often have messes for grub;
In St. James's they feast on the highest of game,
In St. Giles's they live on foul air just the same.

The audience then sang along with:

Officers' wives have puddings and pies,
But sergeants' wives have skilly.
And the private's wife has nothing at all
To fill her poor little belly.

The patterer felt his cheeks flush as he half saw Miss Dormin suddenly slip into the empty seat beside him. He was grateful that the gloom disguised his too-obvious pleasure.

"I'm sorry I'm late," she said. "I had to change and get out of my stage *maquillage*. And the following acts needed help dressing. Did you see me?"

On the spur of the moment the flustered young man lied, "Of course! You were wonderful!"

"You didn't disapprove?"

"Of the Bard? Never!"

But now it was time for Mr. Levey to bounce onto the stage to announce a solo rendition by a lady who had delighted the courts of Europe—Madame Greene. Madame walked slowly to center stage, her green gown and evening turban shimmering in the flickering footlights. She looked pale, especially against the vivid slash of green lacquer marking her lips.

Was she nervous perhaps? wondered Dunne. He marveled at this other side to the Queen of the Drabs. At least he now knew what Levey had meant about the fat lady singing!

Madame announced that she would sing the "'Calcutta Cholera Song,' for all old India hands." Her voice was surprisingly light, yet clear and carrying, although she still seemed under strain, as she sang:

> *Spurn the Hooghly waters,*
> *As the foul miasmas creep.*
> *They steal our wives and daughters,*
> *In pits of lime they sleep.*

> *But raise your rum, be merry,*
> *Ere the depths of hell you plumb.*
> *Pay a toast to those we bury,*
> *And to those with death to come!*

On the last notes she had faltered; now she shook her head as if to clear it, clutched at her belly and took a clumsy step toward the audience. Then she collapsed as if she had been shot.

Barnett Levey ran out from the wings, looked down at his fallen star and yelled, "If there is no surgeon here, send to the hospital!"

The patterer and Captain Rossi, with Miss Dormin at their heels, headed for the evening's most dramatic tableau.

CHAPTER THIRTY-ONE

Come, madam, you are now driven to the very last
scene of all your contrivances.
—Oliver Goldsmith, *She Stoops to Conquer* (1773)

THEY HAD CARRIED THE COLLAPSED MADAME GREENE TO AN
empty chamber (by grim coincidence it was called the green
room, a place where performers could rest) by the time a doctor
arrived. He was Dr. Thomas Owens, wearing, as usual, a long scarf
and thick gloves.

The mood in the room was far from relaxed. The air stank of
sweat, urine and feces. The whoremistress was no longer the dom-
ineering figure she usually seemed. She sat over a chamberpot,
dressed only in a shift; her prized gown had been stripped from
her and tossed over a chair.

Dr. Owens appeared to listen to her chest and back through a
device strange to Nicodemus Dunne, a seemingly simple wooden
cylinder about nine inches long, not unlike a flute without tone

holes. Then he recalled that he had read of an invention by a French physician, René Laënnec, a decade before. The medical procedure was called, he believed, stethoscopy.

Owens frowned. Madame Greene's breathing was labored. "The heart rate is 110, at least thirty beats above normal," the patterer thought he heard the doctor mutter. "She is passing thin, liquid bowel motions and is urinating too regularly."

All the onlookers could see clearly that Madame was sweating profusely, despite the caked *maquillage* on her face, and even though Owens said her extremities were like ice.

Madame Greene pointed urgently to her mouth. It was apparent she could not speak; moments earlier she had complained of a constricted, painful throat. Now she suddenly vomited into the bowl for which she had desperately mimed.

The patterer was ashamed of his sudden urge to flee from the room. He felt discomfort, the common reaction of the young and healthy to illness in another, but there was more; he was afraid. All of which made him amazed and impressed by Miss Dormin's behavior. She was proving more helpful to Dr. Owens than anyone else in the room. With Owens's assent, she used a washcloth to clear off Madame Greene's heavy makeup, then threw away the ruined cloth with a look of distaste. The face that emerged from the gluey mess was of surprisingly smooth complexion, though white as death.

"What is it?" asked Captain Rossi suddenly, articulating Dunne's fears.

"At first glance," replied the doctor, "something so potentially serious that I would not be offended if you all retired."

No one among the observers moved and Owens went on.

"Dysentery presents itself as a prime suspect—the griping

pains, mucous evacuations, even bloody ones, inflammation of the intestinal glands and the mucous membrane. One also has to consider typhus, although, God knows, no one wants to. It's fatal enough. So far, we've been lucky here. It classically breeds in the filth of crowded cities and often in army camps."

His audience needed no reminders. Little more than a decade before, the disease, as much as General Winter, had destroyed most of Bonaparte's 600,000-man Grande Armée in his Russian disaster.

Owens drew breath as his listeners held theirs. An equally dire alternative hovered in their minds.

As if able to read their fears, the doctor continued, "Cholera? That hasn't really escaped from the Indian subcontinent into Europe or elsewhere—"

At that moment, the door to the green room burst open and, eluding the arms of Rossi and Dunne, a small woman dressed all in black charged toward Madame Greene. The patterer and Owens managed to seize her before she could throw herself on the ill woman. "Oh, Madame! Oh, Madame!" she wailed, before collapsing on the floor.

"Who the devil is this?" asked Dunne.

"Why," said Miss Dormin, "I do believe it is Madame Greene's personal maid. Elsie, isn't it?" The woman nodded miserably.

"Yes," said the doctor. "I know her now. She is indeed Elsie." And a very personal maid, he thought. He knew that Madame Greene had long ago lost interest in men, apart from taking their money; physical intimacy with them was unsuitable to her taste. Not that she had abandoned the quest for sexual satisfaction; she now simply had what were discreetly described as "Uranian" or "Sapphic" desires.

Over his shoulder, as he returned his full attention to his patient, Owens asked Elsie about her mistress's eating and drinking habits. He knew (although many of his colleagues did not agree) that febrile fluxes were often transmitted by infected food or liquids.

"Oh, sir," said the maid between wracking sobs. "She is very, very particular—all those soldiers in the house, you know. You never could tell where they'd been. I taste everything myself before she eats or drinks. How could I fail her?" She burst into fresh sobs, then added defiantly, "Nothing passes her lips that don't pass mine. Nothing!" Elsie fell silent, then frowned in deep thought and suddenly burst out, "Oh, I tell a lie, sir! There was something I never tested—the medicines, sir, those medicines you gave her."

The doctor smiled. "Of course you didn't," he said easily. "Those were special medicines, Elsie, to help your mistress."

The woman was stubborn. "Not the lozenge. That wasn't medicine. I saw you give it to her. And she ate it."

Owens waved a hand. "I don't recall a lozenge."

But Captain Rossi had grown impatient. "You haven't yet told us what you think is wrong."

"Patience," soothed the doctor and then asked them all, "Tell me, does anyone notice any particular, unusual odor permeating the room?"

Dunne wrinkled his nose. "You mean, apart from . . ."

"Of course I don't mean those obvious odors."

"Well, there is one aroma, quite pungent, but I'm not familiar with it," Rachel Dormin agreed.

Then Rossi burst in, almost triumphantly. "I know it. It's garlic!"

Owens turned to Elsie. "Did Madame habitually eat garlic—you know what it is? Did she have some today?"

"No, sir. She would never eat"—she looked sideways at Captain Rossi—"begging your pardon, sir, foreign muck."

The doctor laughed and clapped his hands. "I rather thought that was the case."

Before anyone could ask the significance of this exchange, Madame Greene moaned and swayed alarmingly.

"Enough," said Owens. "Now we must get our patient to the hospital."

The patterer managed to interpose one question. "Is there any danger of contagion to others?"

The doctor paused. "I'm beginning to think not, almost certainly not."

While the distraught maid was gently urged to return to the High House, Rossi rigged up a hammock stretcher from some theater canvas and recruited two reluctant stagehands to carry the woman to a carriage. Attended by Dr. Owens, Madame Greene, now drifting in and out of consciousness, was transported the four or so blocks to the Rum Hospital.

———————

THE CAPTAIN CALLED for his carriage and offered to take Dunne, Miss Dormin and Elsie, who was still standing, dazed, in the corridor, to their respective homes.

With four passengers, a driver and a large theatrical costume hamper that Rachel Dormin had commandeered to carry away Madame Greene's bulky discarded clothing, plus luggage of her own, the patterer was glad that Rossi's choice of transport was a brisky, and not a smaller vehicle. The popular open curricle, for example, even with two horses, had room only for two, with a seat at the back for a groom. The brisky, however, was a versatile vehicle that enjoyed widespread approval (the real name was *britzka*, reflecting its Polish origins). Two horses gave it power and its light body, made largely of woven wicker, gave it roominess and speed. It was tough, too. A groaning, sturdy brisky had carried Governor Macquarie and his lady on the first vice-regal traverse of the rocky, precipitous road across the just-conquered Blue Mountains.

The captain announced he would first drop off Miss Dormin.

Damn, groaned the patterer inwardly. He had hoped to sit beside her for longer, pressed close together as they were under the darkened privacy of the closed calash top. Dunne was to be delivered next and then Elsie.

When Rachel Dormin stepped down they waited until she was safe at her front door. As Dunne handed over her bulky luggage— she refused any further assistance—Elsie called, "Good night, miss. Thank you again for what you have done." Then she burst into tears.

Rossi urged his departing companion always to be careful when she was out and about alone after dark. She nodded and spoke softly up to the carriage: "I will not concern myself about calling for the police."

"Well, always think about it; we are here to help," advised Rossi, and was rather put out when all Miss Dormin seemed to do in reply was to frown at him, then hide a smile. The young seem to think they are invincible, he thought testily, as the door closed and the brisky rolled on into the chilly night.

Elsie the maid was still weeping and locked in her private world of misery when she was finally delivered into the sympathetic arms of the girls on Gallows Hill.

CHAPTER THIRTY-TWO

Physicians, of all men, are most happy;
what good success soever they have, the world
proclaimeth; and what faults they commit,
the earth covereth.
—Francis Quarles, *Hieroglyphics of the Life of Man* (1638)

MADAME GREENE DIED DURING THE NIGHT. NICODEMUS DUNNE heard the news when he was summoned to the hospital at about ten A.M. Dr. Owens, his eyes shadowed with fatigue, met him at the front entrance.

"I'm sorry," he said. "She was too far gone."

"What was it?" asked the patterer. "Dysentery?"

Owens shrugged. "Well, there was a flux, as you well know, but not because of one of those tropical or other febrile scourges. There was massive purging and dehydration. And organ failure; her liver and kidneys failed—among other things."

He caught the surprised look on Dunne's face. "Oh, yes, I have already anatomized her. Why? Because, from the start, something about the case troubled me mightily." He took his companion's elbow in a gloved hand. "Come."

"Where to? Not to that death-house again!"

Owens did not answer, just continued to propel the patterer along the corridor. They entered the dissecting room, which looked much as the unwilling visitor recalled from his earlier encounter. There was only one change: The sole examination table now in use had a fresh occupant.

Madame Greene lay under a sheet with only her head exposed, her outlined body seemingly shrunken to a size that didn't tally with Dunne's recollection of her living bulk. Her head was grotesquely haloed by her shock of green hair. They approached the table, Dunne hesitatingly.

"I won't ask you to look at the body," soothed the doctor. "In any case, I imagine it would be a mark of disrespect if you did. My having to is enough. Many women in life are reluctant to let even a doctor see their mysteries. I suppose that one day there may be female doctors—and it will be the turn of the men to be shy. So, we will allow her modesty to remain intact. I will remark about the torso only that there is, and was earlier, an abdominal rash, apart from which the body's skin is as clear as a babe's. Nonetheless, you can directly observe some other important physical matters." He pointed. "For instance, look at the nails."

Dunne looked. They were not worn, split or chipped as were many working women's. But they were not attractive or healthy, and were rather coarse in texture.

"And the face." Even in death her complexion was decidedly beautiful, that of a younger woman. "I just don't know why she caked herself with all that muck," sniffed Owens. "Her eyes see nothing now, but even as I treated her last night they were wide and glittering; her pupils were dilated." He then fingered her hair and remarked that it was shiny but thin to his delicate touch.

"What are you driving at?" asked the patterer, not really understanding what he was being shown. "Exactly what disease are you talking about?"

"Patience," begged the doctor. "There's no hurry. Not now. She is not suffering by my deliberate manner." Then his attention seemed to wander, for he went off on a tangent. "Years ago, a French acquaintance, a very perspicacious artist named Horace Vernet, told me that in all matters—and I take this to apply to medical issues—when you have eliminated the impossible, whatever remains, however improbable, must be the truth. My examination shows that, despite some suggestive symptoms, she did not die of dysentery. The same goes for typhus. True, in Madame's case there was great prostration and a petechial eruption—the red spots I referred to on the belly—but that doesn't always attend typhus, and in this case certainly did not. And although I rule out cholera, there are some similar indicators—puckered lips and a hollow facial appearance—apparent in her case. Please remember that."

"What then," inquired Dunne, "is the truth, the improbable that must be the truth?"

Owens grimaced. "The truth is that she died of acute poisoning."

"Why is that so improbable?"

"Because, my dear young man, I simply have no idea how it could have occurred. I suppose I was reasonably sure of the what—if not the why—when I realized what the unusual odor in the room was. You recall, I'm sure, the smell that Captain Rossi so acutely identified as garlic, which Elsie stoutly denied her mistress had ever touched. A reek of garlic can be a pointer to the presence of arsenic in a body. Very confusing in Latin countries, no doubt!"

"Could it not all have been an accident?" asked the patterer.

The doctor shrugged. "Perhaps. A lot of women take small doses of arsenic to improve their complexion. And deadly nightshade can be used by the ladies to highlight the allure of their eyes. That poison's other name is, of course, *belladonna*—in words other than the Italian, 'fair lady.' Even the late king's doctors dosed him with emetic tartar during treatment for his madness. That nostrum contains antimony, which is commonly contaminated with up to 5 percent arsenic. So you can see that the toxin has respectable medical usage."

"So, in a nutshell, she died by taking too much arsenic," said the patterer.

"'Taking' is the problem word," replied Owens. "Yes, arsenic killed her, but did she 'take' it, in the conventional sense? I tend to believe what Elsie, her distraught lover, told us at the theater—that no contaminated or otherwise infected food or water passed her or her mistress's lips. And the same must be true of poison: Ergo, there is no possible agent in that manner, unless the poison was self-administered."

"You are saying she killed herself, either accidentally or deliberately?" Nicodemus Dunne was not especially religious, but he had a superstitious dread of suicide and all it could mean, of bodies refused rest in hallowed ground and supposedly being buried at crossroads.

The doctor shrugged. "This poisoning was a gradual process. A suicide would surely end it all with one large overdose. And I have recently treated Madame Greene for debilities I now realize were the symptoms of her progressive poisoning. But I believe she was a woman who wanted to live."

Breaking the train of his discourse and pulling the patterer closer to the corpse, Owens poked a flat instrument into the mouth, between the slightly open lips. He withdrew it and remarked, "Nothing." He turned away and continued, "So, to sum up, I have drawn your attention to the rash, the coarse nails, the clear complexion, the once-glittering eyes, the thin, shiny hair—all symptoms of arsenical poisoning, which I have confirmed by postmortem. And . . . ?" He paused and looked at the patterer inquiringly.

Dunne frowned. "Is there any other point to which you would wish to draw my attention?"

"To the curious incident of the mouth," said Owens.

"There was nothing in the mouth."

"That was the curious incident," remarked the doctor.

Dunne did not understand.

The doctor explained, "The deceased's mouth lining and tongue contain dissipated traces of the poison. Most of these traces have been deposited by the passage and residue of vomit—you will remember her retching in the green room? Now, why did I charge you to recall the fact that Madame's face had the shriveled and puckered look associated with cholera—if I also told you that the disease was not involved?"

From the patterer, no response.

So the doctor, slightly irritated by his companion's inability to match his mind, continued. "What is now missing from Madame's appearance, her image as you remember her? And I remind you again of the collapsed face."

Dunne recalled the vivacious, always smiling woman, then he said suddenly, almost shouting, "Teeth! She has no teeth! But how so?"

"Because," said Owens, "*I* have them!" In the dramatic manner of a prestidigitator, he whipped away a cloth from a small mound on a side table. Revealed was a set of artificial teeth for the upper and lower jaws.

"I did not know she had such teeth," said the patterer.

"Neither did I," said the doctor. "Until, that is, I found them beside the commode on which she had been sitting. She obviously took them out when she first called for the bowl, and at the time we were all too busy to notice her putting them down. I only collected them just as we were heading off to the hospital."

Nicodemus Dunne looked at the gleaming teeth, grim ghosts of Madame's smile, now vanished forever. He had never before thought to study such things closely. They were rare; only the rich could afford them. He knew that some supposedly were made of wood—that most famous American, George Washington, was reputed to have had a wooden set—but there were people who said that wood was too fragile for the purpose. He did know that some teeth were carved from whalebone. The best though—if the most ghoulish—were sets made using real teeth taken from the dead.

Dragging himself back to the present situation, the patterer said, "That's all very interesting, but what is the particular significance of the teeth?"

Owens smiled, obviously well pleased with himself. "Before I cleaned the teeth to their current presentable state, I examined their surfaces."

"So?"

"So they were free of any toxin-bearing vomit."

Dunne did not want to say "So?" again and further show his ignorance. He remained silent.

"It proves," said the doctor—rather smugly, the patterer thought—"that no toxic substance passed in through Madame Greene's mouth while she wore her teeth—and that would be all her waking hours. Yet inside she was stewed with evidence of the arsenic that killed her. Thus the improbable conclusion, which must be the truth, is that somehow she was murdered!"

A trick of the light made Madame's teeth seem to smile. She was no soldier, but was the similar death of The Ox somehow linked to hers?

It was not until the patterer had left Dr. Owens and his sad charge that he wondered why, if Elsie could be regarded as trustworthy on the matter of food and drink, the doctor could doubt her story of the proffered lozenge.

Dr. Owens was widely known for his habit of offering the sweets to everyone, including Dunne. And he admitted to dosing Madame. Earlier, too, something about Owens had engaged the young man's imagination. But then he shook his head. If the doctor were in any way connected with the fat lady's death, he would hardly have tried so hard to save her and then have announced, when he could have said it was accident or suicide, that it was murder.

Still, Dunne now half-heartedly entered Owens's name on his list of "Persons of Interest."

And the patterer decided it would do no harm to have a further talk with Elsie.

———————

BUT THAT INTERVIEW never eventuated.

By the end of the day after Madame Greene's death, Elsie, too, lay dead. She was found in a shed behind the whorehouse. Her wrists were slashed and a bloody knife lay beside her body.

Captain Rossi took control of the case, but had to agree that it seemed a clear case of suicide while in a state of despair over the death of her mistress. Out of respect for the two women, he made sure that their full relationship was left out of the report to the coroner.

At least, Dunne and the captain agreed, Elsie would not be left in a legal limbo, unlike the other poor devils who had died, and whose inquests returned "open" findings as the search for the truth went on.

CHAPTER THIRTY-THREE

What dire offence from am'rous causes springs,
What mighty contests rise from trivial things.
—Alexander Pope, *The Rape of the Lock* (1714)

ALTHOUGH LIVES WERE BEING EXTINGUISHED WITH OMINOUS regularity, the patterer determined that his life should go on as normally as possible. Thus he continued his regular public readings of the news, although he was not as driven to work as he had been.

When the demands of the investigation began to eat into his bread-and-butter labors, he confided to several people, including Dr. Owens and Alexander Harris, that his income was declining. Captain Rossi, too, showed sympathy.

His fortunes, however, had taken a turn for the better when he last examined his bank account. Mr. Potts, in his impeccable script, added an extra ten pounds to his usual fee. The only explanation that was forthcoming was that Mr. Potts's principals were very

satisfied with the patterer's service and felt that he had been insuf-
ficiently rewarded for it.

Nicodemus Dunne did not argue, but returned to work with
a new sense of security and a new spring in his step. And so he
went about, bringing tidings of the coming withdrawal from legal
tender of the holey dollar, that strange ring-shaped coin that had,
in its way, solved the colony's currency crisis fifteen years earlier.
Then, there had not been enough English, Spanish, Dutch or Portu-
guese coins to go around, and paying visiting traders for imported
necessities always drained the purse. Promissory notes and private
banknotes, like the famous Waterloo Notes, were of varying value.

Even the arrival from England to the colonial powers of 40,000
coins of that trading benchmark, the Spanish silver dollar (its value
of eight *reales* spawned the legendary piratical label, "pieces of
eight") did not help, because many of them could soon slip back
overseas.

Although it was before his time, the patterer knew the story of
what happened next. The governor, Lachlan Macquarie, hit on a
way to keep the new coins in the colony. And turn a profit at the
same time. Naturally, he asked a convict forger for help. William
Henshall punched out a small disc—called the dump—from each
Spanish coin, leaving a larger ring, called the holey dollar. Macquarie valued the ring at five shillings and the dump at fifteen
pence, so each dollar became worth six shillings and threepence.

Now their death knell had sounded.

Dunne moved on, entertaining a crowd with a letter written
by the architect Mr. Greenway to *The Australian* about his plan to
throw a soaring bridge across the harbor from Lieutenant Dawes's
Battery to the nearest point on the northern shore, a spot east of

Billy Blue's Murdering Point. He had been proposing the bridge for a decade or more. Ten years before, at the height of his powers, no one had listened. Now, in the decline of his career, the idea seemed doomed forever.

To select audiences, the patterer brought news that was difficult to find in the papers. Prizefighting or kangaroo-coursing might be tolerated by the authorities, but of the shadowy worlds of bull-baiting or cockfighting, aficionados could learn only by word of mouth. It was not nice news. He told them how at Brickfield village, the center of many blood sports, a fighting cock still wearing its spur had raked out the eye of its handler.

To more general acclaim, he lauded that famous eccentric and pedestrian, the Flying Pieman, who had recently hauled a gig with a woman passenger over a distance of half a mile. Some listeners asked him for news on a rumor that only recently the pieman had been involved in fisticuffs with wild natives. Hadn't he been defending the honor of a young lady?

As usual, thought Dunne, the gossip was only half right. And the true version was better left untold. So he just shook his head and solemnly professed to have no knowledge of any such fracas.

WITH HIS FINANCES improving, the patterer felt better able to court Miss Dormin lavishly.

He escorted her to a large evening party at the splendid Sydney Hotel, near the Military Barracks. Once inside, Rachel Dormin removed the fur-trimmed overgarment she had worn in the carriage.

"Why, in this climate, does a mantle need a fur trim?" asked the patterer.

"My dear," said his companion resignedly, "it's not a mantle, it's a pelisse. And the fur is— Well, ladies just like fur! Anyway, a lady can't be seen everywhere just in an evening dress."

"Oh?" replied Dunne. "Really? I rather garnered the impression that some modern dresses were meant to show *everywhere*. Only recently I was amused by a witty verse that was reprinted here from an English journal:

"When dressed for the evening, girls nowadays
Scarce an atom of dress on them leave;
Nor blame them—for what is an evening dress
But a dress that is suited for Eve?"

Miss Dormin laughed and slapped him lightly.

Her gown did reveal bare shoulders and décolletage. The bodice was cut off the shoulder and kept up surely by a little whalebone. By gravity, too, decided the patterer; the gravity of what would happen if the dress slipped. Wisely, he kept this amusing thought to himself. One risqué joke was probably enough.

Short puffed sleeves left her arms bare, and her slippers, worn over silk stockings with colorfully embroidered clocks, peeped from beneath a skirt-length shorter than was fashionable by day. The fabric of her dress, she informed her escort, was *gros de Naples*, which meant nothing to him. But he understood and approved that her hair was piled high in an Apollo knot and anchored by a bejeweled ivory comb.

Nicodemus Dunne was no less a picture of sartorial splendor. He had once more consulted Mr. Cooper's tailor—although this time he had been able to pay for the hire—and now he wore a dark blue evening dress coat over a canary waistcoat and tight flesh-colored fine-wool pants strapped to his soft pumps. He carried a cloak and a tall hat.

First, they listened to the band of the 57th play popular airs. When the musicians rendered "General Ralph Darling's Australian Slow March" and an even better-known march by Mr. Handel, the patterer remarked that it was uncommonly civil of the 57th's bandmaster, Mr. Sippe, to perform those pieces. When Miss Dormin asked why, Dunne explained (showing off) that, of course, the governor's march had been composed by a rival, Mr. Kavanagh, of the Buffs, and that the Handel piece was the marching music of that other regiment.

Then the program of the *rout* changed and they danced: waltzes, galops, quadrilles. They sat out the unfamiliar *varsoviana*, Spanish steps in circles or sets of two couples in triple time.

All evening, they deliberately avoided mention of the deaths that haunted them. But memories of them—especially those of Madame Greene and poor Elsie, so recent and so raw—were revived when a plump, perspiring woman whirled past, puffing.

"That could be Madame," observed the patterer, without thinking, steering his partner out of the way. "Sorry."

The announcement of an interval before supper broke the sad spell under which they had fallen.

While Rachel Dormin joined the ladies, a mysterious custom to Dunne, he joined the gentlemen who were retiring to the smoking room. He did not take tobacco, despite its approval by doctors, but he took great interest in its rituals, which were almost as solemn as decanting wine and letting it breathe, or swirling and sniffing brandy, or mulling wine.

This night, there seemed to be no pipes on display—of course, where could a man carry one in his skin-tight evening wear? Most smoked cigars; some (usually older men) took snuff. The patterer observed that these gentlemen carried the powdered tobacco already prepared—again, as in the case of pipes, there was no comfortable place to conceal a grater with which to grind the weed.

He also saw that, whereas on the street one would encounter men with utilitarian wooden snuffboxes, here, adorning officers and gentry, were small works of art, enameled silver or gold.

One thing was certain: No man here chewed. Or spat.

———————

IT WAS REGRETTABLE, then, that the one guest guilty that night of ungentlemanly behavior should be Nicodemus Dunne.

As the parties and couples regrouped to enter the supper room, he steered his partner toward a *chambre particulière*, a curtained-off banquette not meant for use that night. He stepped into one, gently pulled a surprised Rachel Dormin after him and drew the curtain closed.

"I've wanted to do this since I first saw you," he whispered, and pressed himself against her, holding her tightly. He leaned down into her shocked face and forced his lips onto her opened mouth.

She struggled and pulled her face away. "Mr. Dunne!" she gasped. "I beg you. Don't . . . I have my reputation!"

Had she stiffened in his arms in acceptance or rejection? He could not be certain. Then, either by accident or by instinctive design, one of his hands slipped from her bare shoulder onto a breast. He then felt her grow completely rigid before she shoved him violently away. As he moved back she gave him a stinging slap across the face.

His eyes watered. "Miss Dormin, I'm so sorry."

"This is impossible." Her eyes were wide and fearful. She was white to the lips.

"Why is it . . . so impossible?"

"Because . . ." She was angry now. "Because I'm not one of those warm things who tumble indiscriminately . . . who don't give a fig for their good name. Is there no such thing as courtship?"

Dunne looked stricken. "Can you forgive me? Can we forget this and start again?"

Rachel Dormin was suddenly composed once more and spoke calmly. "I always like you better as a gentleman. Let us not speak of this matter again. Please take me in to supper." She opened the curtain.

They supped then he escorted her home as if nothing had happened, and she told him that, yes, they could continue their friendship.

The patterer went to his bed that night a relieved man. He wanted Miss Dormin's acceptance.

But he still wanted a woman. Badly.

CHAPTER THIRTY-FOUR

Night makes no difference 'twixt the Priest and Clerk;
Joan as my Lady is as good i'th' dark.
—Robert Herrick, "No Difference i'th' Dark" (1648)

"HERE'S TO YOU, MRS. ROBINSON." NICODEMUS DUNNE RAISED his glass of rum and saluted the tall, handsome woman behind the bar.

Norah Robinson smiled as she picked up an empty glass and returned the gesture. "And to you, Mr. Dunne." She spoke in the clear Irish brogue heard so often in the town and country. She was no prisoner or servant; the edge of steel that could enter her tone made it clear she was the boss.

The patterer was in an alehouse near Brickfield Hill. Its true name was the Bacchanal but it was known, of course, as the Bag o' Nails, save there was no ironmongery in sight. Or it was called the Bull and Dog because of the bull-baiting held, illegally, nearby.

It was early, not yet ten A.M., on the morning after his dismally failed attempt—if such it was—to seduce Miss Dormin. He rarely drank at such an hour, but now he was on his second dram.

He and Mrs. Robinson were the only people in the taproom. They knew each other as well as any good trader and regular customer do. Or it could be that there was something more. She was a good-looking woman of, Dunne judged, forty or so; perhaps she was still in her late thirties. He was a presentable male. And maybe they flirted sometimes, as men and women in propinquity invariably will.

"You're an early bird, aren't you," commented Mrs. Robinson. "What's the celebration then? Or perhaps it's a small wake?"

"I'm toasting my lack of brains," said the patterer with a shrug. "That and my luck in love—or, rather, the lack of it."

"Ah," was all she said.

"And where's your husband?" he asked after a pause.

"Oh, he's to Parramatta. He's supposed to be loading gin from a still-man there. And buying sheep. But . . ." She leaned confidentially across the bar, in so doing tightening the fabric of her dress against her breasts.

Why the secrecy, thought Dunne, there's no other bugger here. "But?" he prompted.

"But," she picked up her thread, "while I trust him not to sample too much of the gin, I suspect he's making sheep's eyes and tupping a ewe." She laughed.

"Tup," thought the patterer idly. Why, he had not heard the old English word for years. Only rustics and, it seemed, Celtic publicans, used it. Most people now chose other euphemisms for copulation. He remembered the shiver he had felt as a schoolboy (admittedly he had experienced a greater frisson surreptitiously conning *The Rape of Lucrece*) when reading about the Blackamoor Othello "tupping" white Desdemona.

He murmured aloud the lines in which another character tells Desdemona's father, "You'll have your daughter covered by a Barbary horse." He hoped there had been no tupping in Miss Dormin's recital at Levey's theater.

"Pardon?" said Mrs. Robinson, frowning.

His reverie was broken by her puzzlement. "Nothing. Sorry. I was just daydreaming." So, indeed, the Bard had the right of it: The world *is* a stage and there's always passion and lust upon it. Well, I'll act out this play, he decided. "I'm sorry, ma'am, I didn't quite follow what you said."

"Ah, Mr. Dunne! You're a slow rogue, toying with a poor simple woman."

"On my honor, no, ma'am!"

"Well, he has a fancy woman there and I'll wager they're chewing each other's tongues as we speak. If they're not hard at it swiving, that is. Though maybe not that, for I hear he has put her in the family way and there she is now, as big as the governor's stables . . . But what's your worry?"

Here goes nothing, thought Dunne. "Unrequited love," he said.

Mrs. Robinson stared at him. Sure, he was a well set-up boy— man, rather. And she'd heard that he was kind and she knew he was clever. He stared back at her. In the half-light coming through the small windows, her white skin looked almost luminous and her hair made a golden-red nimbus around her oval face.

"Make that one your last," she said finally.

"I beg pardon if I've said something untoward!"

Mrs. Robinson smiled. "No, dear. Just make it your last. In fact, don't finish it. Shut that outside door and bar it. Wait five minutes and come upstairs. There's something you should see."

Dunne did as he was bid. On the level above he found a corridor.

Only one door was open so he headed there. He crossed the threshold into a room dimmed by heavy, drawn curtains.

He heard a sound and turned. From behind the closing door stepped Norah Robinson, wearing only a shift. Shutting off the corridor had lessened the light even more.

"All cats may be gray in the dark, but I'm no cat." She opened a curtain slightly and now there was enough light for Dunne to see her draw the shift over her shoulders and drop it to the floor. She stood still for a moment, almost a ghostly figure in the gloom, but a phantom with very real, high breasts and long legs. Legs that ended in a triangle of dark pelt that looked, he always thought, like a map of Van Diemen's Land.

"Will you love me, Nicodemus?" she asked softly, seizing his hands. "Don't think ill of me. I'm no easy bunter. I haven't had a man for— God! What would it be? A year? More? If you're worried, my husband doesn't share my bed. Not even my room."

"Can't he—doesn't he—claim his rights?"

"Ach! It's my money, dear. He does what he's told. I never loved him and he never loved me. Once, maybe. Besides, I have a long knife handy here always. He knows I'd fillet him."

He licked his suddenly dry lips. "I have nothing with me, ma'am—no protection."

"I'm clean," she said coldly. "And for God's sake, stop calling me 'ma'am'!"

"I'm sure you are," said Dunne. "And I'm not poxed. But I always hope to use armor *d'amour*. And you must not risk becoming with child."

"You're the perfect gentleman, Nick . . ." She drew him over to the bed and from a side table took a box. "If you're happier, here." She opened it. "*Voilà—lettres françaises*, sheaths, an upright knight's armor, call them what you will. I sell a lot to hurried and worried men in the taproom. That's all I sell 'em, mind you!"

She helped the patterer shrug off his shirt and kick off his trousers and undergarment. She lay back as he rolled on a silk sheath and secured the ribbon ties. She held out her arms.

———

DUNNE MUST HAVE dozed. He was woken by being shaken furiously. He looked up at the set face of Mrs. Robinson.

"You bastard!" she hissed. "You talked in your sleep, just as you did when we loved. Who in the hell is Rachel? Some slut who won't give you what you want? Or did she give it to someone else?"

He had already peeled off the silken layer, but that didn't stop him. The bitch! He slapped Mrs. Robinson hard and rolled over and into her.

Even in the half-light he caught the sudden look of surprise on her face and in her widened eyes. "Where is your guardian? You have no armor, no protection!" She arched her hips desperately, trying to buck him off. But he held down her wrists and was too strong.

"Damn protection!" he said savagely through gritted teeth. "Damn Rachel!"

Mrs. Robinson melted. And, for the first time, he said her name: "Norah!"

———

NICODEMUS DUNNE LEFT Norah Robinson sleeping and escaped quietly through the back door.

He returned to the Bacchanal later. The bar was filled and the hostess was busy.

"I'm sorry, Norah," he said when she had a quiet moment.

"Don't be, love," she said. "I'm not."

"You'll be all right?"

"'Course I will. I flushed you out . . ."—Dunne looked around quickly—"And, anyway, I didn't get around to telling you, but I'm unfruitful—as barren as Pinchgut." She smiled sadly. "I don't suppose I can altogether blame my man for playing from home." She laughed. "Ah, well. Will you be having another? Drink, that is!"

CHAPTER THIRTY-FIVE

The unapparent connection is more powerful
than the apparent one.
—Heraclitus (c. 500 BC; translator unknown)

NORAH ROBINSON COULD LAUGH, MUSED THE PATTERER, AS HE nursed the drink she had offered him. And no bad thing. Better that than to leave her crying. He drained his glass, waved because she was busy again and walked out into the sunny street. There was still plenty of life left in the day.

He knew he would go back to Norah, but he still wanted the untouchable Miss Dormin. He tried to dismiss three vastly different feelings tugging in his brain—selfish pride, remorse, self-pity.

He decided to blot out his personal tangles by devoting himself to the murders and soon found that he seemed to be making more progress in a matter of hours than he had in the previous few days. His earlier scattered thoughts were coming together and seemed finally to be making sense.

He reexamined every suspicion or ambiguity, no matter how slight. He studied the lists in his black book. And he trawled through the names of others who raised questions in his mind—notably the governor, whose past still puzzled him. And he had the germ of an idea about the agitating lawyer William Charles Wentworth, whose temper was always cocked on a hair-trigger. Could blackmail perhaps be a motive?

Motive, opportunity and ability. Those were the prime detection yardsticks that had been drummed into Bow Street Runners since the days of the great policeman George Ruthven. So, who could have slashed, shot and poisoned physically powerful men—and, probably by the same hand, one woman, Madame Greene? And why?

To avenge Sudds seemed to be the logical conclusion, but Dunne was sure there was another motive, still tied to the 57th, yet to be revealed.

He knew, of course, that there was usually no science involved in solving a murder. Most killers were caught only if they were seen in the act or if they confessed due to remorse, betrayal or some undeniable physical clue. The smoking gun in the hand would fit the bill admirably.

The patterer also admitted to himself that if the killings were the random work of a cool and lucky lunatic, the cause was near hopeless. But if there were a pattern, he believed that finding the slayer of even one victim would unlock the secrets of the other cases. So, his only chance was to pursue any and all of the few slender leads his observations and instincts had provided.

He turned to the first name in the book: F. N. Rossi. Well, he had arranged to see the captain that evening; any questions would have to wait until then. In the meantime, there were other fish he could fry. With luck he might run across Miss Dormin at *The Gleaner*, although he believed she was spending more time at the dress shop since its mistress had been severely hampered by a fall.

He sought out Dr. Peter Cunningham and asked him outright: had his cryptic warning all those days ago to avoid the Rum Hospital implicated Dr. Thomas Owens? Dr. Cunningham's reply was oblique and unhelpful. He repeated his advice but still refused to elaborate, calling on his professional oath to confidentiality about his patients. But, wondered Dunne, by not denying outright that he was referring to Owens was the naval surgeon implicitly pointing to his colleague? Or was that reading too much into it?

Cunningham would add only one new idea on the subject: "Consider cinnabar," he said. "And its implications." At Dunne's incomprehension, he repeated the word and spelled it. Then, as once before, he nodded, turned on his heels and left his companion, who stored away their conversation then shrugged and moved on to his next line of inquiry.

The patterer and Captain Rossi had been interested in knowing the source of the arsenic ever since it had felled The Ox. And now they must almost certainly add Madame Greene to that equation. It was a common enough purchase. Dunne believed that artists even used it in their colors. And there was no knowing how long ago these recently lethal doses had been obtained. Perhaps years earlier.

The patterer suspected that the poison had come from an apothecary's shop . . . unless, and that was an interesting idea, it came from another possible source: the hospital.

It seemed that Captain Rossi's constables had not turned up the origin of the poison, or else he would have heard. Or would he? How hard had they tried with such a boring, repetitive task?

Besides, these men were not keen Runners. Most had themselves been convicts and were not known for their vigorous pursuit of offenders.

Dunne weighed up the problem. If a constable had been directed to leave the police office in search of a suitable apothecary, how far might he have gone before losing interest or gaining a public house? The patterer decided the answer might well be, not far.

He sighed; there was no alternative. He should canvass himself, from the far end of the town then backtrack. He would have to visit perhaps scores of druggists and chemists in shops and on the street, although he doubted if the handful of itinerant nostrum-hawkers dealt in arsenic.

At only the fifth call, he was lucky. At the first four shops, the attendants had sold no arsenic in the days leading up to The Ox's death. That information did not preclude earlier sales, but at least it cleared the air slightly.

But now he had a lead of sorts. Yes, said the shopkeeper, he had made such a sale on the date in question. He remembered thinking at the time that he expected the customer to buy not arsenic, but oil of cloves for toothache.

The patterer was intrigued. "Why?"

"Because his voice was muffled and he wore a scarf wrapped tightly across his face. But, no, he only wanted arsenic, he said, for rats." The customer wore a severe black suit and had a wide black hat pulled low over his eyes, the druggist added.

"Did you know this man?" Dunne asked.

"Not then—but a few days later I did."

"What happened?"

"He came in again—and once more I thought he'd want something for his teeth. He was still wrapped up around the face. But . . ."—the shopkeeper looked pleased with his skill at diagnosis—"he clearly had facial boils troubling him."

Dunne was puzzled. "How did you know that?"

"Well, it's obvious, isn't it? He bought a lancet, and when I mentioned boils he didn't contradict me, did he? Of course, he could have had other uses for the lancet."

"What made you think so?"

"Well, after all, he *was* a doctor."

The patterer felt a tremor of excitement. "He told you that? What was his name?"

"I don't recall, but I didn't know him."

"Was it Dr. Owens?"

The apothecary only shrugged. "Whoever he was, he should have known better—if he didn't want toothache."

"What do you mean by that?"

"Well, because of all those lozenges."

Dunne was baffled. "The lozenges?"

"Yes," said the man patiently. "The ones he bought. Two bags there were of them, I think. They can rot your teeth in no time."

The patterer thanked the man and left. Come to think of it, however, Thomas Owens was not the only man who could have been the customer. There was another who dressed in clerical black and called himself "Doctor"—Laurence Hynes Halloran.

———

DUNNE DID NOT bother with any more apothecaries, but he still pursued other avenues of inquiry.

Nearby, in one of Sam Terry's buildings, in the rooms of the Australian Subscription Library, of which he was a member, he consulted a general dictionary and found an entry that steered him to a medical tome. The information contained therein made him raise his eyebrows.

The importance of parrots, which had flown in and out of his mind since the day of the fight at Jack-the-Miller's Point, had also gradually crystallized.

He made a visit to the parish offices of St. James Church, where he asked (as a representative of *The Australian*, not quite a lie) permission to consult the records of births, deaths and marriages. It took a while, but one entry yielded satisfaction.

A visit to *The Gazette*, which was regarded as the journal of record, and his evolving theory seemed confirmed.

———————

AFTER ALL THIS activity and progress, Dunne was thirsty, but that was not the only reason he went into the Labor in Vain. It was here that the first soldier had been killed, but he knew this fact wouldn't put off that military man's more fortunate comrades in arms.

So, reasoned the patterer, what better place to pick up a soldier? No fresh-faced recruit would do. His quarry had to be a grizzled veteran who had been with the regiment fifteen or so years. For the price of a drink or two he might explain what both Alexander Harris and Captain Crotty had said casually.

And, indeed, the hunch paid off.

CHAPTER THIRTY-SIX

I met murder on the way . . .
—Percy Bysshe Shelley, "The Mask of Anarchy" (1819)

ON THE WAY TO CALL ON CAPTAIN ROSSI, THE PATTERER MADE A detour to *The Gleaner*. He wanted to see Dr. Halloran—who would perhaps have toothache—and, of course, he might find Miss Dormin there.

Neither seemed to be in, but, as he turned to leave, a man emerged from the composing room and called him back to the counter. It was his informant from the wayzgoose. Dunne recalled the man's name: Muller.

The compositor looked around rather furtively. "You know, something else about that matter has come to me," he said.

Dunne again noticed his German accent, which was now rendered more pronounced by some tension in the speaker.

"Well." The man paused. "You recall showing me that galley

proof? If you can wait about fifteen or twenty minutes, I'll be finished and I can talk to you." He held up one hand, and rubbed together his thumb and two fingers. "Might there be a . . ." He hesitated over the next word. "*Belohnung*?" His look was sly.

The patterer guessed at the meaning from the gesture, but he still waited until the man translated.

"A reward?"

Dunne frowned. "Unfortunately, I can't wait now. Later, perhaps?"

"Come back in the morning." The compositor shrugged. "Early, about seven-thirty. I'll tell you then."

Outside, fortune smiled on Dunne as his newfound friend, Billy Blue, sidled up with a strange story of an unusual group he had ferried during the night of the blacksmith's deadly flogging. This story spurred Dunne to make a quick side trip to see Bungaree . . .

"ARE YOU CALLING me a liar, sir?" hissed Captain Rossi.

It wasn't a very auspicious start, decided the patterer. "Not at all," he soothed. "The fault was all mine that day at the Lumber Yard. You answered me truthfully. I simply asked you the wrong question—about the governor's past involving the dead blacksmith."

"Ah," said Rossi. "And what makes you still think he has an old secret?" He looked slightly mollified, but his eyes were wary.

"The fact," said Dunne, "that I know a new secret. He was in a position on that night to kill the smith. Or to have him killed."

"Rubbish!"

"Well, it's also incontestable that he was seen to attempt to kill another man that night."

Rossi looked at him, aghast. "You're serious!"

"Yes. I am. Deadly serious, you might say."

Rossi sat in silence, staring at the patterer, then finally broke it. "Why would you think that I know any secrets about His Excellency?"

"You worked with him in Mauritius, very closely. And now you are a senior lieutenant here. And you have a known ability to sniff out people's dirty linen. Didn't you have a secret commission from the king, after his succession to the throne, to go to Italy and unearth evidence for a royal divorce? Were you not to be a witness, code named 'Majorca,' against Caroline?"

"Ah, *bella Italia!*" said the captain dreamily. "But"—he snapped back to the present—"of course, I can say nothing about such matters. Except to remark that it was an ill-starred match from the start. First cousins, y'know. Perhaps she should have taken the 50,000 pounds a year we—I mean the government, of course—offered her to go away. Do you know what he said after first seeing his future bride? Well, he said, 'I am not well; pray get me a glass of brandy.' And later he told his sisters that she was 'a perfect streetwalker.' Not true. Ah, poor woman. It was she who had to escape—leaping over sofas!—from her father-in-law's importunements."

"You know a lot about our betters, as I thought," said Dunne.

His companion sighed and looked at him in the eye. "More than you can imagine, lad, much more." Then he clapped his hands briskly. "But enough of reminiscing. That was then, this is now. I agree that you and I now need each other more than ever. So, let us compare secrets. Mind, you must never reveal that I am their source. I will do likewise. If anyone knew what we had done, what sort of spies would we be?"

So Captain Rossi, in exchange for the recent secret Dunne had discovered, truthfully answered the question that Dunne could, and should, have asked days earlier.

———————

THE PATTERER RETIRED that night pleased, but not completely so. So many people, it seemed, had the necessary motives, opportunities and abilities. But which one? Or ones?

———————

AT PRECISELY SEVEN-THIRTY the next morning, Nicodemus Dunne arrived at the *Gleaner* office to find the front door unlocked. No one answered his hail, so he walked through into the silent composing room.

The compositor, Muller, was waiting for him, as promised. But he offered no greeting. He couldn't. He lay on the ink-stained, dirty floor, choking on his own blood, a dribble running down his chin. His eyes were closed.

"Christ!" The patterer knelt and tried to lift the unconscious man's head and shoulders, ignoring the blood that soaked his own hands and forearm. He saw the shallow rise and fall of Muller's chest as his heart pumped blood into an ever-widening crimson bloom on his white shirtfront. The damage centered on a black-edged hole. Muller had been lung-shot.

Dunne's knee stubbed on a hard object. He felt around until he found the obstruction. It was a pistol. He put it close to his face; it still reeked of burned powder. He pushed it to one side.

Muller's face was pale and waxy, but suddenly his eyes fluttered open. He weakly grasped one of the patterer's hands and pulled him closer, smearing more blood on him.

"Don't try to talk. I'll get help."

The wounded man shook his head. "*Gott hilf mir!*" he whispered.

God help you, indeed, thought the patterer grimly.

Muller slowly licked his caked lips and tried again. Dunne caught the words as best he could. They came out—was it German again?—sounding like: "*Chaos . . . alter . . . die blutige Hand . . . Rache . . . Schwein . . . grün . . .*"

"In English, please," urged Dunne. "*Englisch!*"

But the man had fainted again.

The patterer sat back on his heels, thinking furiously. With his smattering of rudimentary German, he had easily translated the appeal to God, but the other words? He thought *chaos* was the same in both languages, and that *alter* could mean "old." And surely three of the words meant what they sounded like— "the bloody hand." *Schwein?* All right. *Grün*: "green"—Madame? One to go.

He heard a groan and bent down. Muller's eyes were open again.

"In English," he asked quietly. "What's *Rache*, in English?"

Muller gave a puzzled look then croaked, "*Rache* . . . is 'revenge' . . . 'vengeance' . . ." Then his eyes and features froze. He was dead.

Dunne gently laid the body on the floor and rose shakily. He picked up the pistol and examined it. It had become as bloody as its surroundings.

He heard a sound from the outer room. Thank God! Now he could send for help. His relief increased as he saw the newcomer clearly. It was one of Captain Rossi's constables and he was followed by a soldier.

But his relief dissolved abruptly. The redcoat was aiming a musket at him, the mouth of the barrel yawning. The ten-pound weapon didn't move and the seventeen-inch bayonet pointed unwaveringly at his heart.

"So," said the man. "The tipoff was right. It was you all the time. Caught in the act! Hand it over. Slowly." He pointed to the pistol.

Dunne handed it over.

The constable motioned to the soldier. "Take him down to the jail. Don't hurt him, not before Jack Ketch can have a chance to top him.

"Oh, yes," he said to the patterer, who was desperately trying to think who had set him up for the fall. "Never fear, my lad. You'll swing for this. High, wide and not very handsome."

CHAPTER THIRTY-SEVEN

I have tried to escape; always to escape as a bird does
out of a cage. Is that unnatural; is that a great crime?
—Dennis Doherty, a soldier transported in 1833 for
desertion and a serial escapee

A BARREL OF RUM SAVED NICODEMUS DUNNE'S SKIN.
As he and his guard stepped down George Street to the
jail, they passed the alehouse called, puzzlingly, Keep Within
Compass, and all hell—in the shape of a 120-gallon puncheon—
broke loose. The giant cask fell while it was being unloaded at
the tavern, smashed open and began to pour its contents into the
nearby drain.

The patterer had always understood and respected the important role of rum in the colony. A roaring convict song (with more
than a germ of truth in it) that celebrated the spirit's iron grip went:

Cut yer name across me backbone,
Stretch me skin across yer drum,

Iron me up on Pinchgut Island
From now to kingdom come.
I'll eat yer Norfolk dumpling
Like a juicy Spanish plum,
Even dance the Newgate hornpipe
If ye'll only gimme rum!

Hard prices to pay, he always thought, when you considered that eating this "dumpling" meant being sent to the hellish Norfolk Island prison, and to dance the "hornpipe" was to dance at the end of a rope.

But even that foreknowledge did not quite prepare Dunne for the scene that unfolded. It was, he thought, almost a colonial miniature of Mr. Hogarth's famous London etching of decadence, *Gin Lane.*

Someone screamed, "Grog ahoy!" and passersby dived at the flowing bounty, scooping it into their mouths with cupped, bare hands. The more enterprising among them came from nearby buildings and captured the golden bonanza with pots, pans and buckets, even a chamberpot. Some stretched out in the dirt beside the drain and lapped like animals. There were women and children among the liquid's looters.

Dunne looked around for his guard and found the man transfixed by the scene, obviously torn between duty and a free drink.

The patterer made up his mind for him. He shoved him under the arms and feet of the scrum of scavengers, where he was instantly swallowed up, then took off along the main street in the direction of the Cove, passing more crowds running toward the rum.

He eased his pace when a ragged file of prisoners, guarded at the front and rear, marched from the jail and slowed to a halt. Both of their guards focused their attention on the drama in the street.

Dunne knew his redcoat would soon raise the hue and cry, and that there were even more soldiers in the nearby barracks. He had to hide somewhere, preferably disappear completely. He had to think.

He had successfully buried his guard in one mess of humanity. The answer to his problem followed: Where better to hide a prisoner on the run than among other prisoners already under guard?

He edged toward the rear of the prison gang. One captive eyed him mistrustfully. "What do you want?" he said softly, out of the side of his mouth, his gaze shifting to Dunne's still-bloody hands.

"Sanctuary," said the patterer. "Bloody help! I'm on the run."

The man studied Dunne keenly. Sure, he looked the part, but could this interloper be trusted? Who was he? All convicts, from harsh experience, were wary of spies infiltrating their ranks, seeking news of uprisings against their masters. The Irish especially aroused fear and loathing among such men as Reverend Marsden, who frequently used the lash to try to uncover imagined insurrections.

"What are they after you for, then?" asked the convict in a soft brogue.

Dunne absorbed the fact that he was pure Black Irish, that different sort of Celt; he was one of those with hair like springy, shiny shards of coal above brilliant blue eyes, a tanned face and a sharp nose that dominated his close-shaven but still blue-black cheeks and chin. Some blamed those looks on shipwrecked Spanish sailors and soldiers from shattered Armada galleons 240 years before. But that did not explain the blue eyes.

Not that the patterer had much time to consider such ancestral subtleties. He simply said, "They'll top me for murder—but I didn't do it!"

The Irishman suddenly, quietly, recited:

Hand in hand
On Earth, in Hell,
Sick or well,
On sea, on land
On the square, ever.

Nicodemus Dunne knew the oath of the convicts' most binding freemasonry, The Ring. He murmured in reply:

Still or in breath,
Lag or free,
You and me,
In life, in death,
On the cross, never.

At that moment another prisoner butted in: "He's all right, he's the patterer." The paddy gave a nod and they dragged him into the heart of the wedge of men.

Dunne's rescuer hissed, "I'll turn you over if it was a woman or a child, mind."

"No, never! On my honor!" Then, with a sudden inspiration (the fact that he was instantly ashamed did not stop him), Dunne added, "It was an Englishman." (Oh well, the German was past caring.)

The prisoner looked hard. "And aren't you just that—English?"

Dunne was quick. "No. I'm Australian."

The man shrugged. "Good enough answer." He laughed. "That is, if you can't be Irish."

Then he turned to a man—not much more than a youth, but he already had almost the patterer's build—beside him. Making sure that the guards' attention was still distracted, he pushed the lad away from the file. "Piss off, Jimmy," he said, and Jimmy obliged.

He turned to Dunne. "That's that, then. You're our Jimmy now."

They hushed as the guards returned to their stations and pushed the ragged ranks into some sort of order. One minder did a quick headcount and was satisfied. "Move on! Move it! Or you'll get a red shirt—and a salty back." A bucket of salty water thrown over bloody lash wounds added to the torment, but the pain was worth it: The wounds would often heal more quickly.

The column shambled south along the main street, past the barracks to the right, and the patterer now had time to take stock. He noticed that some of his new companions were in shackles and wearing canaries, while others were unshackled and in civilian clothes.

"Who are you? And where the devil are we going?" He asked his questions in a murmur and out the corner of his mouth. Dear God, he thought, I've gone back to the black times and the protective habits of prisoners everywhere.

The Irishman seemed cool enough. "Oh, I'm Brian O'Bannion, at your service. And we're today's muster to go on the step."

On the step. Dunne knew what that meant—they were all sentenced to the treadmill, the loathed stairway to nowhere.

CHAPTER THIRTY-EIGHT

. . . and bound him with fetters of brass;
and he did grind in the prison house.

—Judges 16:21

I N THIRTY MINUTES, DUNNE TRUDGED WITH THE CONVICTS THROUGH the main town, past Brickfield, and came almost to the Tollgate, where horse and other animal traffic was levied to pay for the road that stretched toward Parramatta. The reek of Sam Terry's Albion Brewery betrayed their location.

The Carters Barracks loomed on their left. The compound, sealed by twelve-foot walls, lodged and fed 200 prisoners, men whose jobs included driving and handling the government's horses and bullocks—and who sometimes doubled as the draft animals. The barracks also supplied laborers to the Lumber Yard.

Two other buildings completed the Carters complex. Divided only by a party wall were separate quarters for a hundred convict boys. Most were the sweepings of London's rotting tenements for whom thieving and other petty crime had seemed a way out of starvation. The way out, though, had been to Botany Bay.

At the Carters Barracks, the boys were supposed to receive a basic education and learn the rudiments of a trade. Sometimes the lesson was a brutish one. The tawse and cane were applied liberally. And few people were surprised that the boys' accommodation was a sexual honeypot for men starved of women.

Sodomy was an offense with a clumsy official name, "unnatural crime," but a chilling sentence for those who were caught—death (although this penalty was often commuted to life). What threat was "life" to a man who was already a lifer? Only two years before, the patterer recalled, an official memorandum had revealed what most already knew: that prisoners were living "in constant intercourse with the Boys."

Also attached to the Carters Barracks was the House of Correction, home to the town's two treadmills. Everyone knew of their existence—mothers would threaten errant children with "the step"—but this was the first time Nicodemus Dunne had seen the devices close-up. He was impressed, in a chilling way. He scrubbed his hands clean in a nearby trough.

"So we're all here for that?" he murmured to his new friend.

"Aye. Some will stay for as long as a week or even more on the wheels. God willing, you and I are out this evening—Jimmy was only given short time, for dumb insolence to his master."

Before Dunne could ask O'Bannion what he himself had done, a guard waved them into silence and the patterer turned his attention to the treadmills. Looming overhead, they resembled giant, wide waterwheels. He knew that they existed not only for punishment, but also to grind corn, to compensate for the times when there was no breeze to drive the town's windmills. Each unit was reckoned to make the Commissariat 600 pounds through milling each year.

This day, both treadmills were already in operation. On the larger one, Dunne counted thirty-six men, each holding on to wooden crossbars at eye level. They climbed—and got nowhere—from one foot-wide blade to the next. They were stepping at something less than forty paces a minute. Twenty men on the smaller mill imitated these motions.

An overseer and an armed guard watched over each mill. Any man who tried to step back off was threatened with fifty lashes. Once started, the prisoner had to keep going, or he would fall off, or even slip into the gap between blades. There had been many accidents since the steps had been installed five years earlier.

"There are no women," the patterer observed suddenly.

"Oh, aye," agreed O'Bannion. "They don't like to have them here. Like they haven't flogged a woman since '17 or '18. They'll still hang 'em, though."

Dunne must have shown his puzzlement.

"It's the blood, see," explained O'Bannion. "Our masters don't turn a hair at the sight of a bloody back when some poor bastard is married to the three sisters"—he used the convict-talk nickname for the flogging triangles—"and the worst that can happen with someone, man or woman, being turned off is that they'll shit or piss themselves. But they don't care to take the risk with a woman here at this dancing academy. They send them to the factory instead."

"Why not on the step?"

"Why not? Because too many of them have their moon courses while climbing. One keeper complained that they often had not a dry thread among them."

"Oh," said the patterer, who knew as much about menstruation as the next man. That is, precious little. Or nothing.

A batch of men had been stood down from the Great Mill for a spell, leaving empty stations.

"Come on." O'Bannion nudged Dunne. "We're on soon."

"Won't they find out I'm not supposed to be here?"

"No, they'll not care, as long as they have a warm body to make their headcount and lists tally. You stick with us and you'll pass muster. Just answer when Jimmy's called. Remember: Bond's the name—James Bond."

"What did *you* do?"

"Well, apart from those fellows in shackles—they're old lags on secondary punishment—the rest of us are only petty offenders, small beer. Like I said, we're only here for the rest of the day, until sunset. And we're free men—when we're not in places like this! You can tell that some here are soldiers, some are Emancipists, like me, and others are Jimmy Grants. They're in for things like gambling, drunkenness, cockfighting, something like that. Me? Oh, they seized me for riding like the clappers with the hounds of hell behind me down Castlereagh Street, having had a few too many brandies. Furious riding while intoxicated, they called it. Ah yes, I've done all this before."

A guard hustled them toward the big wheel. Now it was their turn to climb. As they mounted their machine, taking up adjoining stations, O'Bannion warned the patterer, "It's terrible hard work, but the boredom can be the worst of it. Don't try to count the steps or the revolutions of the wheel. It can make you crazed. Old hands, brave souls they are, who've done the counting, claim there are 1,440 steps an hour—not that it's really an hour; you do forty minutes then stand down for twenty. And there's an hour for a meal. Bread and gruel, that is. So, if you did an eleven-hour stretch, all told, how many steps would that be? Are you a hand at reckoning?"

Nicodemus Dunne was. He'd had it birched into him at school. With rhetoric and some Latin and Greek. Anyway, he liked numbers. He paused, then said, "15,840 feet. At 5,280 feet to the mile—why, that's—"

"You have the right of it," said O'Bannion. "Three miles . . . perpen-bloody-dicular and getting nowhere!"

———————

THEY CLIMBED TO that routine for the rest of the working day. Dunne and O'Bannion were young and fit. Still, the palms of their hands had soon become slippery on the rail, from sweat and the blood and water from burning, bursting blisters. They felt the muscles of their legs cramp and their hips threaten to seize up. They soon shed their sweaty shirts, but nothing could stop their inner thighs and scrotums being rubbed raw. The patterer now agreed with the men who called the mills "cock-chafers."

At one stage, they felt the blades suddenly become stiffer and harder to depress. They had to use all their strength to make the wheels turn.

"That bastard!" O'Bannion gasped. "He's playing with the brake."

On each machine, a warder started, stopped and, in between, could regulate the speed by releasing or applying a screw-controlled drag on the giant drums. To torment the prisoners, this keeper was slowing the mill. As the men battled the inertia, O'Bannion snorted. "Now you know why they call the buggers 'screws'!"

―――――――

THE DAY'S ORDEAL ended half an hour early for all workers on the Great Mill, but Dunne was sickened by the reason for their early mark. Like the others, he had sometimes not moved briskly enough and had been bruisingly rapped on the shins as he mistimed the next descending steps. But, with the day fading, a man three stations away slipped between the steps. The wheel ground to a halt, but it was too late. The screaming man's leg was broken and mutilated. By the time the shambles was cleared, the day was over.

The names of O'Bannion, James Bond and the other day-men were ticked off and soon they were outside the grim gates. The patterer knew, however, that he was still far from free.

"I have to get back to the heart of the town, but every constable's eye—and every soldier's—will be wide open for me," he said. Then he had an idea. "Will you do me a service?" he asked O'Bannion.

The Irishman nodded. He believed his new friend was innocent of the crime for which he was being hunted.

"Here's threepence. It will buy you a pie at the Hope and Anchor."

O'Bannion frowned. How could food from the pub help? "You want a pie?"

The patterer smiled. "I wouldn't say no to one, but you can have the pie—I really want the pieman."

And he proceeded to explain his plan.

―――――――

WHILE HE WAITED for O'Bannion to return, Nicodemus Dunne was surreptitiously busy.

He made his way to the nearby Benevolent Society asylum

for the poor. Unseen, he filched, from washing still laid out over bushes to dry, a large overall garment and a cap. He added what appeared to be a cape of sorts to his laundry haul. Next, from a shed at the back of the asylum, he wheeled a wooden wheelbarrow. It squeaked loudly enough, he thought, to wake the dead at the nearby Sandhills cemetery. But again nobody challenged him.

Back in the shadows, now by the side of the main road, he settled down to wait. He was weary from his day of fruitless walking and soon felt himself dozing off. A crackle in undergrowth brought him back to alertness. And there it was again; he could not quite pick the direction it was coming from.

"Pieman, is that you? O'Bannion?"

The only response was a crashing blow to the back of his head. A flash like lightning, then pitch-darkness swallowed him.

CHAPTER THIRTY-NINE

Why, was there ever seen such villainy,
So neatly plotted and so well performed?
—Christopher Marlowe, *The Jew of Malta* (1592)

A REGULAR METALLIC SOUND AND A VOICE WELCOMED NICODE-mus Dunne back to the land of the living.

"Snick, snick," went the sound.

"Bugger!" and "Bloody hell!" said the voice.

Through the pain that steadily pounded his head, the patterer recognized the action of a flint and steel—someone was trying to use a tinderbox to make fire. And, it seemed from the oaths, trying unsuccessfully. The tinder, or kindling, would not take a spark from the friction. "Snick, snick" was the last thing he remembered as he again lost consciousness . . .

The clicking and human voice had gone when Dunne woke again from the black pit and blinked his brain back to near full awareness. It seemed to be—still? again?—nighttime and he felt a frisson of cold. At first, that was almost all he could feel: He found he could not move his arms or legs. He flexed his fingers and toes, but movement ended at his wrists and ankles. He did find that he could move his head, though, forward and to each side.

With a sudden fearful thought, he wondered if he had suffered an apoplexy that had paralyzed parts of his body. Then came the realization that, in truth, he was in bondage on the ground, spread-eagled.

One thing: He could see. Out of the corner of one eye, he was able to make out the vague silhouette of the wheelbarrow he had stolen earlier. He could not speak, however; a wad of what tasted like clothing fabric gagged him.

He tried to remain calm. It seemed that he was in much the same area that he remembered before the sudden blow and the dive into unconsciousness. Raising his head as high as possible, he suddenly realized why he felt particularly cold. He was naked; which was also why he could feel the rough ground under his back and limbs.

He must have groaned through the gag. Or perhaps his movement was discernible, constricted though he was. A dim presence—he could not even call it a figure—appeared on one side. A male voice broke the silence: "So, you're awake, patterer . . . Mr. Nicodemus Dunne . . . Ring-master!" The last was said as a jeer.

All Dunne could do was gurgle.

"You should know me," said the voice.

Dunne shook his head. He heard again the conflict of the flint and steel. A spark must have taken in the tinder, for now he could hear the man puffing the glow into further life. Moments later, the captor transferred the flames to a small fire on the ground, too far away to reveal his identity or warm the patterer.

"Yes, you certainly should," repeated the figure. "You smashed me with a rock when you sided with the Indians—you, a white man, taking their part against your countrymen. All we wanted was some fun, a bit of pussy. Their women are all pink inside, just like ours.

"I looked for you all over, you bastard. My two mates were too yellow-gutted; they wanted no part of it. But I wasn't going to forget. I finally saw you in the town and found out more about you. You're no more a Ringer than I am. Just an old lag with a fancy tongue, yapping out the news.

"Then, this morning, near the jail, I got lucky. You appeared and joined that train. So it was no secret where you were going and I only had to follow you and wait outside the House of Correction. I don't know who helped you that morning—yet. Maybe you'll tell me. Don't shake your head. I've got ways. But I'll get square with him, too. And those bloody blacks."

The patterer's chest moved convulsively in a coughing spasm and his breathing through his nose seized up. He began to choke and suffocate.

"Can't have that, can we?" said his tormentor. "You're not going to leave me—yet." He ripped out the gag and Dunne's breathing gasped gradually back to normal.

"What are you going to do?" whispered the patterer. He could barely make himself heard.

"Do? I'm not going to *do* anything to you. Not personally. But my friends here are." Dunne felt the faintest touches on his chest. There seemed a barely perceptible movement, like someone dusting his skin with a feather.

"You know what that is?"

The patterer shook his head. He was still too hoarse to speak properly.

"I'm dropping a handful of bulldog ants on you. There's a nest nearby, almost alongside in fact, and, with a little bit of encouragement, these small fellows, not so small really, will do you in for me. You see? I thought, if I knife you or bash your brains in and if I did get caught, I'd swing. But here's a way that kills you and I won't have harmed a hair on your head."

Dunne knew the red-and-black bulldog ants, which were called soldier ants because of their ferocity and tenacity. They grew to an inch long and had agonizing stings. But could they be killers?

"Now, how good are they?" said the man, reading Dunne's thoughts. "Well, a couple will hurt but not necessarily harm. So here's the help I said I'd give them . . ."

The patterer felt a rain of scattered sensations, even lighter than those made by the ants, fall on his chest and groin. There were two needles of pain, then a third.

"I'll lay a trail from the nest and dust you all over. They'll follow it—to an even tastier meal: you. The bait? Have a bit yourself." Some of the rain fell on Dunne's face and lips.

He tasted sugar.

That fatal calling card—again. His inward groan was stifled by a chilling thought: Was it all just crazy coincidence? Or did it mean that, somehow, the mad mass murderer had turned the tables and caught the hunter?

Then a pitch-topped torch flared to illuminate a face and body standing over the prone prey. The patterer could not recognize the young man he had flattened at the Miller's Point. Something about him was familiar, though.

"You know what they'll do to you?" The voice was excited. "These little buggers will eat you alive. They'll bite you so hard that you'll pray you could tear your skin off. They'll creep into your eyes and into your ears, up your nose and into your mouth. They like sweat and body muck. You'll flinch and struggle and maybe squash a few. That'll only make them angrier. And they'll crawl up your arse and even into the eye of your cock."

"Shit!" said the patterer. It came out only as a strangled sob. His captor nodded and laughed.

Then deliverance came on a divine wind.

CHAPTER FORTY

Where does a wise man hide a leaf?
In the forest.
—G. K. Chesterton, "The Sign of the Broken Sword"
(1911)

THERE WAS THE SMALLEST OF WHISPERS IN THE NIGHT AIR, A THUD. Still holding the torch with one hand, the man suddenly stiffened and gasped. His free hand clutched at an odd, foot-long shaft that jutted out, as if by magic, from his chest. Even in the flare, Dunne could see that the eyes staring down had widened in fearful wonder.

Before the torch dropped to the ground in a cascade of sparks, the patterer saw the man falter and a great gout of shining liquid spout from a silent mouth. The falling figure with its deadly spike narrowly missed Dunne and lay still, apparently pinned to the ground; the other, greater part of the shaft reared up from his back, six or so feet in the air.

The patterer heard bodies thrashing through undergrowth,

then a knife was slashing at his bonds and a voice in his ear was saying, "It's me, O'Bannion, with William the Pieman. And Bungaree's mob. They led us to you. You weren't at the rendezvous so they offered to search for you."

He helped Dunne stand on his shaky legs. "I don't know why, but you've a staunch friend there. I'm not sure who told his man to let fly."

Bungaree helped brush off the ants and sugar. "He wanted to kill you. He got killed." This was all he would say.

The patterer nodded his thanks as he recovered his clothes, which were torn in parts but still serviceable, from a pile on the ground and dressed hurriedly by the light of the torch that William King had saved from sputtering out completely then waved back to life. The stolen clothing from the asylum went back into the wheelbarrow.

The native spearman was recovering his weapon. He put his foot in the small of his target's back and pulled and worried the shaft. The spear came out bloody, with a sucking noise. It had no barb, just a fire-hardened needle nose.

The pieman held the torch over the facedown body while O'Bannion rolled it over with his foot.

He let out a long whistle. "God save Ireland!" he said. "We've just killed James Bond."

———————

DUNNE NOW RECOGNIZED the face as that of the young man who had surrendered his place in the prisoners' line on the street outside the jail. That's why he had been doubly familiar.

"The little shite!" was all O'Bannion could say.

The patterer interrupted. "We've got to get rid of him. Think of it: You, O'Bannion, you're an old lag—an Irish one to boot, with fresh marks on your record—and I'm damned sorry I've involved William. Then there are the blacks. They'll hang them without a second thought—and they're already getting the rope ready for me."

As Dunne rubbed his face free of a stray ant, Bungaree told him the insects would not have killed him—probably—but he was taking no chances. "We could dump him in the bush, but there's always a chance of a dog finding the body."

Brian O'Bannion broke in. "Where can you best hide a body? Why, with a lot of other bodies."

"Like a battlefield," said William King.

"Sure," agreed the Irishman. "Unfortunately, the lobster-backs at the barracks are not likely to stage a battle just for our convenience. But I've got a grand idea. Grab him and follow me."

They loaded the late, unlamented James Bond into the wheelbarrow, on top of Dunne's looted laundry. The strange procession, led by O'Bannion, creaked and groaned as quietly as it could to the Sandhills cemetery. The Irishman whispered to King Bungaree, who sent a warrior silently running on ahead. He soon came back, nodding.

They all pushed on after him and, not much later, came upon an open grave, clearly dug earlier that day and awaiting a burial on the morrow. Even the shovels that would be needed again were still there, sticking out of the mounds of sandy loam alongside the pit.

The patterer read O'Bannion's intent. He gave a shovel to the pieman and said, "You're the strongest. Get down and make it, say, a foot or so deeper. The sand should make it easy." The softness of the cemetery may have been a gravedigger's boon, but it also allowed noxious fluids to leach out to lower ground, some said darkly into the nearby stream, which fed the brewery. And foraging wild animals sometimes found it, as they had the earlier abandoned burial ground, a happy hunting ground.

As a wild dog scrabbled nearby, a warrior's spear thudded into another victim. So much death, thought Dunne. Could the corpse before him be the final piece in the game of murder? He dropped down and riffled through the pockets. Nothing. Now perhaps they would never know. He could hand over all he had discovered—and that was a name—to Captain Rossi and let his men track the dead young man's movements.

But if it were true that the dead man had only stumbled across the patterer that morning, and there was no reason to doubt it, he could not have known of his planned meeting with the compositor. More to the point, at the time of that murder Bond must have been safely in custody.

Dunne knew that his only hope of saving his own neck rested with solving the crimes—and that meant making his peace with Rossi, or at least buying more time. First, however, they had to bury James Bond. They covered him with a layer of rocks to deter any animals, then a layer of infill, until the hole looked much like the original empty grave. Bungaree agreed to leave a native on guard until daylight, hidden but ready to repel scavengers. Then the patterer's rescuer melted away.

"It'll be a tight squeeze," said Brian O'Bannion. "But I fancy neither occupant will complain."

"What if it's a woman?" the pieman queried dubiously.

"If it's a woman on top," replied the Irishman, "well, that's where they all secretly think they ought to be." He struck a pose at the graveside, raised a large rock level with his eyes and declaimed, "Alas, poor Yorick! I knew him, Horatio; a fellow of infinite jest, of most excellent fancy . . ."

"That's downright disrespectful," chided William King.

"Who to?"

"To the man in there—blackguard though he was—and to whoever will be there tomorrow."

"No disrespect intended," protested O'Bannion, throwing aside the rock. "Any road, Master Shakespeare—and he had such a sweet way with the words that he must have been Irish—said, 'All the world's a stage, and all the men and women merely players . . .'"

The pieman wasn't mollified. "He also said that we should not tamper—except at our peril—with the normal way of things. Remember, he wrote:

"Take but degree away, untune that string,
And, hark, what discord follows! each thing meets
In mere oppugnancy . . ."

"Mary!" said O'Brien. "What the devil does oppug . . . whatever, mean?"

William King patiently replied, "Opposition, contrariness, alteration, contradiction—in that a small change can alter the chain of events."

While the two argued, a seed of thought buried deep at the back of the patterer's brain germinated and began to grow.

As if at a distance, he heard the Irishman complain. "Will you let a man have one last little bit of fun?" And in a falsetto he recited, "'O Romeo, Romeo! wherefore art thou Romeo?'"

The seed blossomed and Nicodemus Dunne believed that now he knew the secrets—most of them anyway—of the slayings.

He clapped his hands in delight. "Juliet, I could kiss you!" he shouted.

CHAPTER FORTY-ONE

And immediately there fell from his eyes as it had been
scales; and he received sight forthwith.
—Acts 9:18

"GOD SAVE IRELAND! WHAT THE DEVIL'S THE MATTER WITH YOU now?" asked Brian O'Bannion. He was startled by the patterer's outburst, and puzzled. So, too, was the pieman, but since their companion showed no signs of explaining his sudden cry of pleasure, they both held their peace. He *would* explain, he told them, but later. First they all had much more work to do.

"I must get to Captain Rossi, unmolested—and unarrested," he said. "But I'm guessing there are constables and soldiers still searching for me."

"They were all over the place when we came looking for you," confirmed William King. "And they're sure to be still on the job."

Dunne nodded. "That's why I called for you then, and why I still need you now." He looked to O'Bannion. "The plan stays the same, so let's go over it."

———————

THE PATTERER ENTERED the heart of the town unhindered, just as he had plotted. It seemed an age since he had first hatched his plan, but it was, in fact, a matter of a few hours.

Led by the Irishman bearing aloft a flaming torch, the Flying Pieman wheeled the wheelbarrow at a fast clip, his streamers flying. Dunne sat demurely in the wheelbarrow, clothed in the purloined dress, his face shadowed by the mob-cap and the shawl.

Whenever fellow travelers, late shoppers and other pedestrians appeared—and, for the hour, there was a surprisingly large number of them—O'Bannion would circle the procession, shoving people out of the way and shouting, "The pieman's on a record! Let the bugger through!"

And witnesses—not least patrols of soldiers and constables intent on capturing the escaped murderer Nicodemus Dunne—stood aside, even clapped and cheered.

On George Street, when they were just past the old burial ground and approaching the market houses, William King abruptly dropped the handles of the wheelbarrow. Then he punched the Irishman full in the mouth and the pair began to roll violently on the ground. They were soon surrounded by a cheering crowd.

No one was interested any longer in King's woman passenger, who was spilled to the roadway. And no eyes followed her as she ran down the pathway that led to the rear of the markets—and the police office.

Ten minutes later a disheveled O'Bannion joined Dunne. "I've done this before," he said reassuringly, and proceeded to force a window. He then boosted his companion over the sill into a corridor. "Good luck."

"I'll keep my fingers crossed," said the patterer.

"If you keep those clothes on," replied the Irishman with a chuckle, "you'd be advised to keep your *legs* crossed. You make a darlin' woman."

Within minutes the transformation was achieved, the gown, cap and shawl disposed of, and Nicodemus Dunne was making himself comfortable in the seat of power normally graced by Captain Francis Nicholas Rossi's posterior. He went to sleep and dreamed of ants and murderers.

———————

DUNNE WAS STILL dozing when the room's rightful occupant arrived early the next morning. A speechless Rossi shook him awake. The patterer's first words were, "Who betrayed me?"

The policeman shrugged. "I just don't know. I didn't know anything about the . . . the mess until after you'd been arrested. A message had come to the office early. My man acted on his own initiative, in good faith, I believe. Here's what started it all." He handed over a note that read:

> *He's killed again, there's none that's meaner.*
> *For his bloody new work, go to* The Gleaner.

The script was in the left-handed style they all had come to expect.

"Who delivered this message?" asked the patterer.

"No one remembers clearly. The messenger simply handed it over and disappeared. Who would take any notice—it was just an ordinary-looking note? When its import was realized, it was too late to seek out its carrier." Rossi held up a hand. "Now, you can't blame the constable. You were holding the pistol and were covered in blood. And then you ran—in his eyes, hardly the action of an innocent man."

Nicodemus Dunne flushed. "Do *you* think I'm guilty?"

"Of course not! But you must admit that the evidence is compelling."

"*Is* compelling? Don't you mean, *was* compelling? Am I still a wanted man?"

The captain looked uncomfortable. "Well, it still looks bad for you."

"But that's exactly the reason I had to run! It's a vicious circle."

"I don't quite know what to do with you," admitted Rossi. "The governor is furious. He thinks he's been made to look a fool. You've put him in an awkward position."

"Him? What about *my* position? They'll try to hang me!"

"Oh," said the captain airily. "You won't dance the Newgate jig."

"How can you be so sure?"

Rossi was dismissive. "We wouldn't let it happen to you." He did not elaborate. "But, on a brighter note, Miss Dormin is also on your side. She rushed here as soon as the news had spread. She was white with shock, but I reassured her."

So, she still cares enough, thought the patterer. I must certainly see her.

"But," the policeman continued, "what are we to do to justify my assurances?"

"Captain, I need at least today to clear my name and at the same time finally unmask our murderer—"

"You know now? Who is it?" Rossi broke in excitedly.

"Have patience until I'm sure. But this is what must happen. I give you my parole that I won't escape. What I want in return is a *passeport* so that no one will be able to take me while I'm hunting. And I require a letter from you giving me authority to question any officials and functionaries—don't worry, they'll all be well below the governor's level. I'll call on you later this afternoon. Do we have a deal?"

Rossi pondered a moment, then nodded.

THE PATTERER BEGAN what he hoped would be his last rounds of detection with his hat pulled low over his face. He had his papers of safe passage but he still wanted to avoid wasting valuable time endlessly producing them.

He called first on the apothecary who had made the arsenic sale. There he received fresh information he had failed to elicit earlier: The mystery buyer was much shorter than Dunne. Dr. Owens, noted the patterer, was a tall man. But Dr. Halloran was considerably shorter.

At the building that housed the Colonial Treasurer, Dunne did not find that august gentleman, William Balcombe, who had once been an intimate of the exiled Bonaparte on Saint Helena. As an East India Company official, Balcombe took the fallen emperor in while a rat-infested farmhouse was being repaired for him.

Thus Balcombe's son, Thomas (who rejoiced in the middle name Tyrwhitt), and the defeated Frenchman became firm friends, two lonely figures on the remote island. And it was this young man, now nineteen and determined to become an artist, whom Dunne was pleased to come across.

They talked casually about their favorite artworks of the

colony. Balcombe liked the early paintings and sketches of John Rae, Thomas Rowlandson and George Raper. The patterer praised Joseph Lycett and Augustus Earle, in particular the latter's likenesses of King Bungaree.

"It has been a sad time, with deaths in the art world," said the younger man. "Mr. Lycett is gone, I fear. It seems, no one knows for sure, that a year or so ago, in Bath, he forged some banknotes— unhappy man, forgery is what sent him here originally. Upon his arrest he slashed his throat and then, while recovering in hospital, he ripped open the wound and died. The other death has, of course, been the recent passing of Francisco Goya." Balcombe continued, smiling wryly, "It is ironic that Goya, my artistic hero, used his brush to condemn the atrocities perpetrated by the army of which my old friend, the Emperor Napoleon, was the commander."

On that note, they parted, the patterer to continue his studies in art—only this was the fine art of murder.

CHAPTER FORTY-TWO

Captain Louis Renault: Round up the usual suspects.
—Julius J. Epstein *et al.*, *Casablanca* (1942)

THE COLONIAL SECRETARY'S OFFICE, WHICH WAS MUCH GRANDER than that of the treasurer, was the hub of record-keeping for the colony. There Dunne sought details of shipping arrivals and departures, and their complements, and narratives of incidents on the crossings. Most of the files were voluminous and comprehensive, but sometimes they were not. In one famous instance, the *Anne*, a convict transport, arrived in 1801 with no papers for its human cargo. The lists finally turned up, eighteen years later.

The patterer found the records for the ill-fated *Morley*, which had caused Dr. Cunningham so much pain, but although he failed to find the names he was particularly seeking, he nonetheless left the office feeling greatly enlightened.

———

AT THE SUBSCRIPTION Library, his disguise failed and the attendant coolly pointed out that his annual subscription of two guineas was due. On becoming financial once more, he called for and studied a German dictionary. He also found what he was after in a volume of Shakespeare's works. In his pursuit of the Exodus clue, however, he became bogged down. But Genesis was more rewarding.

As he handed back the foreign dictionary, Dunne had an idle thought. He called for a world gazetteer. When the dying Muller had said the word *Schwein*, had he simply been cursing his killer rather than naming him—surely no one's name began with "pig!" Or did his last breath point perhaps to a place?

In the atlas, Dunne looked for a German location beginning with "Schwein-." He found one, in the realm of Bayern—or Bavaria. There it was: Schweinfurt—ford for swine—which was necessary, as the spot lay on the River Main. But what help was that?

He had an idea, but several of the books he requested next were unavailable. So he moved on to the stationery office and library attached to *The Gazette*. There, Mr. William McGarvie found what the patterer required, including a comprehensive pharmacopoeia—a heavy volume listing drugs and medicines and describing their preparation, uses and effects.

Mr. McGarvie also proudly produced a prize. On the day before his arrest, the patterer had digested a thought-provoking entry in a general medical book. Now he had before him an English commentary on the work of the Spanish poisons expert, Dr. Mathieu Orfila. Dunne recalled Thomas Owens mentioning the expert. The Spanish doctor now spoke clearly to him. The patterer realized that so, too, had the unfortunate Muller. And his message was breath-taking, confirming all of Dunne's suspicions.

Although there was still one gap, that did not put off the imminent denouement—he was certain he had solved the murders. The accidental tomfoolery at the impromptu Sandhills funeral had turned the key to the killing machine's identity.

What a fool I've been, he thought, not to have listened sooner to a dead man. Several such, in fact. And one of them gone to dust two centuries ago.

As DUNNE DREW closer to the waters of Sydney Cove, the tang of salt and mud, even the ships' smells of tar, hot canvas, hemp and, from time to time, carpenters' sweet shavings battled valiantly against the too-often pervading stenches of the dry and thus unwashed town. The drought that baked the colony looked like never ending. Even the seagulls seemed tired.

To the patterer, the strongest smells came as he passed a sentry and entered a Customs Office bond storeroom, which was cluttered with bagged spices and sandalwood from the East, furs from as far away as Canada, whale and seal oil from the southern ocean, rum from India and wine from the Cape. Even the commodities that were tightly sealed somehow managed to stamp their aromatic identities onto the close air. These things and a thousand more were all held in bondage until customs duty was paid.

It was a colorful place, but Dunne thought that it must be duller without the presence or influence of its former chief collector, Captain John Piper. His successors, such as Captain Rossi, oversaw the operations, but more covertly, without Piper's lordly, proprietary swagger.

Of course, nowadays there was not quite the same incentive. Captain Rossi received a flat salary, but when Piper reigned he had taken 4 percent of all duties collected. Originally, his masters expected he might skim off 400 pounds a year, but as business boomed, his fees reached 11,000 pounds.

The patterer well recalled when the customs accounts were found muddled and Piper lost his lucrative post. The collector took it hard and went to sea in his luxury yacht, crewed by blue-and-silver-uniformed sailors who were also skilled musicians. On the open sea, Piper jumped over the side but his serenading sailors fished him out. He then retired across the mountains to hunt kangaroos and wild dogs. In full hunting pink, naturally.

Dunne's daydreams were interrupted by the arrival of the first customs officer he had asked to see. Captain Rossi's letter of introduction worked wonders and the man was eager to cooperate. This fellow enjoyed the title of "gauger," but he could not help the patterer; his function was to work out the quantities of cargo items on which duty was to be applied.

The "tide-waiter" explained that he, suitably enough, awaited the tides' ebb and flow, overseeing ships' arrivals and departures to detect or deter contraband. His colleague, the "landing-waiter," explained that he, on the other hand, waited on the wharf and checked off landed consignments against the ships' manifests.

The patterer thanked these worthies, but passed on. The next—and last—man he interviewed, ah, he was the "jerquer." And he was the man Dunne wanted, for a jerquer examined ships' papers and saw that all cargo was listed and accurately described.

Had he, Dunne asked, seen any unusual cargoes? One from, say, Schweinfurt, in Bavaria? It may have come by way of London, of course.

"Ah, that's an easy one," replied the jerquer. He recalled only one such consignment. But it had come not from Schweinfurt but from another sausage-eaters' city, Leipzig.

The patterer hid his disappointment, but still let the man steer him to the records. Where, indeed, there was a note of such a load upon which duty had been paid. And thus the jerquer was able to name the shipment's contents—and the address, if not the identity, of its recipient. The consignment had gone to the place where the clue originated—the office of *The Gleaner*.

———————

THE PATTERER THEN sought out Brian O'Bannion. "You've shown that you're handy at getting into ground-floor windows—how are you at first-story jobs?"

"Anyone on the premises?" asked the Irishman.

"Not to worry you in the area I'm talking about. I need it done today—so that the item you take will be with me tomorrow morning, early."

"If it's important to you, of course I'll do it."

Dunne smiled. "I wouldn't ask you to risk it if I couldn't look you in the eye and say that lives depend upon you." He told O'Bannion exactly what he was to look for, adding before he moved off, "Be careful near it. It might be wise to wear gloves and a mask."

———————

HE HAD ONE last duty—and it had always been a pleasant one: He called on Miss Dormin at the dress shop.

"You'll be pleased to know that the matter of the murders is coming to a head," he said.

She gasped and shook her head admiringly. "And there's

something I want you to do," he added. "You must tell no one. Not even Dr. Halloran."

"Is it important?"

He took her hand and pressed it. "Oh, yes. It's a matter of life and death."

He made his request and they talked earnestly for a long while. Then, after a squeeze, the patterer released his hold and said, "Now, go."

———————

"WE ARE READY to have a last meeting of the principals involved," said Dunne, handing Captain Rossi a note with a list of names. It was a long list.

"My God, are you mad?" The police chief scanned the names on the note. "They won't all come. And do we *want* all these people? Besides, it will be Sunday."

The patterer soothed him. "Oh, I think you'll find they'll make time if you tell them it's the governor's pleasure that they do. And that they'll meet our quarry. Finally."

CHAPTER FORTY-THREE

It is now rendered necessary that I give the facts—
as far as I comprehend them myself.

—Edgar Allan Poe, "The Facts in the Case of
M. Valdemar" (1845)

So it was that Nicodemus Dunne found himself exactly
where his voyage of death and discovery had all started—was
it really only a matter of weeks ago?—back in the same secluded
room deep in the heart of the George Street barracks.

With him were familiar faces from that first meeting: Governor
Darling, Colonel Shadforth and Captains Crotty and Rossi. Their
ranks were swollen by the attendance, as desired, of lawyer William
Charles Wentworth, Dr. Halloran, his fellow editor Edward
Smith Hall and Dr. Owens. None of them commented on the patterer's
changed status, from fugitive murder suspect to master of
ceremonies. Rossi had evidently calmed those waters, just as he had
briefed those new to the company on the bare bones of the crimes.

"We have until one o'clock this afternoon to put this tragic matter completely to rights," Dunne began. He refused to respond to
the questioning looks that greeted this mention of a time constraint.

Then he lobbed his first grenade, continuing quietly, "In this
affair, most of you have been suspects—" He raised a hand to quell
the hubbub of angry dissent. "All of these men have secrets that
offer motives strong enough to kill for. Each could have killed at
least one of our victims. And, collectively, almost all of you have
also conspired to slay one of your fellows—perhaps even a second." He ignored the renewed buzz of angry objections. "You
must indulge me, as we consider what we first learned about the
murders, in order.

"The soldier outside the tavern? Well, if his had been the only
murder, Captain Rossi's men and the army would probably have
had to file away the facts of his strange wounds and the sugar in
his mouth. The investigation would have gathered mildew and the
letter to the governor, too, may well have gathered dust. For there
were no real clues." He paused. "And, he was, after all, just a poor
soldier.

"But the death of the *New World* printer, Abbot, taxed any ele-
ment of coincidence. He had once been a member of the same
regiment. He, too, was mutilated. There was another mysterious,
wordy 'clue.' Two, in fact. And more sugar.

"The slaughterman's poisoning, although it did not include any
physical violence, finally removed the possibility that the similarities between the deaths were mere chance. The poisoner's instructions were given in the backward-sloping, left-handed writing of
the first letter—and the same regiment was on the march again. It
was lightning striking the same place—a third time. No chance."
He shook his head dismissively.

"Then, the blacksmith's death in the Lumber Yard gave us lashings by another left-hander and more slashing, copying that done to the first victim. And more sugar—albeit dyed green. He was no 'Die Hard' veteran, but still there *was* a military link, which turned out to be a revealing one and about which I will speak more fully in due course.

"I believe the same hand killed all our victims. Could some of them be copycat affairs? I think not. Consider that too much intimate knowledge would be required of cases, but they were never made completely public." Dunne smiled encouragingly at Captain Rossi.

"So, a pattern had emerged—which promptly appeared to be broken by the seemingly unconnected death of Madame Greene. Hers was the most intriguing, until the two most recent murders. And yes, gentlemen, they will be the last in this chain of slaughter. The killing of the *Gleaner* compositor, Muller, was almost the death of me."

Rossi had the good grace to redden at this.

The patterer continued. "I had already harbored certain suspicions, but Muller told me something—although I didn't see it at the time—that lifted the veil on the terrible secrets—"

Wentworth interrupted. His lawyer's forensic mind had already caught an inconsistency. "Sit fast, sir!" he said. "You just referred to 'the two most recent murders.' In the plural. Wasn't the man Muller the last?"

"Chronologically, yes," Dunne replied. "But before him—and uncounted so far—was the maid, Elsie."

Rossi recovered his wits first. "But wasn't she . . . didn't she commit suicide?"

Dunne shook his head. "We were supposed to think so, but she was certainly slain—to silence her—and by our angel of death, no one else. And then someone wanted *me* dead. For getting too close."

Governor Darling spoke for the first time. "So what, to your mind, is the link between the soldiers' deaths and Madame Greene's? And you've thrown in the German and now the maid, for good measure."

"Bear with me, sir," soothed the patterer.

"I still want to hear why you've damned well accused *us*!" interposed Wentworth furiously.

He glowered when all Dunne would say was a curt "All in good time" before continuing. "Until the very last I had trouble making the connection stick. Certainly, Madame was poisoned like The Ox, but where did the others fit in? There seemed no link between their deaths and the Sudds case, which provided a common thread between the earlier murders . . ." He paused and waited while Captain Rossi explained to the uninitiated the concept that the killings were revenge for the persecution of the unfortunate soldier.

Before Dunne could speak again, Wentworth butted in. "What of all the gabble about . . . what was it called? . . . yes, the *zuzim*? And the biblical verse nonsense?"

"Oh," replied the patterer. "I believe the Hebrew rhyme was really just a red herring—although a blood-red one. The sender knew that such horrendous deaths, as they mounted up, would bring ever-closer scrutiny.

"So perhaps the idea was, at least partly, to divert our energies into searching for a mystical Jewish avenger. The Exodus verse? Well, it is in keeping with the theme of vengeance, but it only repeats the threats, shedding no new light on the deaths. It is almost as if something were missing. I thought at one stage that the killer *wanted* to be caught. But, if so, there were more victims to come. Why, after only two, alert us and perhaps cut short the desired cycle? And the whole idea collapses when we consider Elsie and Muller, who were apparent outsiders plucked into the fatal circle for other reasons."

The governor cleared his throat. "Madame Greene?" His reminder was firm.

"Yes," said Dunne. "I could see no link, not until I finally deciphered a coded message sent to us by the doomed printer at the *New World*, Will Abbot." He passed to his listeners the proof of the typesetting found with the body.

"A knowledgeable colleague pointed out to me that the type used was smaller in size than it should have been. Why? Now, Abbot must have had some inkling of his coming death, even before he began to set this material.

"He couldn't write down his attacker's identity, couldn't even set it in type, in the event it was read and smashed. So he did the next best thing—the *only* thing—which was to set a clue by using the *wrong* type. He chose a case of type in a size that was unsuitable, then signaled his intention by setting a first line that indicated the subsequent lines were not set as instructed. Why else would he set such a first line? He already knew, without reminding, that a larger type size was required. No, the message was for some future reader, he hoped.

"Later, Dr. Owens idly asked my observant friend what was involved in a switch of types and he was told that it only required the compositor to select a different wooden case of type. I remember Dr. Owens being told simply, 'The case is altered.' On that deadly day in the printery, the type shuffle would have meant nothing to the killer. Abbot could only hope that someone would one day understand. I finally did. And, as I will soon explain, the murdered Muller gave me the same message.

"First though, I had to remember how, in this very room, you, Captain Crotty, were explaining military nicknames. You mentioned, for instance, how sailors had corrupted *Bellerophon* into Billy Ruffian. And you mentioned another concoction. I called upon a veteran who told me how the 57th and its soldiers had bivouacked during the Spanish campaigns at an agreeable place that captured their fancy so much that from then on they sentimentally attached its name to subsequent comfortable watering holes (in the alcoholic sense) and billets. The name of that Iberian oasis was Casa Alta."

The patterer paused. "Tell me, Captain Crotty, do you know in what rude manner old soldiers render this happy hideaway, Casa Alta?"

"Good Lord! I've heard it garbled as 'the Case is Altered.'"

"Thank you. Now, Colonel. Your turn. Most often, the surrogate Casa Alta for the men has been a public house—there is more than one in Middlesex, the regiment's home territory. Sometimes it refers to a brothel. Here in Sydney we have no tavern or whorehouse bearing the Spanish name, or even its Anglicized corruption. Nonetheless, there is a connection." Calling on all his skills as a patterer, Dunne let the tension build. "Colonel, what exactly does 'Casa Alta' mean in Spanish?"

"Why, ah, 'High House,'" said Shadforth.

"Exactly!" said Nicodemus Dunne. "The very name of the establishment of the late Madame Greene. Abbot was placing Madame Greene conclusively within the fatal circle. But why?"

Captain Rossi nodded approvingly, but William Charles Wentworth only sneered and leaned forward pugnaciously. "So you've connected the brothel-keeper to the others—is that the true extent of your progress? Answer the real questions, the ones you've made such a fuss about. Who among us is a killer?"

"Very well," said the Patterer. "If you demand satisfaction"—at this, he thought he caught a flicker of disquiet cross the lawyer's face at the double meaning of the phrase—"you shall have it. But first, I say that six of you had the opportunity to kill the blacksmith."

The room was suddenly hushed.

"You were all involved in a clandestine meeting and were loose in the early hours of that Monday morning. And there was certainly death on your minds. You were illegally conspiring to kill or at least maim one man; perhaps even two could have died. So, yes, by all means let's talk about what happened . . . at Garden Island. You have a lot to explain."

There was silence. Then, at a nod from the governor, the floodgates finally opened.

CHAPTER FORTY-FOUR

'Tis now the very witching time of night,
When churchyards yawn and hell itself breathes out
Contagion to the world: now could I drink hot blood,
And do such bitter business as the day
Would quake to look on.
—William Shakespeare, *Hamlet* (1601)

A S EACH OF THE ASSEMBLED MEN CONFESSED HIS PART IN THE
escapade, the patterer pieced together the story. In the small
hours of the Monday morning in question, the morning of the
blacksmith's murder, two skiffs stood bobbing at the Governor's
Wharf in Sydney Cove. They had been ordered there during the
previous afternoon.

Apart from its oarsman, one boat already contained its comple-
ment of three passengers; the two men to be carried in the other
vessel impatiently awaited the arrival of their third companion. He
finally arrived, breathless, and boarded with apologies.

"Sorry, gentlemen," puffed Captain Crotty. "I was obliged to
detour to confuse the guard."

His associates either grunted or said nothing. The tension remained.

Without further instruction, one crewman took the lead as the boats quietly moved off, first north past the water bailiff's building and the heaving-down place. They then turned east around Macquarie's Fort on its outcrop, and next crossed the mouth of Farm Cove to Mrs. Macquarie's Point. The last leg of the journey took the tiny fleet farther east, then down to a landing strand on Garden Island. It seemed the long way around, but approach from the town through the Domain and Gardens in the depth of the night was not practical.

Crotty's boat arrived first. His companions, who soon splashed ashore with him, were Dr. Thomas Owens and Governor Ralph Darling. The second vessel then discharged the Reverend Dr. Halloran, Mr. Edward Smith Hall and Mr. W. C. Wentworth.

Although they had remained silent during their ride, they now made no effort to disguise their presence on the island. They knew that the area, which had been given to First Fleet settlers forty years earlier as a vegetable garden and later also used for convalescents and as a quarantine station, would now be deserted.

For this reason, it was Sydney's dueling ground of choice, a place where the town's gentlemen came to settle questions of honor. Its appeal lay in its remoteness, for armed arbitration was illegal. The authorities sometimes turned a blind eye, but duelists were often severely punished. That purest of pure merinos, Captain Macarthur, had been sent back to England in disgrace to face court-martial for seriously wounding his commanding officer. And only four months before, a Garden Island duelist had been jailed for three months for fatally wounding an opponent, as was the man who had stood the killer's second. Sometimes, combatants emerged with bodies unscathed and honor restored. The guns were clumsy and often inaccurate (or the shooters were).

"It's almost a family tradition!" Dr. Owens joked nervously to the governor.

Darling shook his head grimly. He knew the doctor was alluding to the fact that only the previous year his brother-in-law, Lieutenant-Colonel Henry Dumaresq, had felt obliged to challenge that damned Wentworth's partner, Dr. Robert Wardell. Dumaresq had taken umbrage at an article in *The Australian*, "How to Live by Plunder."

The party had arrived at the chosen site, a small clearing. Now all they had to do was prepare for the fight, wait for the first bloom of dawn and let it begin.

Dr. Halloran spoke, by torchlight, as both president and referee of the coming duel. "There is still time to settle this amicably but honorably, gentlemen. Would you repeat the substance of your perceived injury, Mr. Wentworth?"

"He referred to my late father, a pillar of the colony, as a convict, as a highwayman!" he spluttered with repressed anger.

"Governor—your response?"

"No, sir. I merely stated that he had stood trial as an alleged man of the road. As he certainly did, several times."

"Not quite as damning as you seem to believe, Mr. Wentworth," said Halloran. "Is that interpretation suitable to you?"

"Not at all. My dear father was an exile, by his own choice. I still demand satisfaction."

Halloran sighed. "So be it." He turned to the governor. "Will you withdraw and apologize, Excellency?"

"No, sir, I am a prisoner to the truth. I cannot undo it."

"In that case, gentlemen, there is nothing for it but to continue. I am the sole policeman of the rules. You will receive three instructions: to take your marks; get ready, which means have your weapons cocked; and fire. Only one shot each will be permitted. If either, or both, of the firers is clearly hit, then the matter is concluded. So, too, if both shots fail to find their mark, I will consider the honor of both contestants to be satisfied. Your seconds may now approach to examine the pistols and observe their loading. The weapons come from a neutral source. I know you brought your own, Mr. Wentworth, but it will not do, sir."

At this, the lawyer shook his head angrily.

Night had not yet passed and Halloran still needed the flickering torch as he removed the pair of pistols from their plush-lined case. They were beautiful examples of the gunsmith's art, coldly gleaming and ornately decorated. Crotty guessed they were Whitworths. Edward Hall had no idea.

The referee now addressed the seconds: "I can swear to the flints, the touch-holes are clear, the powder dry."

After examination, the seconds handed back the weapons. Halloran poured measures of powder into each barrel and primed the pans. Before dealing with the powder, the party had stepped well away from the open flame, but the dimness did not hinder Halloran's surprising dexterity.

In seconds he seemed to juggle balls, wadding and ramrod into the muzzles. Crotty and Hall took the loaded guns and handed them to their principals before prudently retiring to the safety of the sidelines with Halloran and Dr. Owens.

The referee's first order, "At your marks, gentlemen," was a formality; they were already at the twenty-four paces that marked the boundaries of the killing field. They faced each other, coatless, and turned sideways to offer smaller targets.

Ralph Darling had said he did not want the fight, but it must go on. He was not afraid and was confident of the outcome. In the boat, he had remarked to Crotty that he did not yet intend to meet poor little Edward. The simple truth was that his class's rigid code of honor forced the contest upon him. No gentleman could refuse. All he could do was make every effort to ensure victory.

———————

As THE PATTERER listened to the story unfold, he reflected that it was all so stupid, yet oddly necessary. He understood why officers led assaults in full uniform—as examples. He knew why Nelson had stood in the face of fatal sniper fire at Trafalgar, invitingly displaying glittering stars of the Orders of the Crescent, St. Ferdinand, St. Joachim and the Bath. Men should always show cool resolve. Wellington had calmly ignored small-arms and cannon shot at Waterloo, and General Picton had allowed himself only the protection of a top hat and an umbrella before his head was taken off by a cannonball.

Some had criticized Wellington for allowing Maitland's Guards to conceal themselves behind a slope before attacking on Old Nosey's famous order, "Get them up, Maitland!" (which had been turned by the penny prints into the more commonly known version, "Up, Guards, and at 'em!").

In the matter of the recent duel, Nicodemus Dunne could not help but feel that if there were ever a reason for one, it was editor Hall writing of Governor Darling's "tyranny, surpassed only by that of the Great Moghul, the Czar of Muscovy and the Emperor of China."

The patterer jerked his attention back to the general confession . . .

———————

AT THE SHOUT of "Make ready!", the rivals lifted their heavy pistols, which strained their muscles with every passing second.

But "Fire" did not come.

As William Charles Wentworth raised his weapon, a sudden gust of wind lifted his hanging cravat, flapping it across his arm. Unnerved, he pulled the trigger in a reflex action. Dense smoke coughed from the pan and the barrel. Once the smoke blew away and the ringing of the shot faded, there was a hush, but not a fearful one—more one of embarrassment. It seemed the rogue shot had gone wild. Darling stood unharmed.

"It was an accident," gasped Wentworth finally, appealing to his opponent, who still stood at the ready.

"No doubt," said Halloran. "But the rules are clear. Although uncalled for, you have had your shot. Now it is the governor's turn."

At Darling's shrug of doubt, he added, "You must, sir."

Still the governor held his fire.

"You must obey my call, sir," repeated the referee.

Darling nodded. He saw that his flint was at full cock of the dog's-head as he focused his eye along the barrel at the lawyer's shirt. He made only a minor adjustment, then the muzzle was true at the target. He inhaled deeply, let out half the breath, held it, then squeezed the trigger.

Wentworth staggered, but only in reaction to the explosion. He, too, had not taken a ball.

"I am satisfied, gentlemen," said Halloran. "Are you?"

Both men nodded, Wentworth rather shakily.

"Then let us depart."

Wentworth's bravado quickly returned. He soon seemed to regard his failure as bad luck, Darling's as bad aim. He was heard to mutter, "Not that much better a shot than that damned Dumaresq!"

But the governor did not take the bait. He simply smiled tightly.

With no further discussion, the parties returned to the waiting boats and were rowed back to Sydney Cove. All wanted the matter dead and buried. They would be hard put to explain why they had been involved in a forbidden enterprise that may have killed the king's representative.

Even *being* that very representative wouldn't help.

———————

THE PATTERER, OF course, was not able to piece together the whole strange story. He hadn't been given all the pieces. Dr. Halloran was certainly reticent about some details of the duel. As he spoke, he jiggled in his pocket two small spheres of lead and considered that at least one good thing—perhaps two lives—had come out of his transportation. During the long voyage out, he had instructed shackled shipmates in matters that required his learning. In turn, several had tutored him in their skills as "fingersmiths," who picked pockets; "fogle-hunters," who worked miracles lifting handkerchiefs; and "bung-divers," who purloined purses.

On the recent field of honor it had been child's play for Halloran to palm the ball in the shuffle each time he feigned loading the pistol. He reassured his conscience that he had not lied at any stage. Did not the *Book of Common Prayer* record rewards to "he who hath used no deceit in his tongue"? He didn't recall anything at all in there about deceit with one's fingers.

But the patterer could not understand why the governor had listened to the others tell the tale of this rather shameful incident with such an uncharacteristic smile.

CHAPTER FORTY-FIVE

They [the natives] are the carriers of news and fish;
the gossips of the town; the loungers on the quay.
They know everybody; and understand the nature
of everybody's business.

—Judge Barron Field, *Geographical Memoirs on New South*
Wales (1825, reprinted from the *London Magazine*)

"YOU KNOW, OF COURSE," SAID CAPTAIN CROTTY, "THAT WE WILL deny this conversation ever took place."

"Naturally," agreed Nicodemus Dunne.

"How did you know?" asked the governor, ignoring the pained looks from Colonel Shadforth, who had moved from puzzlement to anger as the tale of the abortive duel unfolded.

"How did you get to the island?" countered the patterer.

"We saw no one on the way," insisted Wentworth testily. "And no one saw us there, or leaving."

"No," agreed Dunne. "You wouldn't see a servant, least of all a black one, would you?"

"Oh, that damned waterman," spat out Captain Crotty.

The patterer nodded. "Also, in the second boat, one of his sons.

And natives followed you and saw it all. They watch us all the time, you know. And they tell me things. Don't even *think* of punishing these people. Cultivating their confidence is far wiser. And, as you can see, rewarding.

"Enough," he continued, more mildly. "We are agreed on one thing: You didn't conspire to kill the blacksmith. But did one of you slip away and act independently? I was interested to learn that Madame Greene was also on the loose that night. She wasn't with you and my spies lost sight of her—which, in itself, is unusual. She was a prime suspect for having slain the blacksmith—until she became a victim. So perhaps we'll never know her movements that night. As I've already indicated, if we know the identity of the killer of any one of our victims, we have the killer of them all.

"Could, perhaps, our slayer have needed to cover the murder he really desired with a deadly smokescreen? Something I learned about the *New World* printer suggested that he could have been a threat to most of you here today, a menace that had to be removed. You see, I found that he was a blackmailer, an extortioner.

"At first I had suspicions that there may have been something of value to him in the past of our Captain Rossi, but everyone seems to know his colorful history. Although I must admit I was, and still am, puzzled as to why he professes not to know the nom de guerre of his old regiment, the Duke of Wellington's 'Fighting Fifth.'"

Rossi interposed. "That's easy, my boy. I served with the 5th only to '03—long before Old Nosey took a fancy to them and bestowed the name."

"The point, Dunne, get to it!" snapped Darling.

The patterer smiled and bowed slightly. "Dr. Halloran."

The black-suited editor gave a start.

"After the murder of Will Abbot, you professed charity among brothers by claiming to have helped him set up shop. But why would you have supported him? Hadn't you dismissed him for extortion? And, in truth, you had a reason to want to be rid of him more permanently: He was yet more unwelcome business competition. *The Gleaner* is failing, isn't it? You are selling only about 200 copies to your rivals' 600 or more each. Isn't that true? Didn't you desperately want to 'kill off' the opposition? And perhaps Abbot made threats to air in public a scandal about your son. Yes, indeed. The man would be a bad enemy to have—alive!"

DUNNE PAUSED TO let his words sink in before continuing. "Then there is you, Mr. Wentworth. A talking parrot led me to suspect you of the same murder."

The lawyer gasped, started to his feet, then fell back into a strangled silence as the charge rolled on.

"During the investigation, I happened across this winged 'witness' in the home of Frances Cox, where I happen to lodge. Your lady was there with your daughter, Timmie. In passing, Mrs. Cox remarked that the child would be three 'come Christmas.'

"When I wondered later what Abbot could possibly have known to your disadvantage—and, pray, don't explode; I have applied my jaundiced eye to everyone I thought possible—I idly pursued the matter of the child, and something did not seem to add up. Church records show that Thomasine—Timmie—was baptized at St. James on January 15, 1826, as the child of 'Sarah Cox and W. C. Wentworth.' Other documents show Timmie was born on December 18, 1825—hence the Christmas birthday.

"Now, I won't duel with you—I think we've had enough of that—for making the following observations. You appeared for

Miss Cox in her breach-of-promise action in May 1825. Your plaint was that she was a respectable girl whose 'reputation had been injured,' a girl who 'kept good company and was never out late at night.' The court supported her case. My ten—no, nine—fingers point to a certain discrepancy of two months."

By this time, Wentworth was choking with rage.

"Now," continued the patterer calmly, "personal affairs are nothing to do with anyone here. But what would the lords of our legal system make of a plaintiff who appeared to perjure herself?—and of a lawyer who, it seems, had already impregnated this paragon of virtue? Perhaps nothing. But again, perhaps, a blackmailer might find it fertile ground."

Mr. Wentworth, though still angry, was pale and silent.

"YOUR EXCELLENCY COMES to my attention, too," said the patterer next.

Darling raised a hand in sudden anger, then let it drop and sat back, stone-faced.

Unruffled, the patterer continued. "You, sir, are all-powerful here and could have had any of the victims disposed of without necessarily lifting a finger. Although, as we have seen, your finger is not above personally pulling a trigger. But that tavern private, or the slaughterman, would have had no power to harm you. And what could a whoremistress and her maid have done to deserve death? The Lumber Yard murder . . . Well, the smith *had* been in the 45th."

Darling looked more animated.

"But I'll deal with that in a moment. The *New World* printer is, again, another story. He was, I repeat, an extortioner. That fact raised the specter of a threat from your past before your rise to vice-regal eminence. But, how are you, the highest in the land, vulnerable?

"Well, in your battle with the Emancipist political forces, especially Mr. Wentworth and Mr. Hall, you must maintain the high ground that being plenipotentiary bestows upon you. What if there were something in your past that would diminish you in the eyes of the Exclusives and thus decrease your power? Something that here and now both snobs and levelers could hold against you and make political capital from? Facts that could alter the delicate social climate here? The shocks could ripple all the way to the Palace. And you do cherish that knighthood. If a blackmailer *had* learned this secret—how could he be dealt with? Paying off is rarely the answer. It never ends. Shall I go on?"

Ralph Darling shrugged grimly. "If you must."

"Then, to put it bluntly," said Dunne, "you, sir, have not always been an officer and a gentleman."

CHAPTER FORTY-SIX

*I now feel that I have reached a point of this narrative
at which every reader will be startled into
positive disbelief.*
—Edgar Allan Poe, "The Facts in the Case
of M. Valdemar" (1845)

THERE WERE GASPS, THEN DEADLY SILENCE, BROKEN ONLY WHEN
the patterer continued. He studiously avoided Captain Rossi's
bland, innocent gaze.

"The Army Lists would show that Ralph Darling first became a
junior officer in the 45th Regiment in May 1793. What is not widely
known is that some years earlier he had joined its ranks as a private
soldier in keeping with family tradition." He looked at Darling.
"You joined your father's regiment in Grenada, as did your brother,
Henry. You were listed on the unit's muster as privates from June
25, '86, to June 24, '88. You became—forever to some—Wellington's
'scum of the earth.'"

The governor interrupted. "So you found someone else from the
45th, apart from that gossip in the Lumber Yard?"

Dunne ignored him. "Often officers' ranks are bought and sold like cattle. Agents such as Cox and Greenwood in London trade in them. What's a captaincy worth in a middling regiment—1,100 pounds and the sale or the equivalent of the buyer's lieutenancy?" He looked to Colonel Shadforth, who nodded. "And a majority costs, what? The sale of a captaincy, plus 1,400 pounds or so?"

Another nod.

"You, Excellency, had no money. But," continued the patterer, "by '93, the extent of war with the *crapauds* was taking its toll on officer numbers. The army found it needed thousands of new leaders, and many came from the ranks, as never before. By the height of the Peninsular wars, about one in twenty officers was not originally of the officer caste. But peace has since revived the cattle market. The blacksmith remembered your humble beginnings. Did Abbot know, too? And was this secret enough to kill for? And kill again and again, as cover?"

Darling started to speak but Dunne allowed him no explanation, no defense and no denial. He moved on relentlessly.

"And now," he said, "Dr. Owens."

The surgeon straightened his shoulders, as if expecting a blow, and nodded slowly.

"Yes, Doctor. What can I say about you?"

————————

ACTUALLY, THE PATTERER could say quite a lot, but he didn't intend to share it all with this assembly. He certainly would not reveal that he had already discussed his suspicions about the doctor with the man himself.

There had been just the two of them. They had met at the hospital earlier that morning and Dunne had begun bluntly.

"You, Doctor, seem to have had a compelling reason to kill Madame Greene. No, don't say anything until I've finished. I wondered about you from the first time we met, and subsequently . . . well, I'll explain as I go along. It quickly emerged that you seemed almost by choice to spend as much time with the dead as with the living. I also noted that you always wear gloves, even in this heat, when you deal with a live patient or make even the most informal social contact. I especially call to mind that you wore gloves with Madame Greene when she was alive, and I saw you without gloves when she was dead. Now, I ask you, what modern doctor would normally choose not to use his bare hands on a patient always, better to feel the problem and gauge the humors?

"Now, I did observe your hands at our first meeting. They were scarred and covered with a nasty rash. I decided idly at the time that you suffered from what I gather are called 'doctor's' or 'nurse's hands,' with common infections from routine contact with septic patients."

Dunne waved away an interjection from Owens. "But progressively I noticed other oddities, although at the time I confess I didn't recognize their import. I also considered the matter of your teeth: distorted and, if I may say so, rather horselike; you bare orange-yellow fangs. You constantly eat scented lozenges, I imagined to disguise bad breath. I was on the right track there, wasn't I?

"I might have put aside all these things, except that, quite unrelatedly, a friend warned me to take care at this hospital. When I asked idly if that involved you, for what could be described as reasons of professional ethics this person gave me a cryptic answer, although not a no. He told me only to consider seriously the import of a word, *cinnabar*. I duly discovered that cinnabar is the most important ore of mercury, or quicksilver. And that the art of the physician offers mercurial treatments, preparations of the metal.

"But these have some nasty side effects: eczema, rash—called, I believe, *Lepra mercurialis*—discolored teeth, degeneration of the gums and walls of the cheek, exceedingly bad breath and excessive salivation. These can be controlled by . . . chewing lozenges, naturally. Mercury treatments are meant to kill infectious organisms, but overdosage can be dangerous, leaving life-threatening, concentrated deposits in animal tissue. That means human tissue. This mercury can, I believe, be administered by pills or injections—sometimes into the penis. Or it can be inhaled in the fumes of heated cinnabar."

"You've not mentioned the underdraws," said Owens.

When the patterer looked puzzled, the doctor explained: "Some patients were prescribed the wearing of undergarments impregnated with the mercury."

"That's very interesting," said Dunne. "If I had known that fact, it may have pointed me earlier to the method used in one of our murders. It stared you in the face, too."

It was the doctor's turn to be perplexed.

"But," continued the patterer, "none of the by-blows I have mentioned is as horrible as the disease mercury is meant to fight—the plague that Columbus brought back from the Pandora's Box he opened in the New World."

"Bravo!" said Owens bitterly. "Your clinical descriptions are broadly accurate if somewhat melodramatic. Yes, we are talking about syphilis. The Great Pox! The disease is commonly transmitted by sexual congress, either connubial or less formalized. It starts with chancres and fever and moves to rashes of the skin and mucous membranes, ulcers, nervous degeneration and collapse. It can lie dormant, but it will invariably kill, once it has rotted the bones, face and genitals."

"Did you blame Madame Greene for this fatal affliction?" asked the patterer. "Or did you, perhaps, regard her as responsible for a diseased girl in her employ—or for any other poxed harlot?"

"You know that the disease may be hereditary?" said Owens.

Dunne nodded. "Yes, I do. And there's one other thing that has been testing my theory. If the disease is passed on sexually, why would you so particularly avoid all, even simple, physical contact? Is not abstinence enough?"

Dr. Owens nodded approvingly. "Well done." He paused. "Have you heard of yaws?"

The patterer knew what Owens was referring to—yaws was a dreaded tropical disease. Discharge from skin sores, not sexual activity, caused it, but it was a scourge almost a twin to syphilis.

"I couldn't be sure it wasn't yaws," said the doctor. "The symptoms and course of both diseases can be confusingly similar. I took mercury to be on the safe"—he paused and laughed wryly at the word that had slipped out—"side."

Dunne hesitated. "Which is it?"

"Take your pick," replied Owens. "Either way, I'm as good as dead." After an awkward pause, he asked, "What do you intend to do with this information—and with your suspicions?"

"With you as a doctor? Nothing. Healing is hard to come by here. Even with such infections, men like you are invaluable if they are careful. And I'm sure you are when you deal with living subjects. God knows, I recall you wouldn't drink with us that day of our council of war because you were later making a consultation. Now, about you as a murder suspect. We'll have to see at the meeting later today."

Dunne justified to himself his special treatment of the doctor. He did not want to punish Owens for his illness, and he liked and admired the man. He thought he was a good person—more than could be said about most of the others he had summoned to the barracks.

But he could not show his hand yet, not to anyone.

————————

IT WAS NOW forty-five minutes after noon and the quiet room was filled with mistrust and tension.

The patterer decided what he would say about Dr. Thomas Owens. "You would seem to be the most likely person, by virtue of training and opportunity, to have killed Madame Greene. Think of it. It certainly wasn't a quick process. Her poisoning occurred over a long period of time—you said so yourself. And you certainly had the necessary access to her. A male figure who called himself a doctor purchased the arsenic we know killed the slaughterman. And we have the evidence from Elsie that your treatment—even your lozenges—broke Madame's usually rigid dietary regime. Admittedly, you were always open and helpful about the medical side to these murders, but were you simply controlling the flow of information to your advantage?"

William Charles Wentworth's confidence had returned and he interrupted again. He shook his shaggy head and snorted derisively. "Is that all you have on him—and on the others you've traduced? Well, sir, it seems you have now besmirched us all with nothing more substantial than your suspicion and with innuendo—and gone nowhere. I note that you have not yet vilified Hall or Shadforth. Is not one of them, in your eyes, guilty?"

Dunne shook his head. "I know nothing to Mr. Hall's discredit. I really asked him here only as an independent witness, a fair broker." To keep the bastards honest, he thought privately. "And

Colonel Shadforth is more likely to have been a victim than a killer." He ignored the stir and continued. "I jest, but perhaps some irate whaling captain may wish to get rid of him, to stop his efforts to have coal gas replace oil for lighting our streets, as in London of late. Seriously, though, everyone I have called here today will soon walk out free. All except one."

But Wentworth would not let go of the bone. "Rubbish! For all your fine talk, apart from some sullied reputations—and it will be all over town by nightfall—the fact is you—and we—are no closer to the truth."

"First," replied the patterer, "none of this need go any farther than these four walls. Each of you should keep any secrets you have learned. That's the action of honorable men, which I'm sure you all are. Or, if you like, it's insurance against your own exposure." Almost as an afterthought, he added casually, "Secondly, as to the murders, of course the mysteries have been laid bare and the killer unmasked."

The governor sat up. "Well, for God's sake, let us into the secret!" he snapped.

"I need only *this* piece of evidence," replied Dunne calmly and raised a hand for silence. And patience. He keenly watched the clock on the mantelpiece as the others in the group fidgeted uncomfortably. Three dragging minutes ticked away until the hands marked the hour.

Almost as the clock struck, there was a sharp rap on the door. "Come!" ordered the patterer. The door opened inward, obscuring from all but Dunne any view of the person on the threshold. He gazed pleasantly at the visitor and said, quite conversationally, "Ah, yes. Please, do come right in and join us. And tell us why you did it."

CHAPTER FORTY-SEVEN

Take but degree away, untune that string,
And, hark, what discord follows! each thing meets
In mere oppugnancy . . .
—William Shakespeare, *Troilus and Cressida* (1602)

OUT OF PURE HABIT, THE MEN ROSE AS RACHEL DORMIN CAME into the room.

She was as Nicodemus Dunne remembered her best, in the same walking-out ensemble she had worn on their first day together, their first good day, the day of the church and the wayzgoose and the cricket match.

Her face was flushed but she was outwardly composed. She carried only the reticule that Dunne also remembered from their earliest meeting.

"Here I am, as you requested," she said in a level voice, dropping a curtsey to the governor.

He, like the others (save the patterer), looked dazed at the dramatic development.

"I'm sorry I kept you waiting until the hour," said Dunne. He was just as even in his speech. "But it was necessary."

Miss Dormin looked around the room coldly. "So I see." She took the seat proffered. "What makes you think that I, as you say, did it?"

"Oh, it all came together. Very slowly, admittedly. I suppose I first realized, early on, that you were left-handed, like our killer. But I dismissed it. Many people are—at least until a schoolmaster or parent has thrashed the sinister habit out of them. Or tied the offending left hand behind their back until they learn to use the proper right hand. Enough of that, though. More important— and not necessarily in this order—I gradually examined all the things I knew about you. They eventually added up to the rather startling conclusion that there really is no such person as Miss Rachel Dormin."

Only he broke the silence that had fallen. "You were no free arrival with independent means. Remember your tale of the aunt who was too poor to escape from the horrors of low Farringdon Street in London? But then, suddenly, she became a lady of means— leaving 150 pounds to you, a similar amount to the Church.

"Official records show all ships that enter the port. There's a good reason for this—they've been levied since Governor Macquarie's time to pay for the South Head Light, and to facilitate customs transactions. Tallies of convict arrivals are kept, too—if sometimes rather haphazardly.

"It seems that Rachel Dormin never arrived. You said that, on arrival, you were met on shipboard by Dr. James Bowman. But he was gone from that duty, to bigger and better things, by the time you say you arrived. Perhaps it's only your timing, not the truth of meeting him, that is at fault. And seeing gold offered by Jimmy

Grants to Bungaree? I have heard from his own mouth that he
only asks for, and gets, coppers—at most a dump or small silver,
never gold."

The patterer paused.

Rachel Dormin remained still.

"Then there is the matter of your treasured painting ... your
extremely professional miniature, executed here and signed 'J. L.'
I am certain it could only have been executed by Joseph Lycett,
who left here for England—in 1822. On the accompanying amateur depiction of your ship of passage, the red-and-white pennant
gives a clue. That whip is the mark of a convict transport, which
brings us to the good ship *Azile*. A friend coincidentally mentioned
to me the transportees' frequent desperate habit of seeking some
sort of solace, if not salvation, by thinking and acting back to better
times, literally trying to go backward. I discovered that one of the
few ships to have made the crossing in about a hundred days was
a convict transport in 1820. This was the *Eliza* ... The good ship
Azile, no?

"Another of your stories falls down, too. No fiancé with such a
serious lung disease would have won a berth with the agricultural
company setting up here. And anyway, he could not have died
here of pertussis in 1826. It wasn't until two years later that whooping cough first entered the colony. And they are just two different
names for the same disease.

"Whoever you are, or were, you came as a convict and almost
certainly served much of your time, before coming back to Sydney,
on a pastoral property. That's why you know so much about sheep.
From your comments, I guess that your master was not an ardent
admirer of the Macarthurs—of Mistress Elizabeth, perhaps, but

not Master John. I also imagine that is how and where you gained your knowledge of firearms—which has proved so fatal."

Miss Dormin waved dismissively. "Even if all that were true, it would simply mean that I created a new life for myself—dragged myself up from adversity. I wouldn't be the first to have done that." She looked around the men in the room.

Most nodded, or murmured agreement.

Nicodemus Dunne bowed his head, then continued. "If that were only as far as you went! You began your killing spree and wrote the *zuzim* note to His Excellency. I thought it was Dr. Halloran, who knew the rare rhyme, but then, of course, you had access to his reference books."

Rachel Dormin sounded more amused than concerned. "But why, pray, would I kill a private soldier at a public house?"

"Why? More of that later. But how? Well, you stalked the streets, trailed him to the Labour in Vain and, without resistance on his part, slashed him to death."

She laughed openly. "My dear sir! How can a young woman do that, unnoticed and unopposed?"

"I didn't know how," replied the patterer, "until I saw a friend recite, in falsetto, female lines from Shakespeare. And another friend, at the same time, remark that if you skewed something, anything, ever so slightly, the outcome was altered. I missed your performance that night at Mr. Levey's theater, but Captain Rossi praised it to me. He even repeated your lines from *Othello*. Later I checked them. They were the Moor's lines! You were playing a male, voice and all. And 'all' meant that you played in black face.

"Thus you killed the first soldier, and took a button as a souvenir, by flitting through the streets made-up and dressed—in a blanket?—as a native. They are always about." He looked hard at the governor. "And we know no white men ever really see them, don't we? The sugar, I believe, was all about Sudds. I don't yet know your connection with him, but you did it."

"Rubbish!" cried Miss Dormin. "I was only play-acting at the Royal."

Dunne pressed on. "Now, let's consider Will Abbot, the *New World* printer. You said that you saw him early in the evening, to deliver the 'copy' for a government order. And you said he was grateful, for he had no other setting to hand and was eager for the work. Then, you say, you picked up the copy for its next destination and this was just before his death and the fire. Now, I believe you *did* make both visits—but you didn't really need to make that second call. For you had retrieved the copy and Abbot was dead not long into your first visit. You shot him.

"You see, normally, to allow you to pick up the copy would require him to make full use of it and set *all* the material. Yet we found next day the only typesetting he was obviously able to do. If he had had all night he would have set much more than the inch and a third we found, unfinished. If a champion compositor could set at a rate of nineteen lines per quarter-hour, let's say that Abbot's fifteen or so lines took him much the same time. I say that he realized very early in the piece that he was in danger— and why. Did he recognize you? He may have. Anyway, he was alerted, although he did not reveal it to you. Somehow he stayed calm and plotted. He was, after all, quite used to being under fire. His chance came when you *had* to let him set *some* type, to confirm your innocent comings and goings. Right?"

The patterer pushed on doggedly in the face of her silence.

"Whatever. Nonetheless, you didn't know that the material should be set in a large type size. And that allowed him to send a forlorn hope of a clue. He altered the case and hoped someone would notice and translate the message."

"What was this famous 'clue'?" asked Miss Dormin. He told her, adding, "It led us eventually to Casa Alta."

He thought he saw a flicker of disquiet cross her face. For the first time.

"Then," he continued, "you made a mistake. For some reason, at one stage—perhaps to stall for time—you asked Abbot what the type he was using was called. Automatically, he answered. An English compositor would have said 'Ruby,' but he said the type's American name, 'Agate'—just what you said to me later when we examined the proof. You couldn't have picked that up at *The Gleaner* or elsewhere—there are no other American printers here and Dr. Halloran has no expert knowledge of the craft. Soon you blasted him when he put down the galley of type. But you *did* come back the next morning. So that you could be seen to continue your normal routine, not to 'find' him.

"Abbot had fallen dying across the guillotine bench. It did not require much effort to roll him under the blade and decapitate him. If it had not been possible, you wouldn't have worried. It was just another touch. You knew that he, too, was—mysteriously to me still—involved in the Sudds affair. So, in yet another odd reference, you poured sugar into his mouth. There was no type form on the press bed and therefore there was room to squash the head. Another touch. Then you fired the building, to cloud the issue of cause and time of death."

Rachel Dormin was still calm, but she no longer smiled.

———————

Dunne took a breath. "Now, as for The Ox. Had it been an isolated occurrence, you may have been safe killing him, even though I found the apothecary who sold you the arsenic. At first I thought it may have been Dr. Owens, then Dr. Halloran. I'm certain that you got the poison to your victim by yet another theatrical deception.

"The flogged blacksmith? Yes, I can see that he, too, had harmed Sudds, through his contraption of torture. You marked that connection with your trademark sugar—though green this time, the first link we could have seen to poor Madame. And your other marks—left-handed ones—were at the Lumber Yard, too. Your scourger's heel, your right one, made a clear indentation in the ground. Of course, even you had to change from the heavy cat to the lighter tawse, but to compensate for this handicap you added injury to insult by attaching the scalpel—the one you bought for 'boils'—to the tawse tail."

"You can't prove any of this," said Rachel Dormin coldly.

Dunne thought he saw Wentworth nodding in agreement with her.

"Be that as it may," he said. "This one I *can* prove. You poisoned Madame Greene over a long period. You talked her into dyeing her hair and introduced arsenic into the coloring mixture. She absorbed the toxin through her scalp. Just as you contaminated her constantly used *maquillage*, with the same results. But your masterstroke was performed in your role as her *couturière*—and I own that you did bring that skill with you to the colony. In doing so, you played up further to her obsession with all things green.

"I've already explained briefly to these gentlemen that Muller, your last victim, guided me, in confirmation of Will Abbot, to the colony's Casa Alta—Madame Greene's High House. At first I thought that his last words were all in German, but only moments before I had begged him to speak in English and, with a few exceptions, he obliged. He did say 'bloody hand' in his native tongue, but he did not say 'chaos,' or *alter* meaning 'old,' as I had thought. He was saying 'Casa Alta.' And, more important, his final words were not *Rache* for 'vengeance.' No. Meaning Madame Greene's killer—and his own—he simply said 'Rachel.' Which, I know now, is why he was so surprised when I required him to translate it as 'revenge.'"

CHAPTER FORTY-EIGHT

What she is not, *I can easily perceive; what she* is,
I fear it impossible to say.
—Edgar Allan Poe, "MS. Found in a Bottle" (1833)

RACHEL DORMIN GLARED DEFIANTLY. CAPTAIN ROSSI AND DR. Halloran, who admired her, wore pained expressions.

The uncomfortable silence that had fallen in the room was finally broken by Colonel Shadforth. "You haven't told us what else this Muller said. It seems there was more."

The patterer nodded. "He offered two more words. I heard *grün*. Whether this was, in fact, 'green' in German or in English, matters little. In the context, that he was referring to Madame seems certain. The other word was *Schwein*. Was this simply a pejorative allusion to his attacker I wondered? I doubted that he literally meant 'pig.' Was it a choked-off longer word, perhaps? Later—in fact, only yesterday—when I was seeking enlightenment on our biblical clue, I came, quite by accident, across a legendary figure whose name plays a part in our mystery."

Dunne saw that his audience was puzzled by this seemingly abrupt swerve from the subject, but pressed on. "Finding that heroic figure sparked in my memory the myth of Medea. In Greek mythology, when Jason abandoned Medea for another, she murdered her rival—with a poisoned garment.

"I was also playing mental games with Muller's word *Schwein*. If it wasn't a pig or a person—could it be a place? I looked in a gazetteer. In Britain, I found Swindon, two Swintons, Swinefleet and of course Swineshead Abbey, near where bad King John lost the royal treasure trove in The Wash 600 or so years ago . . ."

"Get to the point, damn it!" ordered the governor.

The patterer nodded, unperturbed. "Then I found a German link, Schweinfurt. And a book on poisons took me even further."

"What's that got to do with it?" Darling asked, still dissatisfied.

"Everything. It brings together our words *Schwein* and 'green,' which *does* turn out to mean Madame Greene. *And* the manner in which she died. You see, '*Schweinfurt* green' also describes a paste of copper arsenite and starch dried onto dress material and polished to a high sheen. It's popular in Europe, but it can be highly dangerous. Particularly here. In a hotter climate it can be lethal. As it was for Madame Greene.

"Her best-loved gown and turban were made of tarnatan, a muslin originally from Bengal and treated in Germany with the paste. She wore them as often as possible, as well as her shoes covered in the same material, outside and inside, day and night. I'm sure we've all seen her. She danced furiously and sang in sweltering halls, under hot lights.

"Every time, the poison was absorbed through her skin, as was white arsenic from her makeup and the poison in her dyed hair. Minuscule glittering flakes from the material were also shaken into a cloud that entered her mouth and nose.

"That dress, Miss Dormin, was all your work."

————————

"THAT MAKES ME a murderess?" she asked, arch now, unsmiling. "Even if I innocently made the dress in question? I know nothing of this material."

The patterer looked at her sadly. "Ah, but you do. And you were very patient. You had the deadly dress in planning for a long time—allowing for ships' passages, perhaps a year. Which suggests how long you plotted to kill Madame Greene, how far back your grudge against her lies.

"When the dressmaker here from whom you had obtained work made out an order for fabric from Europe, you were suddenly inspired. You secretly added your requirement for some of the poisonous cloth. When the consignment finally arrived, it went to *The Gleaner*. No one there opened it; had you told the office that such a parcel was coming for you? Even if they had pried, the contents would have meant nothing to them. But . . .

"That's where Muller somehow uncovered you. Perhaps he saw you with the material? He was widely read, from the Schweinfurt area and, when Madame died and the description of her strange death circulated, he put two and *zwei* together. Whatever happened, he had to die. But, at the end, he was able to point to Casa Alta, to name your ingenious murder method—and to name you as the 'bloody hand,' ironically in the only German to which he completely regressed.

"Oh, and don't imagine that you can bluff it out here and later destroy the evidence. I have what's left of the consignment—even the dress, which I'm sure Dr. Owens can analyze."

Miss Dormin was wide-eyed now. "But, how . . . ?"

"Rather simply," replied Dunne. "I stole it—or, rather, had it stolen—from your hiding place above the shop, where the disabled mistress of the house has never lately ventured. Recent events guided me. When I was a felon on the run, what better place to hide than among felons? Who would look there? You had applied the same thinking to the green dress. What better place to conceal it than among many other dresses?"

Miss Dormin frowned. "Why would I have killed Elsie?"

The patterer sighed. "Why do you ask that? I've only just informed these gentlemen that Elsie was murdered—you've never even been told." Rachel Dormin paled.

"But, since you ask," continued Dunne, "she was another danger to you. She might find the poisoned *maquillage*. But, more important, she might have asked you to return the dress. Remember, Captain?' he addressed Rossi. "After we left the theater that night, Miss Dormin had the dress. And she kept it. As we left her at her front door, she said something. You took it to be directed at you—that she 'would not call for the police.'

"In fact, she was telling Elsie, who was going back to the brothel, that she 'would not call for the pelisse,' *p-e-l-i*-double-*s-e*. I later learned that this is an overgarment that goes with a lady's gown. This particular example was furred and, doubtless, unpoisoned. And it would seem not to be incriminating. But . . ." He turned to Miss Dormin. "You eventually did want the pelisse. Its existence on its own could always raise the question of the whereabouts of the dress. I also found the pelisse. You killed Elsie, and made it look like a lover's suicide. And you killed all the others, too, didn't you?"

––––––––––

RACHEL DORMIN NODDED, almost dreamily.

"I'm sorry about Elsie," she said at last, softly. "At first she thought Dr. Owens had poisoned her mistress with his eternal lozenges. But then she remembered something: where she had seen me before, in another life. That's why she surely had to die. Yes, I killed them. Every one."

Only the ticking clock broke the silence as she paused.

"I killed the soldier in the lane just as you deduced. He suspected no attack, only had time to invite me to urinate with him, then ask what I was doing there. Will Abbot at the *New World* also died much as you said. I don't regret telling him that he was about to die, even if he was more cunning than I could have imagined. I waited until he paused to fiddle with the tray of type, then I stepped behind him, clapped the pistol to his face and fired. I took back the document for setting and, on the spur of the moment, decided to leave another significant, yet confusing clue. And, yes, more disguises delivered The Ox to me."

She rushed on, brooking no interruption. "The Lumber Yard blacksmith? Male vanity and lust sealed his fate. Again in my first disguise, I played the tart and made up to him as he went to work. He greedily accepted my offer of some *bhang*. What danger could a native harlot pose? With the promise of my favors, I persuaded him to demonstrate the workings of the flogging apparatus. I secured him there and . . . you know the rest. You're correct about the tawse and the scalpel. The green sugar? Oh, I accidentally spilled hair dye."

"Why?" Mr. Hall got in a word. "Why, in God's name, mutilate him in that horrific manner—even worse than the others?"

Miss Dormin's fierce frown returned him to fascinated silence. "I chose the way that bitch, Madame, died quite deliberately. I wanted her to sicken slowly, not go out quickly. You were right, in the main, about Elsie," she said to Dunne. "But only partly correct about Muller. His main offense was to know the same secret that sealed the maid's fate. But neither of *them* deserved the mark of sugar," she added cryptically.

"What the devil has any of this got to do with Sudds?" asked the governor. "And what is the truth of your messages?"

Miss Dormin eyed him steadily. "The business of the *zuzim* was just something I came across, but somehow it summed up my mood and plans. I wanted someone to know what was happening. Did I want to get caught? Perhaps. Who knows?" She gave a brittle little laugh. "My attempt at typesetting was rather a failure."

"What were you trying to say?" asked Mr. Hall gently.

"Oh, I meant to set 'Exodus 21:22.' But I couldn't find the piece for a colon. That last number '3' was meant to be followed by the words *more to come* or at least the printers' abbreviation *mtc*, to indicate three more killings. However, it all became too hard. I had only *played* with type at *The Gleaner* and, of course, I didn't think about the right way to put the pieces in place. I just went to the case Abbot had been using. 'Exodus' came out with a small *e* rather than a capital *e*, simply because I couldn't readily reach the upper—the higher—part of the case. And it all turned out garbled. I wonder you could make any sense of it."

"What *is* verse 22?" asked Wentworth.

Rachel Dormin replied curtly, "'If men strive, and hurt a woman with child, so that her fruit depart from her . . . he shall be surely punished.'"

Dr. Halloran frowned. "Is that the full verse?"

Her eyes glittered. "It is the only interpretation that I care to recall. It represents, gentlemen, what this whole sorry saga is all about. Those four men who were executed—I won't say murdered—raped me. And that rape left me with child. And the lady in green made me a whore. And she had my baby killed, before it was even born."

CHAPTER FORTY-NINE

Truly My Satan thou art but a Dunce,
And dost not know the Garment from the Man;
Every Harlot was a Virgin once . . .
—William Blake, *For the Sexes. The Gates of Paradise*
(1820)

THE MEN SAT DUMBSTRUCK AS MISS RACHEL DORMIN CONTINUED. "I did arrive in Sydney in 1826 as I told you, Mr. Dunne. But by road, not by sea. The actual sea-landing *had* taken place, but six years earlier. That's when I came to begin seven years of punishment—for stealing hair!

"Back home I had worked hard as a seamstress—although even then I longed to be on the stage—but it was barely enough to keep me and my poor aunt out of the poorhouse or the debtors' prison. One day a lady inspected our wares and absentmindedly left behind a hatbox. I opened it, simply to seek some identification, and found a beautiful wig, made of real women's hair. It was very valuable. Wigmakers, you know, seek hair, usually from poor girls' heads, but there's never enough. Thieves attack women in the street and even steal tresses from hospital patients and dead bodies.

"I did nothing, but I was still accused. I'd put away the box, anticipating the customer's gratitude on its return and then forgot all about it. One day, however, I came from an errand to find the shop's mistress confronted by the angry customer, who was accompanied by a constable.

"The box had disappeared and the woman accused *us* of stealing the hairpiece. She eventually believed my mistress. That left only me. Despite my protestations, I was arrested and charged. Together with a young man, who stood accused of stealing a brood of oysters, I was sentenced to transportation."

She nodded to the patterer. "Upon my arrival in the colony and after induction at the Factory, I was assigned to a distant pastoral family, as you thought. They were kind to me, in a rough-and-ready way. And yes, I did learn to shoot—for we were always afraid of outlaws and blacks—and to ride, side-saddle *and* astride. It was there that Mr. Lycett, who was visiting, painted my miniature, adding it to the rude rendering of the *Eliza*.

"After four years, I received my ticket and determined to start a new life in the town. How could I have returned to London? And why? God knows, my poor aunt was probably dead without my companionship and help. So, although I was freed, I was still in a prison whose bars were the sea. Thus, following a period sewing in Parramatta, I did arrive, but by cart, on a spring afternoon. With little money, certainly not 150 pounds.

"I was set down from the cart in George Street, near the Lumber Yard and spent some time wandering the nearby streets, enjoying the rediscovered bustle of a town. I then sought directions to

St. Phillip's, where my kind country mistress had always said I could receive advice on where to stay. Dusk was falling by then. Beside the main guardhouse, I asked directions of a soldier and explained my quest. Both actions were my undoing. He seemed drunk, but soldiers often are. Nevertheless, I allowed him to guide me toward a street he said led to the church."

Miss Dormin's voice did not waver. "Near a vacant allotment he suddenly pushed me over savagely and dragged me behind a shed. Before I could scream or attempt to fight, he knocked me unconscious. When I awoke, I was trussed and gagged. And it was darker.

"Four men came for me. All except for one, whom I made out to be a black in civilian clothes, were white soldiers in uniform. They tore at my outer clothes and chemise, held me down and . . . forced me, in turn, again and again. I wanted to tell them that I was a maiden, that I had fought to keep pure on the voyage and afterward, for God's sake! But I couldn't speak. Oh, how they tore me!"

She trailed off, tears glazing her eyes. No one dared speak or move. "I fainted from the pain and the terror. When I awoke I feigned unconsciousness, but it didn't stop them. They ceased only when another soldier came upon them and ordered them to stop. At first they ignored him and laughed, but he attacked them. He struck out so hard that I heard the stick he had taken to them snap.

"The three soldiers backed off and he set me free. The black brute seemed to disappear. 'Go up the hill, lass, to the church,' urged my rescuer. 'Hurry!' I started to stagger away, covering myself as best I could with what was left of my bloodied clothes, but I had gone only a few yards when a hand seized me. It was the black man. 'I'm not finished with you, little missy,' he said. And then he hit me and everything went black again."

———————

"WHEN I AWOKE I was in a strange bed, one with which I was to become familiar. Too familiar.

"That's when I first met Madame Greene. The black man had, for a reward, brought me to the High House to become a captive whore. It happens often, I later learned, no different from a towns-man being impressed as a sailor. When I resisted her scheme, Madame called on the black man's services again. It emerged that he was her expert in bringing reluctant and recalcitrant girls to heel. He was a 'breaker,' akin to a man who masters horses. He broke me in by performing on me every physical indignity and obscenity you can imagine. I won't describe them to you, but it is the reason I left him so abused."

She took a deep breath. "I still have nightmares, and even when we did *Othello* I thought of him when the play talks of Desdemona being 'covered by a Barbary horse' and a 'black ram tupping your white ewe.'"

The patterer felt a shiver at the parallel, having remembered the same lines at Norah Robinson's.

"So, I learned to behave," Rachel Dormin continued. "I was too broken and ill to fight back anymore. And who would miss me? All that talk about a fiancé was just that, talk. I was left alone for quite a long while, to recover. I think Madame thought that some cus-tomer with a conscience might report a whore who had been too badly beaten. Perhaps she had high hopes of my eventual worth.

"Certainly, when I began my new 'career,' though I was never let out of the building, I was fed and dressed well, and Madame insisted that the men who bought me should take . . . precautions. Which is why, when I found I was missing my courses, I knew only my rapists could be responsible. It was the evil seed from their ravishment that had taken possession of my body."

She was almost shouting now, her lips flecked with white spittle. "And I felt in my heart that it was likely to be the fault of that blackamoor, who had taken me the most. So." She laughed bitterly. "I had sailed 15,000 miles to get a black child in my belly!"

CHAPTER FIFTY

Malvolio: I'll be reveng'd on the whole pack of you.
—William Shakespeare, *Twelfth Night* (1601)

CALMER NOW, MISS DORMIN CONTINUED HER CONFESSION. "I was more determined than ever to find out all about those animals and punish them. From words dropped by Madame and her faithful Elsie, and from horror stories told me by other girls, I had learned that the 'breaker' was a blacksmith at the Lumber Yard.

"Now, one rum-sodden soldier—I don't know how he afforded me, but the gods did us both a favor—boasted to me how three of his mates had raped a foolish young bunter and got away with it. Only two had been punished—for having dirty uniforms! He stupidly named all three; my hunt could begin."

"Dear lady," protested Colonel Shadforth. "The regiment didn't know of your plight. Or of the men's dereliction of duty. They could have been flogged . . . shot!"

Rachel Dormin looked at him scornfully. "Would anyone believe a convict girl, that she was forced? Besides, two of them finished their enlistments soon after. Abbot went back to being a respectable printer and The Ox became a slaughterman. The others stayed free. Who was I, a whore, to complain?

"Then the soldier in my bed laughed that the man who intervened had been punished for losing equipment—a cane, the stick that I had heard him break. And then he said that this man was dead, anyway. That was the first time that I, locked in my prison room, heard the name Joseph Sudds and learned the details of his fate.

"Gradually I realized the amazing coincidence, that the men who had despoiled me had also played parts—some minor, one major—in the destruction of the only man who had shown me any kindness. I had dreamed of vengeance on all my tormentors. Now I vowed I would take some measure of retribution for poor Sudds.

"The child quickened within me and Madame Greene soon found out. Her response was swift and direct. A child is a liability for a whore. It had to go. For once I agreed with her, but not with her methods. She never let Dr. Owens, who checked all her other women, come near me—she said he was too 'straight.' So, first she fed me some potions, but they only made me sicker. Then, while that black bastard held me down, Madame forced rounded shapes of raw, dried wood into the neck of my womb. I gathered that the wood was supposed to swell with bodily moistures and encourage the expulsion of the child, but I only expelled the wood, amid a welter of blood. What do you make of that, Doctor?" Her aside, delivered unemotionally, almost conversationally, surprised Owens for a moment.

"Well, I'd say," he replied, equally clinically, "that Madame's choice of abortifacients was unwise. The failed oral mixtures may have been something derived from Queen Anne's lace, or rue. Or perhaps from juniper; a common attempt to shed a fetus is by massive ingestion of gin, in a very hot bath. You allude to a wood suppository used vaginally. The traditional wood used for this purpose comes from the elm, although Hippocrates himself recommended the cucumber."

Governor Darling coughed. "Must we have this distasteful detail?"

Miss Dormin rounded on him. "For a soldier, you have a delicate stomach, sir. I am not finished. There is worse to come."

Darling snorted, but fell silent.

Barely above a whisper, she continued. "Madame then had the blacksmith beat my belly until the child dropped."

At this Mr. Hall looked close to tears.

"I almost died . . . and I wanted to. But I slowly gathered strength and a new determination. All the while I showed compliance and I noticed the restraints on me gradually slackening.

"One afternoon, while the other girls were resting and Madame, attended by Elsie, was out showing off in some manner, I stole clothes and money—a lot of it—from where I had learned it was hidden in the bitch's parlor. Money's a wonderful, persuasive friend—it's all that really counts, isn't it, gentlemen?—and it bought me a new life.

"I became the Rachel Dormin you know, the comfortably situated immigrant, successful seamstress, amateur thespian of note, with an inquiring mind and a respectable mentor, Dr. Halloran.

And I got my revenge—and laid, where I could manage it, sweet memorials to Joseph Sudds.

"But Elsie eventually saw through me, if no one else did. I had avoided her successfully until her charge into the green room to see her lover. I'd even managed to escape her when she had come with Madame Greene to the dress shop.

"Then Muller became a problem, too. It seemed that he had been a customer at the High House and had seen me there. It meant nothing to me—there were so many men—but one day at *The Gleaner* he discovered my secret. He came upon me in a spare room that Dr. Halloran had allowed me to use. I had forgotten to lock the door and he surprised me—with the dress and the fabric remnants. And the bill of lading. Whether he realized what I had done from the start, I can't say, but any suspicions he did have were heightened when he saw me in a new light and recognized who I had been."

Mr. Hall now asked the question that had vexed several of the listeners. "Muller could see through you. Why, in heaven's name, didn't Madame Greene recognize you when you fitted her and primped and preened her hair and face?"

"Why should she?" replied Miss Dormin. She turned to the two soldiers. "If you came across one of your hundreds of private soldiers, but one now with a new moustache, say, and dressed smartly as a fellow officer, in different regimentals, and now taller, would you still know him?" She could see they still had doubts. "How do you think I passed so readily as a native?"

"You used theatrical makeup, as Dunne suggested," ventured Wentworth.

"Yes, but how could I disguise *this*?" She shook her golden mane. Then she quickly grasped a handful at her forehead and peeled off the long locks. Underneath was only a stubble of short-cropped brown hair. She laughed at their shock. "Suitably, a wig—one of which had brought me low in London—helped save me in Sydney. And Madame's money paid for it. I cut off my dark hair and wore higher heels.

"But the wig is hot, and when Muller intruded on me he saw my bare head. He wanted to see more, much more, but I put him off. Then I overheard him talking to you, Mr. Dunne, and I knew I could never trust him."

She smiled at the patterer. "Haven't you wondered where both Muller and I learned about the poisonous fabric? It was just another of the strange conjunctions in this matter. A dispatch about it had appeared in *The Gleaner*. He had typeset it. I had read it. Is it little wonder that our paths crossed? You really didn't need all those fancy reference books."

"So," said Nicodemus Dunne when Rachel had come to the end of her confession. "We are at the finish."

"Almost. Not quite," Miss Dormin corrected him. She reached down into the reticule that had never left her side.

Then, for the second time in two days, almost as if by some magnetic attraction, the patterer had a gun pointed at him.

CHAPTER FIFTY-ONE

Look in my face; my name is Might-have-been;
I am also called No-more, Too-late, Farewell.
—Dante Gabriel Rossetti, *The House of Life* (1881)

RACHEL DORMIN'S LEFT HAND WAS ROCK STEADY AS SHE AIMED the small pistol straight at the patterer's heart. He noted with surprised detachment that the serpent's-neck was at full cock. She had said she could shoot. And she had proved it. Twice.

"Why me?" he asked. It was a question loaded only with calm interest. He wasn't begging. Not yet, he thought grimly. "Why did you set that trap for me?"

Her voice was as coolly controlled as his. "It had to be you—you were getting too close to the truth. And suddenly I didn't want to be caught. Perhaps, at the beginning, I didn't care what happened to me, but then I grew to like my life as Rachel Dormin—and her power. Who knows, maybe I could even have taken Madame's place. Why not? I served my apprenticeship there.

"But you spoiled it, and now the bill must be paid. Death is the price. I promised myself *that* when I realized why you must have summoned me here." Her tone softened. "I more than liked you at first, I really did. You seemed old-fashioned in your manners, and a gentleman. You were nice, if there's such a thing as that.

"Even when I waited that night to go to the Lumber Yard, with my arms and face blackened and my wig discarded, I even girlishly, foolishly, thought that one day we might become more . . . intimate . . ." She broke off. "But it was not to be. And, in the end, you turned out to be like all the others. You couldn't help touching—no, *pawing*—me. And I knew I could never let myself be soiled again."

She glared at the men. "How many children did it take to kill your first wife, Dr. Halloran? Was it a dozen?" she asked her old friend, who could only shake his head, stricken.

"Even you, Excellency. Like a rooting dog, you can't leave Elizabeth alone, can you?"

Darling flushed brick red.

Distract her, thought Dunne; delay her until salvation presents itself. But even the soldiers are paralyzed. Think, damn you! Keep her talking. "Of course," he said, "there was always one clue staring me in the face right from the beginning. I own that it slipped completely past me."

"And that was?" prompted Rachel Dormin, distracted.

"Why, your very name."

He turned to Dr. Halloran. "But this is *your* field, Reverend. Doesn't Genesis talk about a 'mighty hunter before the Lord'?" He raised a hand to stop Halloran answering too soon. "And I believe the Targums, those Aramaic interpretations of the Old Testament, say the name in question is that of a 'sinful hunter of the sons of men.' More modernly, Mr. Alexander Pope agrees, in his 'Windsor-Forest,' that the name refers to 'A mighty hunter, and his prey was man.'"

"Get to the point, Dunne," said the governor testily. "This is not a damned schoolroom."

"My apologies, Excellency," murmured Dunne. "Your thoughts, Dr. Halloran?"

The minister nodded. "Your hunter, of course, was Nimrod."

"Exactly. Nimrod. Which, backward, is Dormin."

Their Nimrod nodded approvingly, adding, "They say his tomb is in Damascus and that rain never falls on it."

"So, we have captured the angel of death," said Mr. Hall sadly.

Miss Dormin looked at him intently. "Yes, sir, but the *zuzim* verse is not quite finished, you know."

He frowned at her as she continued.

"I'm sure you believe in God, in a higher being?"

He bridled. "Of course!"

"Well then. The last line—I know it comes first, but it is the end of the cycle—the last line of the riddle has the Most Holy killing the angel of death . . ."

"The hangman will do that job for the Most Holy," interrupted Darling coldly.

"I won't hang!" said Miss Dormin fiercely. "I know what would happen. I won't be forced into canvas underdraws to save my executioner offense as I drop through the trap and lose control of my bladder and bowels. I won't have any dirty man's hands pulling at my thighs to finally strangle me if he's misjudged the drop and failed to break my neck cleanly. I know that happens." She turned the pistol to her own breast. "I never said *who* would die!"

The patterer's satchel was beside him. He swooped it up and

hurled it at Miss Dormin, to distract her. But his desperate move failed. The bag deflected her aim, but only downward. In reflex, she squeezed the trigger.

The crash of firing echoed through the stone-walled room and battered the eardrums of the shocked witnesses. As the smoke cleared, Rachel Dormin slid to the floor. When Dunne reached her, so much blood was already pumping from the area of her thighs, and so fast, that her blue dress was soaking with a glistening stain. The very fabric seemed to pulse.

The patterer moved in and bent low. Her face was contorted in agony and blood oozed through her fingers as she pressed her hands to her thigh and weakly tore at the dress.

"You could have got away, Rachel," cried Dunne. "I tried to warn you. Doctor, help her, for God's sake!"

Owens pushed the patterer aside and knelt beside the dying woman.

Those who were nearest heard her say, "Do you want to save me for the noose?"

The doctor held her hand and looked up. "The ball has hit the femoral artery. It may even have gone right through the thigh, without breaking the bone. But there's no way of staunching the flow. She's lost, I'm afraid."

Only the clock broke the hushed deathwatch.

Dunne took her limp hand from Thomas Owens's grasp and squeezed it.

She gazed up and smiled crookedly through her pain. "Do you remember my goats? . . ." Then she fell back and lay still.

The doctor felt for a pulse, shook his head, then gently closed her eyes.

THE GOVERNOR TOOK charge while Shadforth and Crotty stolidly surveyed the scene; they were no strangers to violent death. The civilians, however, were shattered. Even the usually blustering firebrand Wentworth was pale and silent.

"Colonel," ordered Darling. "You will ensure that there is no record of this matter. Put your heel on any loose talk. It seems that no one has heard the shot—keep it that way. In a moment, put a sentry on the corridor to keep others out. The rest of you—except for Captain Rossi and Dunne—will disperse quietly. The whole matter is now closed. I think you will find it in your best interests to remain silent."

There was a murmur of agreement, punctuated by nervous nods.

Nicodemus Dunne sat shaking, with his head in his hands, saying brokenly, "I killed her. But I had to do it."

Captain Rossi at last eased him to his feet.

CHAPTER FIFTY-TWO

For secrets are edged tools,
And must be kept from children and from fools.
—John Dryden, *Sir Martin Mar-All* (1667)

"LET US ALL GO OUTSIDE FOR A WHILE," SAID ROSSI. "DR. OWENS will attend to Miss Dormin." He gently ushered the patterer out of sight of her body.

"I want her, Rossi," said Dunne. "At least I can see that she's not shoveled like a dog into a pauper's hole at the Sandhills. Or buried in a lime pit." He seized the captain's shoulder. "And Owens—or any other surgeon—can't have her to rip open on the anatomizing table."

Rossi shrugged him off. "You shall have her. Intact. Never fear." He turned as the governor called him into another room. "Wait here for me."

The patterer did as he was told. All other members of the party had drifted off, shaken and mindful of Darling's stern admonition to hold their tongues about the day's events.

The barracks hallway was silent. Only the armed soldier standing warily at one end and the fading smell of burnt gunpowder in the air testified to the fact that anything out of the ordinary had happened.

After some time, the governor bustled back into the corridor, alone. He gave Dunne a grim glance, nodded curtly and marched off past the watchful soldier, who stiffened to attention.

IN THE ROOM, Darling had been sharp with Rossi.

"Does he know?"

"Dunne?"

"Of course, Dunne!"

"If you mean what I think you do, Excellency, then the answer is that he doesn't. I'm sure of it."

"Doesn't he wonder where the money comes from, why he was given the status of a Special, why I haven't taken away his ticket— even had him flogged—for his disrespect?"

"It seems not."

"The question now is, can he be trusted to keep his mouth shut about this business—in particular, the business of all our private affairs? Not that we have anything nefarious to hide."

The captain nodded sagely.

"However." The governor waved a manicured hand. "It is better for all if a veil is drawn over some events in the past. I think that is already understood by the gentlemen who were here today—and you can reinforce the concept, I'm sure. All except Dunne. He can be silenced on two fronts, I believe. First, tell him he can have the girl's body in exchange for silence."

Rossi did not think it wise to mention that he had already given away that advantage, so he simply nodded. "And the second front, sir?"

"Tell him the darkness in his own past. See how he likes the idea of people knowing *his* family secrets!"

"Do you think that wise?"

"I do." The governor rose. "You can keep me out of it, of course."

Of course, thought Rossi. That's how Darling keeps his hands so clean. But he said nothing, just bowed slightly.

"Oh, and Rossi." Darling paused. "See if you can track down the man from the 45th who talked out of turn."

With that he was gone. He missed Rossi's small smile.

———————

CAPTAIN ROSSI BECKONED the patterer into the side room from which the governor had just stormed. He motioned him to a chair and sat down opposite him.

"You've made some bad enemies here today."

"It had to be done." Dunne shrugged and looked bleakly ahead, with the thousand-mile stare of the dying or the hopelessly distressed. I gave her the chance to escape, you know. Yesterday, when we talked, I made it clear to her that the game was up. I asked her here today, but she didn't have to come. There are plenty of ships a pretty girl could have slipped away on. The others—even you—think I lured her here to her final exposure. But I think she really did just get sick and tired of the whole sorry business. Perhaps she simply came to the end of her madness and anger. She genuinely did regret killing Elsie and Muller, I'm sure." He rubbed a hand wearily across his face. "It doesn't matter now, anyway. There are too many unhappy memories here. I'm going home. To England."

Rossi sighed. "Ah, well. Strangely enough, that's what the—what I want to talk to you about. The truth is that you can't go home, lad."

The words penetrated Dunne's mind after a moment. "Why the devil not?"

"Because," replied Rossi, "home doesn't want you."

"What does that mean?"

"Consider," said the captain gently, "most of us here are embarrassments to England. I know *I* am, with my funny ways and accent, and the baggage I carry professionally. But *you*—you are particularly embarrassing."

"Why, in God's name?"

Rossi paused. "Because, lad, enough people believe you are the king's nephew."

CHAPTER FIFTY-THREE

Curses are like young chickens, they always
come home to roost.
—Robert Southey, *The Curse of Kehama* (1810)

Nicodemus Dunne gaped. Then he laughed. "The king's nephew! Jesus, Captain, am I hearing you right?"

Rossi nodded. "Yes. A bastard, certainly, but still his nephew. Come to that, if we lived in earlier, less enlightened times, and if somehow you were legitimized and acknowledged—and if certain other people died—why, you'd be the heir to the throne!"

Dunne shook his head, like a man mazed by too much rum. "This is madness, man. That means my father would be one of the royal dukes. Which one?"

"The rumors say Cumberland sired you. And that you were born in Weymouth in the summer of 1800."

Dunne barely took in Rossi's last words as his mind raced. Wasn't Ernest, Duke of Cumberland, a notorious man-lover?

Which deviation—most whispered it, though others recklessly spoke and wrote it openly—may have led to murder. For many years he had been popularly dubbed "Deadly Ernest," after one of his male servants was discovered with his throat cut. A coroner found for suicide, despite the clear evidence that the victim could not have inflicted the wound upon himself. Most chose to believe that the man had died resisting the duke's overtures or that it was an amorous affair gone wrong, terribly wrong. Either way, poor bugger, thought Dunne.

Then his attention turned back to what Rossi had been saying. He stared at the captain. Weymouth. The year 1800. "Are you saying that Mrs. Dunne, respectable Mrs. Dunne, steadfast wife of an honorably retired army officer, was not just my guardian's wife? That, as well, she was a royal paramour and my mother?"

Rossi shifted uncomfortably. "No, she wasn't your real mother."

"Then who was?"

"Well, the rumors say it was the princess Sophia."

It took moments to sink in. "But you're talking about brother and sister. Christ, that's incest!" He paused. "How could the princess keep such a secret?" After all, bastards by royal males were usually acknowledged in some way, but this fantastic story . . .

"Oh," said Rossi. "She went into a long retreat from public and Court view—that's how Weymouth came into the picture—and everyone, even her father, the old king (and he wasn't yet mad enough not to have seen the growing problem), was fobbed off with the story that she had left London suffering from dropsy. But a thing like that . . . well, enough people know that secret, or at least some of it."

"How do you know *I'm* the one?" insisted Dunne.

"Yes, well, the Palace and all governments, from Pitt's then to

Wellington's now, have kept an eye on you. In fact, they could have saved you from your troubles over Caroline's funeral. The main parties are alive, you know. But, in the end, someone decided it was a stroke of fortune—you know, out of sight, out of mind. At least, that's what all would like. And so far it has worked out thus."

The patterer was ashen and growing more and more agitated.

The captain raised a hand. "Calm yourself. It may not be as bad as that. Other rumors say General Thomas Garth was the father."

Garth! Dunne remembered the name and the man from his childhood. Christ! What a day—what a mess!

Rossi was still talking. "Either way, it must remain a secret here. It is a powerful weapon that already hasn't served you badly. Darling daren't push you too hard—he'll treat you with respect, just in case, even if with his usual disdain. And he'll keep secretly slipping you money. Don't you see, however, that in England there are enemies of the king—men who want a republic—who would, if they got wind of your story, offer it as an example of how corrupt, depraved and ultimately worthless the monarchy is? Then there are king's men who would kill you to get you out of the way. Other men would exploit you here, too, or kill you for their own reasons. What of the thousands of convicts and Emancipists who are Irish and loathe the Crown with a passion?"

A vision of Brian O'Bannion flashed before Dunne's eyes. Would his friendship stay warm if he knew the truth or would it turn to hatred? He looked at Rossi and said calmly, "I will try to forget I ever heard those names. As far as I'm concerned, we never had this conversation." But deep down he could not help but wonder if the bad seed of incest really ran in his blood.

There was a knock on the door. "Come," said the captain.

Thomas Owens entered and looked at the patterer. "I've cleaned her up as best I can. She looks as though she's sleeping." He paused. "You were right, you know. I'll be careful and still useful."

Dunne thanked him and held out his hand. After hesitating, the doctor took it in his, as always, gloved fingers. The patterer nodded to Rossi and walked toward the door leading to a Sydney that could never know his secrets.

CHAPTER FIFTY-FOUR

Now cease, my lute! This is the last
Labour, that thou and I shall waste;
And ended is what we begun:
Now is this song both sung and past;
My lute! be still, for I have done.
—Sir Thomas Wyatt, "My Lute Awake" (1557)

DEATH HAD COME EARLY FOR MISS DORMIN, EVEN IN A WORLD IN which the average life span was (according to those men who conned such things) fifty-eight years. In particular, ill-treated servants, convicts and women in childbirth died too soon. But the most cruel mortality figures were for infants. Survive birth and childhood, however—say, overcome croup, scarlet fever and the like and attain the grand age of ten—and then, with further luck, reach adulthood, and you could live out the allotted three score and ten, perhaps more. Such luck was elusive, though.

People countered the fearful omnipresence of death with morbid gallows humor, whistling in the dark, even at the graveside. Dr. Peter Cunningham, dogged by death in his trade, liked to repeat an epitaph he found in a Parramatta graveyard:

Ye who wish to lie here,
Drink Squire's beer!

Even the pioneer brewer thus maligned apparently saw humor in the slight and would repeat it regularly.

Funerals in the colony had many facets. Few bodies went to an ornate, or any kind of vault. Some, especially away from towns, went into the handiest hole, which was often unmarked; perhaps an impermanent wooden cross might be raised, at best a cairn of rocks.

Even in town, interment could be a casual affair. There was no call for a doctor to certify death. Someone had only to register a death and deliver a body for burial, not necessarily in that order.

Some ceremonies, however, were grand affairs, with mourning mummers and black-decked hearses and horses. When old D'Arcy Wentworth, who may or may not have been a highwayman, had died the previous year, hundreds of people from Sydney traveled miles to follow his cortege in Parramatta. In Van Diemen's Land, an acting governor was dismissed for spending 800 pounds on his late superior's burial. In Sydney, a lady publican requested that her coffin be accompanied to the cemetery by a dozen white-gowned virgin barmaids. They raked up two, with few questions asked.

Rachel Dormin—and now that would always be her name—went to rest very simply.

———

IN THE DUSK, a handcart, with its box-shaped contents shrouded in canvas, was wheeled by a lone figure to an empty jetty at Jack-the-Miller's Point.

Between the Military Barracks and the spot where the cart now rested, it had halted only once in its progress, at a carpenter's shop in Cumberland Street.

There's that damned name to haunt me again, thought the sweating patterer. "I want it in cedar, no cheap pine," he directed the carpenter.

They found one ready-made that was to his liking. Dunne then borrowed a hammer and nails, and the use of a shed. He already had a pick and a shovel in the cart.

Now, at the jetty, he waited patiently. About thirty minutes passed before a splash announced the approach of a skiff. It came from the northern side of the water, from Murdering Point. As it pulled up to the jetty, lamplight helped reveal its occupant. A dark-skinned old man in a top hat was at the oars. Looking up from the boat bobbing on the tide, he waited for Dunne to speak.

For several moments, the younger man was silent, gazing into emptiness. It's strange, he thought. Or is it just right and proper? For all the twists and turns, the biblical clue and both riddles had ended truly. By and large. The men who had hurt a woman whose fruit thus departed from her, they were surely punished. And take the *zuzim* parable. If there were a God, then, as Miss Dormin ensured, the Most Holy *did* slay the angel of death.

He considered, too, the children's rhyme that Dr. Halloran had likened to the *zuzim* theme. And he noted wryly that their story—his and Rachel's—had now ended at John Leighton's mill. And wasn't that, after all, a house that Jack built?

He finally spoke. "Commodore, I need that favor repaid now. I need to go to an island."

The old man nodded.

ON ANOTHER, SUNNIER day, Nicodemus Dunne stood in easy silence on the harbor shore near Lieutenant Dawes's Battery. Alongside him, in his familiar eye-catching breeches, jacket and streamered hat, stood William King. "I often walk out along the South Head Road, to the Light, and I look out," said the Flying Pieman dreamily. "I know she's out there somewhere."

"Yes," said the patterer. He gestured to a drought-browned mass rising on their left from the sea. "I know she's out there somewhere, too." He wondered if the goats missed the rain.

As the two men walked back along George Street into the town, they were met by an excited Captain Rossi, who leaped down from his carriage. "Dunne, I've been looking for you everywhere," he exclaimed. "What luck! They've robbed the Squatters' Bank! Come on!"

The patterer put his arms around the shoulders of his companions as they all moved to clamber aboard the carriage. "The Exclusives robbed!" he cried as the carriage lurched off. "You can bank on the wails!"

EPILOGUE

CORONER'S INQUEST. An inquiry was held before Major Smeathman, Coroner for Sydney, on Saturday week, at Bax's Australian Hotel, on the bones of a woman. It came out in evidence that the men employed at Goat Island to cut stone, on Thursday last dug up an old cedar coffin, at the depth of about 14 inches from the surface, containing the bones in question. The jury returned a verdict, "That the bones were those of a female, which had been interred in a secret manner, about two years ago, but how, or by whom, to them unknown."

—*Sydney Herald*, June 13, 1831

AFTERWORD

Pluck one thread, and the web ye mar;
Break but one
Of a thousand keys, and the paining jar
Through all will run.
—John Greenleaf Whittier, "My Soul and I" (1847)

WHAT WAS TRUE? WHO WAS REAL?

I can only echo Michael Crichton, who wrote of his work *Next*, "This novel is fiction, except for the parts that aren't."

My story began with the accidental discovery of the factual, terse inquest report—possibly not dusted off for more than 175 years—which is reprinted here as the Epilogue. Who was this dead woman? I wondered. What could have happened to her only a few years earlier?

And so I stepped back to the dusty streets and into the lives of long-gone people to create this other 1828. People and events are frozen forever in the amber of old letters, journals and reports. Some of the dialogue I have given my real-life characters are words they actually spoke or wrote when they lived.

No solutions to the original mystery of who the buried woman was could be too improbable; the time and the place involved were ripe with intrigue and violence. The entirely "new" country, on the other side of the world, a world turned upside down, was populated by little that was familiar: unknowable native "Indians" and weird, unfathomable fauna. Consider the platypus.

What were strangers to make of a duck-billed, furred mammal with webbed feet—a beast trapped halfway in evolution between reptile and mammal, laying eggs but suckling its young? Science then gave it a suitable name, *Ornithorhynchus paradoxus* (since altered to *Ornithorhynchus anatinus*), but most in Britain thought it a fake, a trick by taxidermists.

And Australia *was* a place so out of this world that some convicts imagined they could escape across the nearby mountains to China; others really did believe that walking backward could return them their lost freedom.

Informed by many threads, this tale took to heart Shakespeare's pronouncement: "Untune that string, and hark! what discord follows . . ." The story became neither all fact nor all fiction—call it instead *friction*, in which real events, places and people (plus some mischievous inventions, suggestions and interlopers) collide. The result is fantasy and actuality tossed together.

The central characters of Rachel Dormin, Nicodemus Dunne and some of his immediate associates, notably Norah Robinson and Brian O'Bannion, are figments of my imagination, as are the murder victims and Dr. Owens.

But I have drawn much from historical reportage. The backgrounds, secrets and troubles discovered by the patterer about the governor and his lady, Captain Rossi, the Flying Pieman, the Wentworths, Doctors Cunningham and Halloran, Alexander Harris and editor Edward Smith Hall involve the real concerns of very real people.

I have taken some liberties with their lives; I have, perhaps, rearranged their actions and compressed or shifted them in time to advance the story. For instance, Captain Rossi's various posts, while factual, did not overlap quite so neatly. And Dr. Halloran's failing newspaper receives a stay of execution in my fictional universe. Mr. Levey's theater had a longer, more difficult birth. The epitaph on page 301—a real one in the old Parramatta cemetery—critical of Squire's beer, of course has no bearing on today's brew of the same name. The cruel and unusual punishments for theft meted out to Privates Sudds and Thompson, however, are very painfully factual and unvarnished.

Is it plausible to cast Nicodemus Dunne as the bastard son of royalty—with his father a murderer to boot? Ernest, Duke of Cumberland, was widely regarded as the murderer of his servant. He was also said to have been implicated in an attempt on the life of the Princess 'Drina (later Queen Victoria), who stood in the way of Cumberland succeeding King William IV.

As shocking, and more guarded, were allegations that he had broken the ultimate taboo: incest. Gossip claimed that Princess Sophia, the fifth daughter of King George III, gave birth to an illegitimate child in August 1800, and that Cumberland was the father. Other versions, however, said that Thomas Garth, a royal equerry, was responsible. Perhaps Garth was just a smokescreen? It is impossible that the real Darling and Rossi could not have been aware of these scandals. Whether they reacted to them in any way remains unreported.

Dueling had been forbidden by 1828, yet records show it still flourished, and that the governor of New South Wales would fight over a matter of honor is eminently feasible. Even the highest in the land at "Home" in Britain did it.

Not a year after our story, the Duke of Wellington, war hero and First Minister, faced a political critic, Lord Winchilsea, over an insult. Their confrontation in a London field was as deliberately undamaging as the Garden Island affair. Wellington aimed well to one side, his opponent shot in the air and apologized. Just as in our duel, game over. And for the patterer to have remarked on it in 1828, the Duke of Wellington must have referred more than once to his soldiers as "the scum of the earth."

The assertion (that the truth may seem improbable after eliminating the impossible) attributed by Dr. Owens to the artist Horace Vernet coincides with the words used more than half a century later by Mr. Sherlock Holmes in Sir Arthur Conan Doyle's *Adventure of the Greek Interpreter*. And the curious incident of Madame Greene's teeth predates a similar deduction by Holmes, regarding the dog in the nighttime, in Doyle's *Silver Blaze*.

The explanation is elementary: Vernet's life (1789–1863) was contemporary with that of Owens. And Holmes, of course, at one stage revealed that *his* grandmother was that very artist's sister.

I have used the common spelling of Bungaree (who, like Billy Blue, was a living person), although in contemporary records there are at least thirty variations. A French artist, Jules Lejeune, once even rendered his name "Buggery." His kingplate, or gorget, does not survive (although Queen Cora's does) and there are varying versions of its inscription; there may in fact have been more than one plate. His wide recognition may have spawned the word *boong*, eventually the enduring pejorative slang for Aboriginal.

At least I can assure readers that, in the making of this book, no *Ornithorhynchus paradoxus* was harmed, although a few sacred cows may have been skewered.

WHATEVER HAPPENED TO . . . ?

Governor Darling was recalled to England three years after this adventure, to a promotion (to full general) and a knighthood. Less pleasing had been his farewell. W. C. Wentworth roasted an ox for a jubilant celebration and an illuminated sign in George Street spelled out, AWAY, YE DESPOT! An official English Parliamentary Inquiry cleared Darling of blame in the Sudds affair. As Captain Rossi foreshadowed correctly, the old lag Patrick Thompson had returned safely to Ireland and traveled to London to give evidence at the inquiry. Oddly, perhaps, he was never called.

Dr. Laurence Hynes Halloran's newspaper, *The Gleaner*, lasted for only a handful of issues, as the patterer accurately anticipated. Halloran died in 1831.

Mr. W. C. Wentworth could look forward to a long and successful, if checkered, career, and to the start of a famous family line. His early, seemingly democratic leanings were to be compromised by his unrealized dream of creating a local hereditary peerage, dismissed derisively as a "bunyip aristocracy." He died in 1872.

Captain Crotty, like all old soldiers, faded away.

But **Colonel Shadforth**, who died in 1862, became a leading light, literally, in the colony. He played a key role in the introduction of gas lighting in the town, as did our *Gazette* editor, the Reverend Ralph Mansfield.

The "Die Hard" **57th Regiment** (to which our tale's rapists did not, of course, actually belong) and the **39th** soon made way for relieving garrisons. The last British troops to march out of Sydney, in 1870, belonged to the 18th (Royal Irish) Regiment. But there were no longer any new Irish prisoners to guard. Transportation to Sydney had been abolished in 1840.

Editor and cleric-baiter **Edward Smith Hall**, fined and jailed for his pugnacious publications, died in 1860, honored as a champion of the introduction of trial by jury and of freedom of the press.

Dr. Peter Cunningham, remembered for his medical successes and keen social eye, left the colony in 1830. His wanderlust undiminished, he served on the Royal Navy's South American station, based in Rio de Janeiro.

Captain Francis Nicholas Rossi remained a leading figure on the Sydney crime and justice scene until his retirement in 1834. He died on his country estate in 1851. He never talked publicly about the case of Rachel Dormin or many other intriguing matters.

"Old Commodore" Billy Blue sailed on until his death in 1834. He may have exaggerated his grand old age. London trial records gave his birth year as 1767—if so, he died at sixty-seven, not the eighty-six indicated by the census. And, to cloud the issue further, the Blue family bible entry claimed he died at a hundred! Murdering Point? The name became as forgotten as any crime there. It became, simply, Blue's Point.

Sadly, his comrade in arms, **Bungaree**, is largely forgotten. Death, speeded by drink, dethroned the "king" at an indeterminate age, four years before Billy's passing. **Cora Gooseberry** lived for another twenty years.

Alexander Harris lived in Australia until 1840, when he left for the United States, Canada and England. His legacy was his vibrant book of recollections, *Settlers and Convicts* (1847). He died in 1874.

William Francis King, the Flying Pieman, continued his career of astounding athleticism, becoming more and more eccentric until his death in the mid-1870s.

Ernest, Duke of Cumberland, became ruler of Hanover and died in 1851.

Princess Sophia never married and died in 1848.

There *was* a convict named **James Bond**. From Lancashire, he arrived on the transport *Albion* in February 1827, and went to Hyde Park Barracks. He was caught as a runaway on April 7, 1828—but soon disappeared again. His fate is unclear. That Dunne and Queen Cora's young attacker shared the same name is pure coincidence. Or a case of identity theft?

Dr. Thomas Owens's name seems to have been removed from all colonial medical records—perhaps a transgression after the facts related in our story merited this. Certainly, his grasp of medicine may seem quaint and crude (even dangerous) by modern standards, but he was, after all, a man of his times. Nevertheless, his diagnosis, long after the event, of Joseph Sudds's condition was astute, as was his clever conclusion as to the cause of Madame Greene's death.

There were, no doubt, many Irishmen in the colony named either **Brian** or **O'Bannion**, or both, but our man seems to have slipped from officialdom's gaze. We do know that many convict records were incomplete to start with and also that many criminal records were lost in the great fire of 1882 that destroyed the wooden Sydney Exhibition Building, where they were stored.

Or, perhaps, **Owens, O'Bannion** and **Norah Robinson** simply lived quietly and productively—except on those occasions when they were inveigled into more mischief and mayhem by . . .

Nicodemus Dunne, who regularly found he could not keep out of trouble. He is last heard of—perhaps?—in the mid-1850s. A business directory then refers to a Nicodemus Dunn (sic), a maker of ginger beer and soda water. Were they one and the same person? For the Nicodemus we knew, it would have not been an inapt career change. The patterer would always have agreed with Lord Byron, who wrote in *Don Juan*:

> *Let us have wine and women, mirth and laughter,*
> *Sermons and soda-water the day after.*

Some of the few physical reminders of the patterer's time are the Hyde Park Barracks (now a museum), parts of The Rocks, St. James Church and the nearby courts, part of the Rum Hospital (now inhabited by well-nourished State politicians) and a rebuilt replica of Macquarie's lighthouse. Rachel Dormin's beloved Goat Island, surrounded by millions of Sydneysiders, is today as silent as, well, the grave. It is little used and unloved.

The Squatters' Bank—and who robbed it? Ah, well. That's another story . . .

SOME SOURCES

Ashdown, Dulcie M., *Royal Murders: Hatred, Revenge and the Seizing of Power*, Sutton, Stroud, 1998.

Australian Dictionary of Biography, sequential volumes in progress, Melbourne University Press, Melbourne, 1966–.

Bell, Gail, *The Poison Principle*, Picador, Sydney, 2001.

Bennett, Samuel, *Australian Discovery and Colonisation, Vol. II: 1800–1831*, Currawong Press, Sydney, 1982.

Brewer's Dictionary of Phrase and Fable, revised by Ivor H. Evans, 14th edition, Cassell, London, 1992.

Cannon, John & Ralph Griffiths, *The Oxford Illustrated History of the British Monarchy*, Oxford University Press, Oxford, 1988.

Crowley, Frank, *A Documentary History of Australia, Vol. I: Colonial Australia, 1788–1840*, Nelson, Melbourne, 1980.

Cumes, J. W. C., *Their Chastity Was Not Too Rigid: Leisure Times in Early Australia*, Longman Cheshire, Melbourne, 1979.

Cunnington, C. Willett & Phillis, *Handbook of English Costume in the Nineteenth Century*, 3rd edition, Faber, London, 1970.

De Vries, Susanna, *Historic Sydney: The Founding of Australia*, Pandanus Press, Brisbane, 1999.

Flannery, Tim (ed.), *The Birth of Sydney*, Text, Melbourne, 1999.

Fletcher, Brian H., *Ralph Darling: A Governor Maligned*, Oxford University Press, Melbourne, 1984.

Fraser, Flora, *Princesses: The Six Daughters of George III*, John Murray, London, 2004.

Hughes, Robert, *The Fatal Shore: A History of the Transportation of Convicts to Australia, 1787–1868*, Collins Harvill, Sydney, 1987.

Joy, William, *The Venturers*, Shakespeare Head Press, Sydney, 1972.

Murray, Venetia, *An Elegant Madness: High Society in Regency England*, Viking, New York, 1999.

Ritchie, John, *The Wentworths: Father and Son*, Melbourne University Press, Melbourne, 1997.

Scott, Geoffrey, *Sydney's Highways of History*, Georgian House, Melbourne, 1958.

Smith, Keith Vincent, *King Bungaree: A Sydney Aborigine Meets the Great South Pacific Explorers, 1799–1830*, Kangaroo Press, Sydney, 1992.

Tyrrell, James R., *Old Books, Old Friends, Old Sydney: The Fascinating Reminiscences of a Sydney Bookseller*, Angus & Robertson, Sydney, 1987.

Wannan, Bill, *Dictionary of Australian Folklore: Lore, Legends, Myths and Traditions*, Viking O'Neil, Melbourne, 1987.

Ward, Russel & John Robertson, *Such Was Life: Select Documents in Australian History*, Jacaranda, Brisbane, 1972.

MEASURES AND MONEY

Imperial measures have been retained in this story, since use of the metric system would have been out of character. Some approximate equivalents are:

1 inch	2.54 centimeters
1 foot	12 inches or 30.5 centimeters
1 yard	3 feet or 0.914 meters
1 mile	1.61 kilometers
1 acre	0.405 hectares
1 ounce	28.3 grams
1 pound	16 ounces or 454 grams
1 stone	14 pounds or 6.36 kilograms

| 1 pint | 0.568 liters |
| 1 gallon | 4.55 liters |

Money, unlike weights or measures, makes for more confusing conversions. It is difficult to accurately weigh and relate monetary values in the late 1820s with today's. It helps to know, however, that there was one penny, twelve of which made a shilling. And twenty shillings made a pound. Now, consider that tobacco then cost three shillings to three and six a pound, eggs one and six to three shillings a dozen, bread two and a half to threepence a pound, and mutton six to seven pence a pound. A man's good suit cost nine to ten pounds and a dozen bottles of claret thirty shillings.

A tradesman could earn about six shillings a day. A female servant, fed and clothed, cost ten to fifteen pounds a year. A farm laborer received twelve to twenty pounds a year, plus weekly rations of seven pounds of beef and a peck (fifteen pounds) of wheat.

And what price a human life? In Britain until 1827, a child could be transported for life, even hanged, for grand larceny—which meant stealing personal property worth more than a shilling.

ACKNOWLEDGMENTS

To all those authors, past and present and too numerous to be mentioned, thanks for the memories that informed this tale.

I owe a debt to Robert Sessions, Penguin Australia's publishing director, who overcame his initial shock at being confronted with a manuscript knocked out on an old manual typewriter and talked me out of abandoning the project when my confidence flagged.

My editor, Nicola Young, was a rock of calm, cool and courteous professionalism. Certainly, she worked wonders on my German and French. I hope my grammar improves. *Bonne chance!* My thanks, too, to Anne-Marie Reeves for her superb design and Michelle Atkins.

My old friend from the *Women's Weekly*, the now so successful author Di Morrissey, urged me on. I also thank Peter Klimt for invaluable professional advice and Bert Vidler, too, for guidance.

My wife, journalist Julie Kusko, put up with my panics, toned down my tantrums, read and researched with me and, when I had two eye operations, became my seeing-eye dogsbody.